A Race with a Rogue

VOTES FOR WOMEN

REBEKAH JOHNSON

Paperback ISBN: 979-8-9880941-9-7
Library of Congress Control Number: 2025909294

Cover art elements commercially licensed from Veris Studio, designed by WSIB.

hello@rebekahjohnsonbooks.com

For my first editor, who told me my female lead characters were uninspiring and lacked agency.

Point taken.

You have to make more noise than anybody else, you have to make yourself more obtrusive than anybody else, you have to fill all the papers more than anybody else, in fact you have to be there all the time and see that they do not snow you under, if you are really going to get your reform realized.

— Emmeline Pankhurst

Content Note

A RACE WITH A ROGUE is a work of historical fiction and includes open-door, non-explicit romantic scenes between consenting adults.

This book reflects the U.S. political landscape in North Carolina in 1908, and the contemporary reader should note that the positions taken by Democratic and Republican officials in this era differ greatly from the modern platforms of those parties. This story addresses political and social matters, including the 1898 Wilmington Race Riots, in the framework of the time. For more information, please see the Afterword.

Chapter 1
Maudie

For more than a year, I have dreamt of Tobias Shaw kneeling before me, begging me to do him the honor of becoming his wife. Somewhere on the journey from dream to reality, the message was mangled— and now here I sit, screaming in his face while he clings to the bench in my back garden and pleads for me to calm down before my parents hear me.

"I don't care if they hear me!" I shriek. "They ought to hear me! And you ought to hear yourself, you cad. How could you do this? You are a scoundrel of the lowest order, Toby. Mr. Shaw."

"Maudie, please."

"Do not call me that. We are no longer so familiar."

"Aren't we? Maudie, I was going to ask you to marry me."

"I should count myself lucky you didn't get around to asking months ago and then spring this horrible news on me so I'd have to take it all back."

He sweeps his sandy blond hair back with a boyish smile, then tries to take my hands. "My darling. You are reading far too much into this. It's just politics, sweetheart. It's strategy. You know that."

"Whose strategy? Whose brilliant idea was it to remove women's suffrage from your platform?"

"It doesn't even matter. We won't vote on the matter at the state level anyway. It's just pandering to bring it up at all."

I will not be placated. "Ten states had referendums on women's rights in the last year. It is gaining traction and you know it."

"It's a temporary, strategic move based on my advisors' assessment of my potential competition."

I speak slowly and glare, relishing the growing panic in his dark eyes. "But whose idea was it, Mr. Shaw?"

I won't call him Toby anymore. I refuse. Whether he is doing this of his own accord or in compliance with his father and advisors, it is a betrayal. He knows this is the cause dearest to my heart. He knows the world is unjust and he has a responsibility to fix this part of it, at least, since I cannot vote or run for office myself.

"My father suggested it."

"This tells me a great deal about how much he respects your mother. And how he expects you to respect me."

"My mother's role is to support his platform and his interests. He's the one who needs the votes, and men are the ones who vote, so of course he is the decision maker."

"Is that the dynamic you would have expected for us? Goodness, how things have changed." I shove some errant blonde curls out off my sweaty forehead. Even in the shade of a towering lilac bush, I am steaming.

He throws up his hands. "Maudie, why are you acting as though we've never talked about this? You have always been so supportive, my darling. It's one strategic move for the platform. That's all."

"That's not all. If you would let go of the cause that matters most to me, one you said mattered a great deal to you, then you and I have fundamentally different values. It is just your platform changing, isn't it? Or do you no longer believe women should have the vote?"

He is silent—as silent as I suppose he expects me to be.

"Did you ever believe it?"

No response.

"You're a man, aren't you, Mr. Shaw? You're allowed to speak your mind, so speak it."

"All of your friends would vote like their husbands anyway, so why do they need to vote on their own?" He rises and begins to pace, not looking my way. "Ellen would certainly vote however Spencer does. Georgia would follow Leo's guidance."

Did I ever kiss the lips that uttered such nonsense? My mouth waters and I bite my lip to keep from spitting in the dust at his feet. I haven't spit since I was a little girl, but I've already given up all pretense of maturity by screaming at him until I broke a sweat, so why not?

"And as for you and I, Maudie—"

"Do not presume to think of me as your wife. Not in the same breath that you reference men who respect women's brains," I snap. "I see that in a true politician's style, you cannot give me a straight answer. That tells me all I need to know. You may go, Mr. Shaw, and I do not wish to see you again."

He drops to his knees in front of me and the year-long daydream snaps back into focus when he opens a blue velvet box. The sunlight catches the diamond ring and nearly blinds me when he lifts it up.

What on God's green earth is wrong with this man?

This is the moment I've dreamed of since the first day we sat together at a football game, when I got a terrible case of the anxious giggles and he snuck a hand next to me, squeezed my fingers, and told me he adored me already and I should relax.

I cannot relax now. Every muscle in my body tenses tighter the longer I look at him, and my fingers curl into claws as the diamond flashes in my eyes and the man I thought I knew speaks the beautiful words I longed for.

"Maudie Hamilton, I love you. Be my wife and see this through with me. I cannot conceive of a sweeter woman to have at my side, not for this campaign, but forever. Things like the platform will change. That is the nature of this job. We must shift and adapt to make our way up, but the love I have for you will never fade or falter. Marry me, my darling, and we will work through this and every obstacle ahead together, as husband and wife."

It is nearly silent in the garden. Only the late spring breeze rustling the foliage breaks the quiet after he finishes speaking and awaits my answer. I cannot take my eyes from his, searching their dark depths for the mischievous winks and adoring gazes that captured my heart so quickly last year. We had plans together. We had dreams. He's still in there beneath this posturing politician. I know he is. He has to be.

"What happened to changing the party from within?"

"I will, darling. But not yet."

"Just put women's suffrage back on your platform. You

don't have to make a fuss about it, but go on the record supporting it."

Toby, please. Be the man I think you are. Be the man I think I know. Please.

His shoulders slump. "Maudie, I cannot."

Despite the roaring of my heart in my ears, I stand and lift my chin with the unshakable poise that won me "Miss Perfect Posture" at school three years in a row. I draw back my skirts as though he were made of mud and I do not wish to soil my hems with his presence.

"I am neither honored nor flattered by your proposal. I will not sell out my principles to win you a vote I cannot cast." I jerk my head in a curt nod and catch his gaze—jaw set in stubbornness, hand quivering as he holds the blue velvet box. "Good day, Mr. Shaw."

Chapter 2
Cooper

I am not a religious man, but I am also not a stupid one, and I have the good sense to wake on a morning like this and send thanks to the heavens for this charmed life I lead. Is there a finer day than one's college graduation? A finer place than this beautiful campus canopied by ancient chestnuts and crowded with the finest family and friends here to celebrate at my side? This glorious slip of paper in my hand declares that Cooper Truxton is a college graduate with a degree in engineering, class of 1908, a man who can do more than call a play and throw a football.

I did it.

I finished something.

And, to be clear, I never finish anything.

Engineering is my third major. Football is something like my ninth sport. Maybe my tenth, if you count bowling, but nobody counts bowling. Please don't make me count how many girls have bored me in a matter of weeks—some in a matter of minutes. My good manners have their limits, and I learned early in my days bearing the mantle of "eligible bachelor" that it's better if I bow out gracefully before I offend anyone.

This degree is more than a game, more than a touchdown. Those victories belong to the team I led. This is mine alone.

I suppose it's partially thanks to my parents for paying for everything and more or less bribing me to finish.

It's partially thanks to my sister Georgia, who through some magic convinced them to do that instead of cutting me off when they thought I ditched class to save trees.

It's partially thanks to her husband, my best friend Leo Rigby, for forcing my nose into my books when I was daydreaming about a life in the Forest Service.

All right, so my degree was a team effort, too—paper proof from East Piedmont College that I have been granted second, third, and fourth chances by so many people I hold dear. It's my stepping stone to a program at the North Carolina State College of Agriculture and Mechanic Arts. A&M is younger than I am and brimming with energy and new ideas. I am the last person any of my instructors, from grammar school to thermodynamics, would expect to pursue more time in the classroom. But here I am, packing up my dorm room for the last time, ready to move to new bachelor's quarters in Raleigh at the end of the summer.

"It's the end of an era, Trux."

I look up and spot Leo in the doorway, a wry smile on his face as he surveys the empty room he shared with me until he married my sister. "I still cannot quite believe it, Rigs. You and I, college graduates. You, a married man, and I—"

"Not celebrating alone, I am sure."

"I have no plans for that kind of celebration."

He raises a brow, but I twirl my hat in my hands and don't meet his eyes. "It's been a while since I visited Miss Ada's establishment. I'm in no hurry to go back."

"What about Ella?"

"I'm sure she has already found a new man to adore her. The infatuation ran its course and we parted on fine terms."

Leo frowns. "Is it really all so transactional?"

"It's clear, that's what it is. No games. Mutual satisfaction with no attachments."

"Nonsense. You liked her a lot."

"I do not wish to get married any time soon, if ever. That much has not changed."

Leo has always been a hopeless romantic and has spent most of his life besotted with my sister. He does not understand my visceral aversion to the kinds of girls one must marry because no one would use him for his name or his income. He's a better man than I by every measure, but he is a third son, a little shy socially, and never had much interest in society's games.

I, by accident of birth, am quite a prize.

For the last five years, Hillside's debutantes have been reminded that Truxton is an old name and a sound one, thanks to my grandfather's foresight in railroad investments and my father's careful management of our funds in steel and shipping. All of that will be mine one day, they think—mine to offer some empty-headed young lady who, in return, will embroider fine linen, host parties, and bear children.

I like parties and I suppose I would like children, but that still seems like a poor deal to me.

I wonder how my stock would plummet next season if I stood on a chair and announced that I plan to move north to work with the Forest Service, where I will drain my coffers curing the blight of the American chestnut tree.

"Perhaps someone will surprise you at the party tonight," he says. "You ignored the latest crop of debutantes and claimed you were studying all season, which no one believed for a minute. Dance with each of them once tonight so your mother stops pestering Georgia and me to make you remember your courtesies. But try not to be too charming unless you intend to call."

"It's impossible not to be charming with my natural wit."

"You're a natural nitwit."

"And you act as though I haven't done this for four previous crops, as it were."

"And every year, you manage to get some poor girl's hopes up."

"I don't see how that is my fault. I might parry a little clever banter with someone who can keep up, but those girls are mostly Georgia's friends who are far smarter than I am and like to use me to make their lagging suitors jealous. As for the rest, I don't make promises. Rigs, you know me. I don't even make hints. What people do with their hopes is no business of mine."

He slaps the side of my head. "It's the curse of being born the eldest son in a family of means, and a handsome idiot to boot. Be open-minded. I may be biased in my domestic bliss, but there is much to be said for a happy marriage."

"Tell me though, when my sister had her coming-out, which of her desirable feminine traits stood out so much you selected her from the crop? Her lemon tarts, her swanlike posture, or her embroidered tea towels?"

"Trux."

"Ah, I remember." I snap my fingers as though I'd forgotten. "It's because she can fix bicycles and helped you with your homework in chemistry and fluid dynamics. She can do all those things they say a lady should do, but she is true to her interests, her humor, and her dreams. Why does every girl I am required to dance with strive so hard to be a paper doll of a wife?"

"How will you know if anyone is more than a paper doll if you don't speak with them beyond a spin around the floor?"

"I'm not inclined to chance it."

Leo snorts a laugh. "One of these days, you will get in over your head with someone who makes you chance it. Not now, and maybe not soon, but it will happen."

"I'll give you this: a woman with distilling skills would pique my interest." I nod at the stack of newspapers on my otherwise-bare desk. "I've been stirred to activism lately. I've written a hundred letters to Ambrose Shockley and every other representative whose district touches Raleigh."

While the rest of the country bickers and debates this impossible notion of a federal law on temperance, our vote on statewide prohibition takes place next week. I still cannot fathom this blanket ban on alcohol throughout North Carolina if it passes.

"Whatever happens, we'll manage fine at home," Leo says. "I'll be back and forth between here and Virginia at least once a month for my new job, so I'll get whatever we need and be a generous brother to you."

"As you always have been."

He leans on the doorframe, shaking his head. "But it is short-sighted how Shockley and the rest support this. The legislature wishes to placate the League of Women Voters with temperance in order to hold off the suffrage movement, but this is going to backfire."

"Are there no women who wish to vote *and* drink? Surely there are." I scoop up the newspapers and drop them into the last open box. "How strange it is. The fight may take many more years, but women will have the vote, that much is sure. They already have it in other states, so why not here? Why not now? If temperance wins, they will flatten an industry and destroy jobs, but it only delays the inevitable."

He eyes me. "It might not hurt for you to find affection in a different manner than you are accustomed, in any case. Houses like Miss Ada's may not do much business without liquor."

"Perhaps not." I pick up the box just to busy my hands and disguise the nervous jitter in my fingers. "But it is a quieter house than most in Raleigh. The law will go after the bawdy houses with cabarets before they bother Miss Ada and her girls."

He scoops up the last two boxes and we scan the room one more time. Its blue striped wallpaper, marble-topped oak dressers and spindle-framed beds were our home away from home for three years together. This past year, since Leo and Georgia set up house in town, his old side has been occupied by our teammate Brent Hayes.

But Hayes moved out yesterday, so today it is the two of us once more in this empty room with its bare mattresses and spotless floors. The only evidence we ever lived here is the tiny notches in the doorframe where we marked our heights on move-in, when I swore I'd catch up with him.

Leo catches me looking at them and drops the boxes back on the bed. "We never finished this, did we?"

"Don't bother. You win." I try not to smile. "It's obvious I must look up to you forever."

Flicking open his pocketknife, he stands with his back to the doorframe and lifts his chin.

I scrape a small line slightly above his first one, then stand in his place while he measures me.

"Done."

I step back and follow the glint of the blade where he's pointing to a new gouge half an inch above the one we carved my freshman year.

"How about that," he says. "You grew up a little, Trux."

"A little."

He snaps the pocketknife shut. "That alone is worth a hell of a party. Let's go."

Chapter 3
Maudie

I pace my best friend Georgia's childhood bedroom, fanning my cheeks to cool an angry flush. My evening gown is a lovely, warm rose, one of the finest colors for my complexion, but my cheeks seem set on matching it every time Toby Shaw crosses my mind—and for two solid weeks now, that unprincipled rat keeps crossing my mind.

"Maudie, are you sure—"

"I am here to celebrate and have fun," I declare, whirling around to meet Georgia's concerned gaze. "And so I shall. I was momentarily flustered."

She squeezes my hands. "You are so strong, Maudie. No stupid man has ever spoiled such a beautiful party for you, and you-know-who will not spoil this one. Let me distract you. You must see what Mama and Caroline have done."

With Georgia's steadying hand on my arm, I take a final glance in the mirror, relieved to see my cheeks have calmed to a becoming shade of pink. I expect her to lead me to the staircase, but she turns right instead of left and takes me to the end of the hall where a cozy window seat looks over the backyard.

The view is breathtaking.

Georgia and her brother Cooper Truxton's childhood home backs up to Leo Rigby's, and for the boys' graduation, their parents have opened the new double gate between their yards to host the party in both houses. Gas torches light the way along a path of heavy rugs laid for the occasion, and through the window I can see guests traipsing through spring flowers in both gardens. Mrs. Rigby's greenhouse is strung with lanterns and lit from within, glowing like a moon plucked from the sky for our enjoyment.

"Dancing is at the Rigbys' since they have the double drawing rooms," Georgia says, leading me to the stairs. "Dining is downstairs, and there are tables for cards and conversation."

"I need to dance tonight. I don't have to think when I dance."

"Then you shall dance. You will see many friendly, familiar faces tonight, darling. Old friends. Trusted friends."

I catch the eye of Angeline Berger, an old schoolmate with a new engagement ring, and I bob a quick greeting. She has her arm around her little sister Catherine, a debutante with an elegant updo and a nervous smile. "Old friends, indeed," I sigh. "Georgia, I waited for that awful man for too long. I am twenty-two, and when I am ready to open my heart again, I will be in competition with seventeen-year olds like Catherine Berger."

"Any man who would select Catherine Berger is not man enough to marry you," Georgia says. "Catherine is a sweet, empty-headed girl. You are a sweet, clever, talented woman. You are not that malleable, nor should you be."

"A malleable woman would be in greater demand," I mumble. "No. I will not turn my thoughts that direction. Do not mind me. I am determined not to speak of him tonight."

"I have one more distraction for you." Georgia takes my hand and taps her stomach.

"Are you sure?" I clap my hand over my mouth as soon as I squeal the words. "Are you sure?" I whisper, trying not to hop like a little girl with a secret.

"Shh. I am entirely sure. Leo and I haven't even told our parents yet, but I wanted you to know tonight."

I can hardly keep from crushing her in my embrace. "Darling, this is the finest, happiest news I could hope for this evening. Thank you for telling me. I won't breathe a word until you're ready, but—oh, I am delighted for you. You have put a spring in my step, and I will enjoy my dances tonight so much more. You will be the perfect mother, and you'll have everything you and Leo dreamed of."

Her blue eyes shine as she glances across the room and spots her husband in conversation with her father. "Wouldn't it be funny if one day Leo and I have his parents' home, and Cooper has this one? Our children would grow up together as we did."

"That would require a woman willing to take him on."

"I recall a time not long ago when you were a willing volunteer for that role."

I snicker. "That was all in fun. Cooper is a lark. He will never be serious about anyone or anything. As a matter of fact, he owes me seven dances I have saved up from the last three seasons because he kept disappearing from events when he got bored. I may cash in on that debt tonight so I don't have to worry about being bright and witty for my partners. He will excuse me if I seem glum and will do his best to amuse me with off-color jokes. I am quite looking forward to it, if he'll grant me a few minutes."

"Well, he's not allowed to leave early tonight. May I recommend seeking him out after he does his mandatory turn with Catherine? He'll need the intelligent conversation."

After a lively cotillion, I excuse myself from Anderson Oliver's efforts to escort me to the punch table. Mr. Oliver is a friend of Leo and Cooper's but also a close friend of Mr. Shaw's, and his company is unremarkable but comforting in its familiarity. He is a paper doll of a good man, and I have no complaint of him other than that he bores me to tears despite the many pretty compliments he offers on my dress, my hair, and my company. Perhaps I should nudge him to ask Catherine Berger for a dance.

I escape to the terrace alone for a view of the torch-lit gardens.

Caroline Rigby's beloved greenhouse is aglow so guests can visit her prize-winning blooms. The entire scene is one of peace and light. With Georgia's beautiful news about the baby still singing in my ears, for the first time in the two weeks since that final, disastrous meeting with Mr. Shaw, my heart truly lifts. Something good lies ahead for me, too. I can feel it as though the air around me is warming with hope.

"Tell me where to find him, and he's a dead man."

I try to whirl around and am stayed by a hand on my arm. The voice is one I looked forward to hearing. "Hello, Cooper."

"Hello, Miss Maudie."

He remains behind me, hands on my elbows, and leans his head against mine so he can look where I am looking. "The gardens are lovely tonight, I see."

"And you are most familiar this evening." I push him off me, and he scoots right back.

"I mean it. I'll kill him, if you like." His whisper is warm next to my ear, and I can't keep from smiling because I know he is grinning like an idiot.

"How very gallant and absolutely antique of you."

"Do you doubt my ability to avenge a lady's honor?"

I step back and turn to face him. "My honor is quite intact, and you may assure my brother of that in your next letter. There is nothing to avenge."

"Your honor is, in my eyes, entirely yours to do with as you wish." He bows. "But leaving that aside, your feelings matter to me a great deal as well. A certain person was most unkind to you. If your brother Jeremiah were here, he'd have called him out. I would be honored to act in his stead."

"Just what everyone needs is another meddling older brother who thinks duels are still legal and he can decide what is best for his sister." I adjust my hair where he messed it up leaning against my head. "Interfering in Georgia's affairs should have taught you a lesson."

"Well, I never was especially bright."

The twinkle of the lantern light in his eyes makes me smile. "Did Jeremiah even tell you why I sent that man off?"

"'That man' was stupid enough to rat on himself. He had the gall to complain to Ollie that you spurned him over a little tiff, and you know Berger—he overhears everything, and of course, well..."

17

"Oh, no." I cover my mouth with my hands. Matthew Berger, Angeline's brother, is her coworker in a rumor mill that is far-reaching and rarely wrong.

"And as fate would have it," Cooper continues, "my room-mate Brent Hayes is quite the cartoonist, and has whipped up a glorious comic featuring Lady Liberty standing on a rock labeled 'Suffrage' and sporting a banner labeled 'Principles,' while a tweedy little man waving a Confederate flag and a ballot prostrates himself at her feet."

"Well, I rather like that. But a Confederate flag? Why?"

"Because standing against women's suffrage is a ruse to stand against equal votes for all races as well as sexes, and a clear call to return to the days of the votes in only the hands of the white landowners." He glances around the yards. "Our dear little Hillside emerged fairly unscathed from the wrong side of that little conflict fifty years ago, so perhaps we have forgotten how far passionate people will go to fight for equality. You are in good company, Miss Maudie."

My heart does a little flip, and I cannot muster a reply.

He clears his throat. "In any case, that clever cartoon will make its appearance in the final run of the school paper next week, and I shall save you a dozen copies, if you wish. You are a stunning Lady Liberty, by the way."

"I should look for Mr. Hayes tonight to thank him for his flattering likeness."

"I helped."

"You are an artist now, as well as an athlete?"

"Well, I told him where your dimple is." He pokes my cheek. "And when I didn't think the petulant smirk on your face was petulant or smirky enough, I waxed poetic about the shape of your lips. I think he got it right."

"How I have missed you, Cooper. Thank you for cheering me up."

"You have a spine of steel behind that tender heart. I have always admired your tenacity, Miss Maudie." He gives me a smile and a salacious wink my brother would not approve of, and I cannot help but giggle.

"I suppose today I should applaud your tenacity as well. College graduation. I must confess, I was not sure you had it in you. Congratulations."

He offers his arm, and his eyes light up when I tuck my hand in the crook of his elbow. "You and I have always thought alike. I also thought it unlikely I should ever finish my degree. And here I am, all set up to pursue another one."

"We never know what the earth's next turn will bring. Perhaps I will have such a surprise in my future."

"You would make a delightful coed. Come with me to the football games this fall. I will be miserable since I can't play anymore, and you always lift my spirits."

"Georgia and Leo and I will be there every weekend we can get away."

"Psh. I don't need them. Only you."

I am enjoying this so much. Cooper Truxton really is the finest sort of good-natured man, rogue that he is, and he is impossible not to like. With a voice as caramel in tone as his eyes are in color, a little banter is more pleasant with him than with any other man. My dearest friend's brother, safe and familiar and oh-so-funny, is exactly who I needed to see tonight.

"While my devotion to you is unquestionable, dear Cooper, I can hardly go alone."

"I meant you should come to school. To the women's

college in Raleigh. And join me at all the games, naturally, where I will whine to you that I would have been the best quarterback the school has ever seen, were it not for me breaking my wrist twice last year."

I flutter my lashes at him. "You believe I should sign myself up for a college education just to cheer with you and listen to your grumbles at football matches."

"Yes, that's what it boils down to, I suppose." He winks again. "I told you, we are often of like mind, Miss Maudie, and now that I have plopped that idea into your pretty head, you won't be able to escape it."

"I cannot decide what looks more desperate. Chasing you to Raleigh to be your personal cheerleader, or demanding payment in full tonight for all the dances you owe me."

"Plundering all my dances would be most unladylike." He gently turns me back toward the house where the orchestra is beginning a song. "And I do love an unladylike lady."

"My reputation will be in tatters if I dance seven times in a row with such a rogue."

His hand slips to my waist as I lift mine to his shoulder, and even though we are still on the terrace, we fall into the steps without thinking. "You will do wonders for my reputation, though," he says. "That the impeccable Maudie Hamilton, so choosy she has declined not one but three proposals of marriage, should grant me her attention immediately elevates me from rogue status to a mere cad."

An embarrassed flush rushes into my cheeks as the faces of the men I declined flicker past me in a blink. I twitch my head, shaking them out like cobwebs as I force a smile.

"Propose to me now and we'll make it four, so the old ladies have something to talk about until the season begins."

"I could never aspire so high."

His wicked smile sets me giggling. "I suppose you'll have to remain a rogue or a cad, then. Have you a scale for such things?"

"I have obviously never stooped so low as to be called a villain. Slightly above that, though, is a varmint, then a brute. Then a rake, a rogue, a scoundrel, and a cad." He tickles my hand with his fingers. "After that, it's onward and upward to respectability."

We spin in the steps of the dance on the terrace among the trees. "I disagree with that assessment. I would use each of those terms for a man who was ungentlemanly in different ways, so it is not a natural scale from bad to worse."

"An example, please."

"A villain is obviously a law-breaker. A varmint may have committed grave moral offenses in an underhanded manner. And a brute is one who is violent."

"Go on."

"A rake is a term somewhat out of fashion. But he is a man who has many women and lives only for his pleasure at the expense of others. His eyes may seduce, but his lips smile only for himself. I would not place a rogue next to him on your scale."

"'Rogue' is the term I hear most often applied to myself."

"And it suits you. You are an overgrown, naughty boy who plots his own course and does not wish his waywardness to cause anyone harm, but you are slightly libertine in your beliefs and habits."

He shakes with laughter. "Miss Maudie, you are an angel to honor me with such a generous description. But to be clear, I should not strive to be a scoundrel or cad after all?"

"Absolutely not. A scoundrel is a cheat and a cad is a liar."

"It seems that if one is not a gentleman, a rogue is the next best thing to be." He seems very pleased with this idea and continues to chuckle under his breath. "You have challenged my way of thinking, and I believe this construct of yours will occupy my mind for some weeks. When I have all the nuances defined, I will seek you out with a treatise for your approval before we publish it in the paper."

"Just in time for me to request your assistance with my college applications, then."

He whirls me in his arms and smiles, a devilish light in his eyes. "We have known one another so long that I feel strange playing at formalities with you now. Do you know, you are the one unmarried woman at this party that I completely trust is not after me for my name or my income?"

"Have I ever called you Mr. Truxton? I want nothing from you but my dances. And I imagine you are the one unmarried man at this party who does not include pity in his list of reasons to dance with me."

"Utter nonsense. In addition to your cleverness and charm, you are radiant tonight. Truly magnetic."

"May I tell you a secret?"

He breaks the formation of the dance and pulls me a little closer. "I love secrets."

"Flattery may set me swooning tonight. A rogue is an exceptional flatterer, and I thought you should be warned."

He eyes me curiously. "Is it just flattery you want? I believe you could get that anywhere. I noticed Ollie and Berger both seemed quite taken with you when you danced with them. Did they not satisfy you?"

The way the word *satisfy* rolls off his tongue is pure silver, and my breath catches in my throat.

"No."

"Perhaps tired remarks about your dress and pretty smile are not what you need."

"I am ready for a change."

"The freckles on your nose are like a dusting of buttercups in a lovely spring meadow."

I smile and twirl in his arms, and he tightens his grip on my fingers.

"And your one crooked tooth is a Tahitian pearl in a strand of perfect Italian ones."

"You are a delight, Cooper."

"But you have not swooned yet." He spins me again and lowers his voice. "And I am bold enough tonight to tell you I have long thought the line of your lovely neck must be the perfect fit to the shape of my hand. The desire I feel to touch you there has overwhelmed me to the point that I just might do it."

The heat in his brown eyes is no longer the warmth of the savvy flirt or the old friend. He is not teasing. He is smoldering inside, and I am tired of hints and implications and assumptions.

I am so tired of wondering and waiting on men.

I clasp his hand in mine and lead him off the terrace into the shadows along the side of the house where we cannot be seen.

"Do it."

The press of his palm to my neck sends tingles through my body as his fingers glide into my hair with a tender massage. I grip his coat, leaning into his touch like a cat savoring a caress, and when I look up at him, his eyes are closed.

The possessive pressure of his fingertips loosens my hair at my nape and he twists a curl tight, startling me into a gasp.

He opens his eyes.

"Is this what you want?" he asks, his voice low and shaky.

"Yes." I pause. "Is this what you want?"

I can barely make out his whisper.

"I want you to touch me, too."

I walk my fingers up the lapel of his coat and drag them lightly over his shirt. I have never touched a man like this, not even Mr. Shaw, who I only held around his shoulders in our most passionate embraces. He certainly tried to touch me more than once, but attraction never overrode my fear. As I pause to tease the corners of his tie, Cooper's heart thuds beneath my palm as though I could reach through these layers to the core of who he is.

He has always been appealing and a little dangerous. Tonight, he is intoxicating.

I am no fool. He knows exactly what he's doing as he slips his hand over my waist, edging closer to me as he tightens his grip on my hair. I don't push him away as his breath grows raspy and he bends forward, forehead against mine while I trace his jawline with my fingers.

"I cannot swoon for this," I whisper, my lips only an inch from his cheek.

"Is this not enough?"

"If I faint, it will end. And I do not want it to end."

"Maudie, I will not take advantage of your heartache."

I press a finger to his lips. "I don't want anything from

you. I want just you, for a moment or whatever suits us. Be a rogue or a gentleman. Just you."

His lips meet mine and I lose myself in his kiss—in the taste of brandy on his tongue, in the sweet, urgent pressure of his mouth—tender, almost tentative, but hungry. I slide my hands under his jacket without shame and rake my fingernails over him to jolt his senses, and he caresses my shoulders with the gentlest of strokes, lowering his fingers to graze across the neckline of my gown.

I catch my breath.

"Is that enough?" He moves his lips on mine as he speaks, a kiss between each word.

I shake my head.

He tucks a finger inside the lace and glides it over my breasts as my breaths come harder, pressing me against him.

I was afraid to let Mr. Shaw undo a single button, let alone touch me beneath my clothes as Cooper is doing now. Yet when his finger curls against me, so slow and deliberate I feel the ridges of his fingerprint as hot as a brand on my skin, fear and propriety melt away and I hold him tighter.

"Is that enough?" he asks again, and to my astonishment, his voice is shaking.

I look up and meet his gaze.

"No."

He smooths his hands with a firm grip over my hips and then around my backside, squeezing as he teases my lips with his tongue. Wobbling at the knees, I lean back against the wall when he brings his hands forward to press on my thighs, pulsing gently as his thumbs creep closer and closer together.

"Is that enough?"

"No."

Those three words set me trembling each time he says them, and the only answer can be no, it's not enough. His eyes are hungry and vulnerable, almost a stranger's eyes, for although the movements of his hands are steady and experienced, I have never seen him so unsure of himself. He strokes my legs through my dress and kisses me again when I cannot hold back a whimper. "I want you to touch me," he says, his breath hot on my cheek. "If it's not enough for you, it's not enough for me."

"I want to. But I have never touched a man before."

He licks his lips as his mouth curls into a satisfied smile. "Then go exploring, Maudie. See what you find."

Looking up into his eyes, I press my palms to his chest. "I want to find you. Whoever you are under all this."

He sucks in a sharp breath when I slide a hand up his shoulder and into his hair, twisting the light brown tendrils tight between my fingers like he did to me.

He likes that.

I scrape one fingernail down the back of his neck and tuck it inside his shirt collar, then graze it back up over the curve of his ear. He shivers.

Oh, he likes that, too.

I bring my hand to his waist, and, scooting his waistcoat aside, glide a finger over the edge of his trousers, like he did on the neckline of my dress.

The rumble in his chest is like a purr.

Anyone could stumble on us here. Any loving couple in search of a little privacy could sneak into these shadows as we have and see his hands all over me, and my stomach turns cold when I think of what that could do to both of us. I just want to feel something. I want to feel him, not marry him, and he is not a marrying man.

"We will be seen," I whisper as he pulls me close for another kiss.

"Then dance with Berger again. I must take my mandatory spin with Tabitha Jeffries."

I straighten. "What?"

"She's the last of my requirements for the evening, and I imagine Berger's awkward flattery will give you a headache and you will need to excuse yourself to rest for a bit."

No one will think twice to see me ascend the stairs alone to powder my nose in Georgia's old bedroom. No one will think twice to see him roaming the halls of his own home.

"Should I go to her room to rest?"

"Only if you don't remember which room is mine."

Chapter 4
Cooper

"**Y**ou are a delightful dancer, Miss Jeffries," I say to my partner. She can't be more than seventeen years old and is blushing red as a beet, but the set of her jaw brings me a smile as I recall Georgia's determination to make our parents proud when she had to engage in this dreadful ritual. It is my job to drive the conversation with superficial topics and set her at ease until I can get the hell out of here and upstairs into Maudie's arms.

"Thank you, Mr. Truxton. It is quite easy with such a skilled partner."

"Have you enjoyed your evening so far?"

"I have indeed."

"What are your politics?"

She nearly missteps. "Excuse me?"

Everyone should be able to talk about politics a little, so I'm helping her, really.

"Your politics, Miss Jeffries. The state legislature is about to vote on statewide prohibition of alcohol. How do you feel about the matter?"

"I—well—" She looks around for help as though I've propositioned her. "I do not know much about the legislature. What are your thoughts?"

She's doing well. It's always best to be honest when you haven't a clue what you're doing.

"I enjoy a good brandy, so of course I am against the measure."

"Oh, well, I am sure the—the legislature will see it your way and vote for it."

"Against it."

"Of course. Against it."

I shake my head as we circle the floor, narrowly missing Maudie and Berger, who is holding her a little too close for my liking. I should have suggested she dance with Hayes. Or Leo, since he's the only safe one. My lips still tingle from kissing her.

"What about trees?" I ask.

"Trees?"

"Do you like them?"

"Very much." Miss Jeffries' embarrassed flush fades. "I heard you are interested in conservation, Mr. Truxton. Our flowering dogwood is in bloom. You might like to see it."

I should say something pleasant, like *how delightful*, but when Maudie giggles and Berger snickers at some private joke, pleasantries escape me. I'll run Berger into a wall if he gets in my way tonight.

"Did you know every chestnut tree in America is likely to die in the next forty years?"

She skips a step and corrects herself. "Oh, my. That's terrible."

"Indeed, and so far, it is impossible to stop. Imported

chestnuts carried a blight from Asia, which they can resist but the American chestnut cannot. It's infecting every tree it touches with great sores on the bark that strip the life from it and then murder the tree from within."

She grimaces.

"And there is no cure," I continue, watching Maudie's blonde curls bob through the sea of dancers. "The forests of Appalachia will be devastated. Already, up north, farmers are clear-cutting chestnut groves that have thrived for hundreds of years."

"That's terrible," she says again, glancing around the room to avoid meeting my eyes.

My words flow faster. "It is. And it is driven by greed for the timber harvest of the last American chestnuts, disregarding the fact that clear-cutting wipes out any chance we have at developing a resistant strain. Yes, it takes more time, but one must remove the infected trees one by one and let the healthy ones stand in hopes that even one of them might survive it and prove useful in propagation. Why does no one understand that? Why does no one care?"

Miss Jeffries stops and I stagger to a halt as the orchestra releases a note into silence.

Half the room is staring—including Maudie, Berger, and Miss Jeffries' irate papa.

I clear my throat and my awkwardness echoes.

"Miss Jeffries, I beg your pardon," I say, bowing. "The matter of forest conservation does get me unbecomingly excited at times. Please forgive me."

She smiles when I lift her hand and barely brush her glove with my lips, and her father's frown relaxes. "Of course,

Mr. Truxton. It is plain you care a great deal about the trees, so of course you are very passionate."

The word sounds profane in her high, child-like voice. I am only twenty-three years old. This girl, supposedly the right age for me to court and marry, wouldn't know passion if it landed in her lap. She is sweet and amiable, just like all the rest of them—a perfect match for someone bland and respectable like my friend Anderson Oliver. But her mother has coached her to catch my eye by inviting me over to see a dogwood, of all things, because I am interested in trees and surely one is as good as another.

I look again for Maudie and spy Berger handing her a glass of punch, and I am about to lose myself in a jealous simmer when I realize he is looking over her shoulder into the Rigbys' front hall, his face darkening with fury.

"It was a pleasure to dance with you, Miss Jeffries, I hope you have a delightful evening." The words tumble from my mouth as I turn away and hurry across the room, yanking my sister away from a conversation.

"What do you want?" Georgia asks.

"Get Maudie out of here," I say. "Toby Shaw is here and we are going to ensure he knows he is not welcome."

She blanches. "Cooper, don't do anything foolish."

"Please take Maudie away. We will deal with him."

"I'd like to know what you mean about dealing with him."

"He is not welcome here."

"Who is not welcome where?" Leo asks, catching up to us. I peer around him and catch Berger's eye again, then elbow Georgia in Maudie's direction.

"Toby Shaw has invited himself to our party, Rigs. What do you think of that?"

"I think I will politely tell him to leave. You've got steam coming out of your ears, Trux. Please don't shed blood at my parents' house."

As soon as Maudie is on Georgia's arm and on her way to the terrace, Anderson Oliver scoots by us to the hall and gets in Toby's face before we can.

"Out, old boy. They don't want you here." He places a hand on his back to steady him.

"I just want to talk to her. Her father won't even let me talk to her."

He's plainly drunk.

"She doesn't want to talk to you," Berger says, scowling over Ollie's shoulder. "The lady has been quite clear about that. Run along."

Toby's eyes light up when he sees Leo, who he called a friend after so many outings together with Georgia and Maudie. "Rigby," he calls. "Delightful party."

"It is a delightful party, but I am afraid you were not invited."

"Sure I was."

"You would have been welcome as the guest of my dear friend, but as you are not with her, I must ask you to leave."

"Come on, Rigby. I just want to talk to her. It was just a little spat. You know Maudie. She got a little emotional. There's been a big misunderstanding."

"Perhaps you could write her a letter and explain everything," Oliver interjects. "That would be the surest way to explain yourself. I'll deliver it personally so you don't have to speak with her father."

Ollie is so damn nice, and my fists are already twitching.

"A letter's a great idea," Berger says, hulking over my right

32

shoulder. "There's nothing like a love letter to soften the heart of a woman who wants your head on a pike. You're going through all of us if you think you'll see her tonight." Leo is at my left, and with Oliver at his side, my teammates and I make as formidable a front in evening dress as we ever did on the football field.

Toby tries me next. "Trux, come on. I need to see her."

The alcohol on his breath could knock out the General Assembly. Down with temperance—this is almost amusing.

"What's so important you must say it tonight?" I ask. "This is half Rigby's party and half mine, and he clearly doesn't want you here. I like Ollie's idea of a letter."

"I just want to apologize."

"And put women's suffrage back on your platform?"

"Ah, no."

"Then there's no misunderstanding. Good evening."

I turn around and lock gazes with Oliver as he steps forward to remove his drunken friend.

"Now, wait a minute," Toby says.

"Yes?"

"I love her."

I whirl around and drop the smile. "I am sure you have great affection for her, but so do we. And your actions have spoken louder than your words when it comes to your respect for her or any woman."

He snorts. "That's rich coming from a man who buys whores. Does it really serve your pride if you must pay them to say how splendid you are?"

My gut churns. "I am honest with whoever I am involved with and I do not take anyone's feelings lightly. You drop hints and make promises as it suits you, then change the terms with no care for who you hurt. In that regard, I will always be a more honorable man than you."

He staggers forward and Oliver catches him around the shoulders.

I ease him aside and smack Toby's back to force him upright. He jolts a little when he looks at me through bleary eyes as though he's forgotten we were just speaking.

"Hey, Trux."

"Come on, old boy. Let's have a walk."

"I want to see her."

"Well, maybe she's around here somewhere."

I lead him onto the terrace, praying Georgia has taken Maudie out of sight. On the opposite side of the party, in front of my house, a row of carriages waits for guests to hire. I intend to deposit him in one and give the driver a large tip in advance for dropping him off a bridge.

Maudie's brother in Washington, D.C. writes me often and tells me he is no friend to the Shaws and their politics. He's thrilled his sister's mésalliance is at an end, and it is no surprise to either of us that Toby should turn out so faithless. His father served several terms in the assembly before procuring a seat in the House of Representatives, and the Shaws' cunning and shifty ambitions are well-known. Toby has his eye on his father's old seat in the Wilmington district and will bend with the breeze on any subject to get his foot in the door.

Maudie must have fancied a life at Toby's side as the dutiful hostess but also an influential voice in political conversations. God, what a picture he must have sold her. What a cheap bill of goods it all was in the end when he yanked the rug out from beneath her dreams.

He picked the wrong girl to tolerate disrespect. I'll dump this drunken oaf in a carriage and run to Maudie, lock the door, and give myself up to anything she wants. She says she wants no rules or expectations— but perhaps she has no idea what she's doing. My stomach is unsettled when it occurs to me that right now, neither do I.

This is my sister's best friend. She's a lady—exactly the kind of woman I have avoided since I was eighteen—and I am near ready to fling myself at her feet for another kiss.

"Maudie'll understand," Toby slurs.

"I don't think you understand her very well if you think she'll accept you back."

"Oh, I understand her. About as well as a man can understand a woman, you know."

I halt and look around. We are only a few feet from the open gate, and Leo, Berger, and Ollie are several steps behind us. Georgia and Maudie are nowhere in sight.

"You know, Toby, you might rub my indiscretions in my face all you like." I sling an arm around his shoulder like we're old friends. "We are very different men. But when I politely offered to kill you earlier, Miss Maudie assured me that you did not dishonor her. She was most discreet about this entire sad affair. I trust her. Therefore, I think you are a liar." I raise my voice just enough for my friends to hear. "In fact, I would be most offended to hear you make any further assumption that you understand her in a familiar way."

"I'll say what I like. I want to see her. She can come tell me to shut up."

Leo doesn't want bloodshed on his parents' property, and I respect that. I'm sure my father feels the same. But he's not here to remind me and I don't have his scruples, so I shove

Toby Shaw through the gate and welcome him to my back garden with a fist to the face.

And so, it all fell apart.

I have suffered an entire month now. I have woken each morning splayed like a starfish and stiff as an iron rod, staring at my ceiling and counting down days until I can leave Hillside, move down to Raleigh, and never disgrace myself in front of Maudie again.

In all my youthful follies, it never occurred to me to take a woman to my bedroom under my parents' roof in the middle of a party. I have never been so reckless—and this from the idiot who nearly lit the altar cloth on fire one Christmas balancing burning Advent candles on my nose. She melted my brain like wax with her innocent words, and, fool that I am, instead of taking my cue and asking to call on her like any decent man would, I pawed her like an animal in the shadow of the Rigbys' forsythia.

Certainly some of her behavior was due to her heartache over that bastard Shaw. That desire could not have been all for me. I've felt that frustration—the hurt of being misunderstood and unappreciated. Wanting to be wanted. Oh, I have felt that.

The sky is pink outside my curtains and the floor creaks in the hallway as my parents make their way downstairs for breakfast. I heard Mabel and Victor arrive an hour ago to begin the day's work, but even the smell of coffee hasn't lured me from my bed and my self-pity. I uncurl my fingers one at a time, cracking my knuckles as I open my fists and relive that night again. Toby was soft and drunk and not really worth fighting. I could have slung him into the gutter without a scene and found my way upstairs into Maudie's arms.

I am not surprised my parents let me off with only a few stern words once they learned what Toby implied. Southern chivalry is a fine excuse for a man who can't mind his temper. Jealous men, please join us in old Dixie where we are immediately forgiven—nay, celebrated—for punching a man who once dared lay a kiss on the lips of a woman we think is above his station. How we love to cloak our rage and insecurities by defending women who don't need it. Even if a lady went with such a man willingly, he might find himself on the wrong side of a fight.

And oh, the gut-wrenching irony of what I would do if she went with me willingly.

But as soon as I broke free of the small crowd that gathered around the scuffle, I raced upstairs to find my room and Georgia's empty.

The next day, Hayes edited his cartoon and added one more figure—a comical little version of me in evening dress, ironically labeled 'Honor,' sucker-punching the supplicant at Lady Liberty's feet. The powerful woman standing on her principles while a man cowered before her was relegated to the background and the focus shifted to two pathetic boys.

It should have been her triumph, and with one entirely unnecessary swing of my fist, I ruined it. I saved her a dozen copies of the paper as I said I would. It's just as well that she left with her parents for their annual seaside vacation the next day because I can't bear to give them to her.

A knock comes on my door. "Breakfast, darling."

"Thank you, Mama, I am not hungry."

She swats my foot. "What has happened to your appetite? Mabel is making French toast."

"I'll be down in a minute."

I yawn and glare at the ceiling once more before rolling off the bed and inspecting my bloodshot eyes in the mirror. My hair is spiraling in ten different directions. I look like a walking hangover, and I didn't even drink last night.

Oh, and the wretched temperance measure passed and the entire state must comply in a matter of months. Many businesses have already stopped or reduced the sale of alcohol, citing restrictions from suppliers.

I cannot even have a drink in a dark pub and pour out my misery to my best friend anymore. I doubt this will ever leave my mouth sober. Telling Leo I've laid hands and lips on Georgia's best friend might make his perfectly pomaded head explode. Then, after piecing his brain back together, he would drag me to a jeweler's for an engagement ring so I might make amends for my disrespect.

If I ate a slice of cake and didn't like it, would I apologize to the baker by swearing to only eat that cake until the end of time?

If she regretted what happened and thought I disrespected her, why would being stuck with me for a lifetime be a suitable apology for my disrespect?

This entire thing was reckless and unconscionable and completely out of character for her, but from the moment she dragged me off the terrace and demanded I touch her, I was lost. I was so far gone I begged for her hands, something I have never done with any woman. I have always been in

38

charge. But in the time it took her to say *be a rogue or a gentleman, just you* I wanted to give myself to her entirely.

It shattered something in me.

I don't know what *just you* even means, except maybe it's the man she thinks she'll find when she touches me. I don't know who the hell he is, and I need to sleep somewhere I haven't imagined her undressing me and telling me she wants to see every part of my soul.

I need to forget this. I am not a marrying man, now or perhaps ever, I think.

I thought.

I don't know.

What I do know is that there are lines I must not cross again if I wish to keep my status as rogue and not reduce myself to a varmint.

She's due back from her family vacation tomorrow and I still have twenty-seven days before I can pack my trunks and move into a boarding house in the city where there are thousands of beautiful women who have never kissed my lips, played with my hair, and said they wanted me just for myself.

Chapter 5
Maudie

Papa wrangles his spectacles from their case and peers over my shoulder. "Registration ends August twentieth," he reads, "and after that, you have four weeks to withdraw from a course if you wish. That seems very reasonable."

I murmur agreement and flip a page. I sent away for a booklet about the women's college in Raleigh shortly after we arrived at the seaside for our vacation and I didn't unpack so much as a hairbrush before snatching it from our pile of accumulated post when we got home.

"Does it say whether you must declare a course of study?" he asks.

"There is an option to take general studies courses for one year."

"That could be useful."

"Yes, Papa."

My most productive conversations on this matter have been with my brother, who was with us on vacation, and Matthew and Angeline Berger. The Bergers have a vacation home near ours on the Outer Banks, and I am used to seeing all seven of the brothers and sisters in and out of sandy beaches, dusty verandas, and salty waters. Matthew is a year younger than my brother, and while Angeline and I are the same age, we have never been especially close. Yet this summer, she seems to have mellowed in her recent engagement, and we spent many evenings poring over her wedding plans and discussing this tiny tickle of an idea about going to college.

Matthew reminded me that he will be in Raleigh this fall as well, starting his legal studies. And between him and Angeline, they rattled off a dozen more friends from Hillside who I would know either in the college itself or elsewhere in the city. My brother Jeremiah wholeheartedly endorses the entire thing, even if he does joke a little too often about college being a fine place for me to snag a rich husband.

I hope he enjoys the sand I dumped in his trunk.

Mama joins me on the settee and for her peace of mind I flip to the section of the booklet about living arrangements. "Men may not visit ladies in the dormitory, Mama, unless they are family." I point out a photo of a cozy room with twin beds, tidy desks, and lace curtains. "Visitors must check in and out."

"How does that work if you have a gentleman caller?"

"I believe there are common areas for meeting. I shall find out, if it would set your mind at ease."

"I'm sure you will not go unnoticed, darling."

"Who will be around to notice me? I look forward to meeting my classmates, and since all meals are in the dining hall, I will not have to go out and about off campus much. If I do, I'm sure I will have many friends to accompany me. Look at all the clubs I could join. There will be so much to do right there. Who needs gentleman callers?"

"Matthew will be close by," Papa says. "And Cooper Truxton. Either of them could escort you home on weekends, if you wish. They were both home often when they were at East Piedmont."

Turning a page with a trembling hand, I keep my head down so they don't see me blush.

Mama looks up from the booklet. "What is Cooper doing in Raleigh?"

"A program at A&M, apparently." He turns to me. "Didn't Georgia think at one time he might not finish college at all? And now he's going back for more?"

"She said he had a hard time focusing his energy for a while." I bite my cheek, trying to recall the flighty boy he'd been and not the young man whose tender kiss still simmers on my lips. "He's quite excited about his new agriculture program, though. He says with President Roosevelt's new Forest Service, there are many opportunities to use his engineering degree along with whatever he learns next."

"Mmph. How do you find a roommate?"

"The school can assign one, or I can make a request. Angeline suggested I reach out to Victoria Harper. She attended last year but her roommate got married."

That's another thing about the Bergers. Not only are there quite a lot of them, they know everything about everybody. It's thanks to their good-natured rumor mill that everyone we grew up with knows at least a little about Cooper's reputation from his college days. No one shares details, but Angeline once told me that when it comes to gossip, sometimes what we don't say is more powerful than what we do say. Cooper's friends call him a rogue and he laughs about it, so whatever he's done obviously isn't degenerate or worth casting him out of polite society. It certainly hasn't stopped good families from flinging their daughters at him like bait to a lazy, uninterested fish.

Satisfied with my response, Papa moves on to questions about coursework and I exhale in relief, glad to be done with Cooper. I dread the moment he finds out I am going to Raleigh for school. I'll look like a silly girl vying for his attention and anxious to show my devotion at his side at the football matches. That's not why I'm going, but oh, it will look like that.

He will tease me about it all being his brilliant idea. I do want to thank him, but I don't need to look or feel any more desperate.

I've spent weeks trying to put the night of the party out of my head, pretending he never kissed me and that I have never seen his eyes so raw with emotion. That naked yearning is not what I expected from someone with the experience people say he has, and I wonder sometimes if I am making some sort of girlish projection and looking for feelings that aren't there. Every night when I dress for bed, I feel his hands glide over me and my thoughts race to what might have happened if Georgia hadn't pulled me away when Mr. Shaw staggered in and ruined everything.

The scoundrel is back in Wilmington now, no doubt, and good riddance. I have now turned down marriage proposals from two decent, boring men and one absolute cad, and I will do more with my life than wait on any man to propose ever again. I will join the League of Women Voters and the tennis club and the Horticulture Society. My friends are getting married and having babies, and I will take courses in biology and government and commit myself to finding out what's best for me.

If someone comes along, whoever he is, he's going to have to fit with me this time, not the other way around.

But Cooper's hands fit me so beautifully, and that's proving very hard to forget.

Chapter 6
Cooper

Leo has proven true to his word and brings back liquor every time he goes to Virginia for work, building up a decent stash so we'll have a cushion for our bad habits when the state ban on alcohol goes into effect. As skittish suppliers clamp down on shipping to North Carolina, this backward state is somewhat less annoying when we are in our little makeshift speakeasy in his home. Georgia, in her early days of pregnancy, is often tired early and does not stay up with us, but she welcomes me and our friends with open doors and an open heart. During the month Maudie was at the seaside, we developed an informal schedule of drinks and dinner twice a week with old friends.

On the day everyone came home, we added Angeline Berger and her fiancé, her brother Matthew, and Maudie.

Hugs were given, cheeks were kissed, and formalities dropped among friends. Our parents' rules seem so foolish in the privacy of our generation's homes, and when Leo opens a bottle of the same fine brandy my father prefers, we feel quite grown up and in charge of our own destinies.

I keep my composure when I greet Maudie and ask about her vacation, and she smiles warmly as though I am merely her best friend's brother again.

"I hear you have taken me up on my idea about college," I say when I can find a quiet corner to speak with her.

Her jaw drops. "How did you know?"

"You know your brother and I correspond regularly."

"Silly me, of course. Well, I thank you for the fine idea. You were right that it stuck in my head, and now I am quite excited to begin a new phase of my life."

I cannot hold back a grin. "I am pleased to be of any service to you. I may not have been the most admirable student, but college was a wonderful experience that expanded my mind and perspectives, and I think you will enjoy that as well."

"I am staggered by the list of opportunities for courses and clubs. I should have looked into this much sooner."

"There is a Chinese proverb that states the best time to plant a tree is twenty years ago. The second best time is today."

Her smile is so kissable. "What a perfect proverb for a tree man. And perhaps for me. I thought of you the other day when Papa had the papers from New York. Your poor chestnut trees at the Bronx Zoo. My heart ached for you a bit when I saw how bad it's gotten."

"You are so kind to remember how that matters to me." My pulse quickens. "I mean it, Maudie. Not many people take that very seriously about me. I know it is a bit of a wild obsession, but it captivates me and I cannot let it go."

She looks down. "You are a passionate man. I am not surprised in the least."

Angeline chooses this moment to cut in on our conversation with her fiancé Gregory Anson. She sips a glass of white wine and offers one to Maudie, who accepts it but does not bring it to her lips as Angeline dives in with a long ramble about wedding plans as though I am not standing there.

"Are you one of Angeline's bridesmaids now?" I ask when the couple finally turns away.

"I am. She and I had a lovely time at the beach going over her wedding plans, and I think we have become better friends."

"She was not always especially nice to you in the past. Gossip, and all that."

I take a swallow of my brandy and savor it on my tongue. Its forbidden status makes it all the more delectable these days. Maudie shrugs, still not sipping her wine. "Anyone can change, and I like to look for the best in people instead of holding grudges. Angeline has found her direction in life with Gregory, and her happiness shows. Even her gossip is a little less sharp-edged these days. I am quite thrilled for her."

"You always do this, Maudie."

"Do what?"

"You are always so happy for your friends' happiness and never begrudge them what they have, even if it's something you want. You are never jealous or spiteful. I am in awe of how you do it, for it is not something that comes naturally to me. It is no wonder they hold you so dear."

She blushes prettily. "That is very sweet of you to notice, Cooper."

Suddenly, I cannot meet her eyes, and I have to grip my glass tighter to keep my hand from shaking with all my pent-up need to touch her. I might be imagining it, but she seems to be trembling as well.

"May I speak with you a little more privately?" I ask. "Just over there, maybe, so no one thinks much of it."

She sits on the third stair in Leo and Georgia's front hall, spreading her skirts to keep me at a distance. "What do you wish to talk about?"

"I would like to offer an apology for my disrespectful behavior at the party."

"No apology is needed. I did not feel disrespected."

"I am grateful you feel that way, but—Maudie, it's not only when we—" I stumble and take another sip of my brandy for courage. "I made a scene with Toby, and in fighting with him, I not only ruined the possibility of spending more time with you that evening, I ruined the statement your cartoon was meant to make about your principles and convictions. I reduced it to brawling boys like we were fighting over you."

"Georgia told me what Mr. Shaw said. He lied. I appreciate that you corrected him."

"I could have corrected him more quietly. But you had just told me you'd never done anything with him, so to hear that from your lips and then to hear such a lie from his infuriated me beyond belief. I should have handled it differently. I am sorry."

"What's done is done. I have tried not to dwell on anything that happened that night."

My heart sinks. "Of course. So have I."

"I'm glad we are friends, Cooper." She adjusts her skirts again. "And I am glad I might see you in Raleigh from time to time."

"Any time you like." I clear my throat to keep my voice from wobbling.

She only nods in response.

"All of the football games, remember?"

She flicks a wave. "It's a shame I cannot watch you play again, but I'm sure I shall find someone else to hold my attention."

"I am bereft." I fall back into the familiar banter, and it's almost as good as it was.

"I would still like to come. You and your friends made me a fan of the game. I see there is even a Football Boosters Club at my new school, and Matthew said he may accompany me as well when his schedule allows."

"But I asked you first."

"You more or less demanded it." She arches a brow. "It's more fun to have a group, anyway."

"Lucky for me then that his course schedule is much more strenuous than mine. What are you taking?"

We talk of mundane things, classes and programs and clubs. I notice eyes on us from time to time: the Bergers and Leo specifically. My glass is empty, and I don't leave for a refill even when Matthew lifts his glass to signal I should top off with him. I cannot drink another drop tonight. I cannot lose control of my tongue or I might try to slip it back between her lips before begging her to touch me again.

Chapter 7
Maudie

By late July, my plans for college are falling into place, and the fresh start energizes me every morning when I reach for one of my old schoolbooks. I am determined to re-read everything from my last year of high school to get my mind back in shape for the classroom. I may be a few years older than most of the freshman class, but I will not fall behind. I might major in anything from mathematics to nursing to history or education—my world is a blank slate today, and I want to take it all in before declaring a program next year.

Cooper called one day when I was out and left a stack of newspapers with articles marked about a suffrage rally and the upcoming college football season. *Not kidding*, he scrawled in black ink next to a circled list of dates. I am glad we cleared the air at Georgia's house, but we left what happened between us rather open-ended, and I am a little bit ashamed of how glad I am about that. I think of it. I dream of it. But I won't run after him to pursue it. Football games are fine as friends, but it will be best to put some space between us. This college experience is about me, not about a man—until Matthew Berger shatters my peace with terrible news.

He presents me with a posy of daisies as though he's making a formal call, but as soon as I invite him to sit, he starts to pace my sitting room.

"Your daisies look a lot happier than you do," I observe. "Something is wrong."

"I have news you will not like, and I wished to deliver it with some haste so you do not hear it anywhere else."

My thoughts shoot immediately to Cooper, wondering if someone saw us the night of the party and is now spreading rumors. I swallow thickly and nod at Matthew to go on.

"Toby Shaw is not qualified to run for office in the Wilmington district as he planned because he was resident in Hillside and voted here for all four of his college years. Ambrose Shockley has announced he will not seek re-election here, and Toby is going after his seat."

My mouth hangs open like a fish and I flop back against the settee in an ungainly slouch. Matthew rushes to sit by me and grabs both of my hands. "I thought of you immediately and wanted you to know. To prepare yourself, somehow."

"That was so thoughtful of you." My voice seems to echo. "I appreciate your consideration for my comfort."

"I would have punched him if Cooper hadn't. He betrayed an important promise to you, Maudie. We all know that, and a man like that is not to be trusted."

"We should campaign against him." I sit straighter. "We must. People should know what kind of man they are electing. He will compromise on any of his so-called principles. He wasn't for temperance until it was widely popular, you know. Suffrage, obviously, is a sticking point for me. But many times he talked with me about taking varying positions for advantage in different voting populations."

"Yet so far, he looks to be unopposed."

"I don't suppose you have time in your schedule to join the state legislature."

He offers a wry smile. "I am honored you consider me qualified, but no. It is the sort of thing I might consider after my law degree and a few years in practice. It's a damn shame, pardon me, that you cannot do it. You could tear him to pieces."

I could. For a year and a half, I was Mr. Shaw's confidant and learned more about his political scheming than anyone outside of his father's advisors, who have been plotting his path since birth. He fancied himself so smart, telling me how he would strategize this and that. Fool that I am, I didn't realize that the things I thought we held dear together might be strategized out for his convenience.

"We must know someone who would make a viable candidate to go against a carpetbagger," I say. "I shall write to my brother about the men he was in school with here. Perhaps one of your other classmates would be interested. Mr. Oliver would be very suitable were he not also new to the area. He is most personable."

"Ollie's nice, but he's bland." Matthew shakes his head. "A new man on the scene should make a splash. No one talks when they haven't got someone interesting to talk about. Are you going to Leo and Georgia's tonight? We'll put our heads together and come up with something."

"Someone," I reply. "We must come up with someone."

That afternoon, I am the first to arrive besides Cooper, who is sprawled on a sofa in Leo's study with his nose in a magazine about forest conservation.

"How are the trees?" I ask him.

"The hickories and beechnuts are trying to fill in the gaps," he says, not looking up. "I approve."

I leave him to his trees and spend an hour flipping through the college booklet with Georgia before the Bergers arrive, along with our friend Brent Hayes and his new lady friend, Angeline's neighbor Emilia Dodd. Around the table, my friends' faces look like mine did, mouths agape, when Matthew delivers the update on Mr. Shaw and his campaign.

"It cannot stand," I announce. "Not only is he opposed to the causes we all support, he will not do right by our friends and neighbors. They deserve better. We must find another candidate to support so he does not sail into the legislature unopposed when Mr. Shockley retires."

"We already talked about Ollie," Matthew says. "He might do well, but he's an outsider like Shaw when it comes down to it, and I think a local would be better."

Everyone murmurs agreement.

"I asked Gregory," adds Angeline. "He said he will think about it, but he's new on the job at the bank and his supervisors may not like it."

"His supervisors report to my father," Leo says. "Perhaps we could work something out. If Papa were a more personable sort, I'd recommend him."

"Georgia, what about your father?" I ask. "He is so well-regarded here and in the city. Your family has been here for generations and has a familiar name. He is a moderate, which I think would play well against Mr. Shaw's more radical platform."

"We could certainly ask him." Jabbing Cooper, who is idly flipping pages in his magazine as he thinks, she jolts him from his silence. "Would Papa do it, do you think? Or will he make the standard 'tired old man' complaint to retire early each night as he has done lately?"

I hold up a finger. "No."

The whispers around the table stop and all eyes turn to me.

"Cooper's going to do it."

Jaws drop again and he looks up at me, laughing. "Oh, of course. On my way to Buckingham Palace, I'll drop by the governor's mansion and share my opinions."

"I mean it. What are your politics?"

He holds up two fingers. "I'm a Roosevelt man, and he's on his way out. He gave me forestry and football. That's not a platform."

"You have your family's name and history, just like your father. You are young and charismatic and can connect with people."

"And I'll be in school full-time, so when will I campaign? All the work that must go into it, from fliers to debates and door-to-door canvassing... listen, even if I were a good candidate, I cannot commit to all of that."

"You *are* a good candidate, come to think of it," Matthew says. "You'll get every vote out of EPC because you're a football hero, and Shaw can't hold a candle to that. You'll get most every vote out of A&M just because you're one of them now. Students lean progressive."

"A Truxton will get every vote in Hillside over a stranger, regardless of party," Angeline adds.

Cooper sighs heavily, shoulders slumping as he leans back in his chair. "Your faith in me is very flattering, but to the ladies in the room, please forgive me, it is no secret that I frequented brothels for several years. Although I have not done so in months, this is something Shaw knows and would use against me. We should ask my father. We should ask Leo's father about Gregory. This will not work."

His admission of his visits to brothels doesn't shake me. I suspected it was something like that, even though women are not supposed to know. It's a thing some men do, or at least that's what we're given to believe. While ladies may not like it, they generally do not raise a fuss.

This is far more important than how I feel, so, I will not raise a fuss.

"Everyone loves a redemption story, Trux," Brent says, patting his chest. "And you've got your own personal political cartoonist right here if you want to do a little muckraking in the press. I know people who will print what I draw, and if you've got a little money to throw into leaflets and the like, whatever he slings at you, we sling back."

Cooper lowers his forehead to the table and groans. "I don't want to sling anything else. I already punched him at a party."

"Defending a lady's honor," Matthew says. "That sells well around here. Telling that story will speak to his character."

He looks up at me as though I'm the only person in the

room. "Football and forestry. How do I run a campaign on that? I don't know how to run a campaign at all."

"But I do."

The buzz around us fades when his eyes spark with the same naked emotion I saw the night of the party. *What are we doing?* he asks me, deeply unsure beneath his sarcastic, confident mask. *What am I doing?*

"You'll have classes too," he says.

"I'll also have the Ladies' Republican Club, the League of Women Voters, the Horticulture Society…" I reach for my booklet, which Georgia and I were reviewing before everyone arrived. "The Botany Club, the Football Boosters, the Raleigh Parks Supporters, and a host of others who align with your interests."

"But they can't—"

"Add suffrage as a talking point and you'll have some very persuasive ladies going door-to-door talking about how grand you are."

Matthew lets out a low whistle and mutters something about never underestimating women.

"And do you know what else you have?" I cannot believe this is only now occurring to me, and suddenly I'm patting the table in excitement. "You've got North Carolina jobs that depend on trees. The furniture industry is so important to this state. We need chestnut timber and the current clear-cutting practices have got to stop or people will lose jobs if they flood us with supply and then have nothing left. We can't replace old trees with hickory and beechnut saplings fast enough. Cooper, there it is. It distracts from your past and focuses on the future, on a topic very few people have probably ever considered because right now, it's far away.

Platforms are practical, but votes are emotional. This could be both."

The room is silent as I hold his gaze. His uncertainty has vanished and his brown eyes are warm with amusement. "Bull's eye," he murmurs. "You know my weaknesses, Maudie."

Cheeks burning, I shake my head. "Your passions are not weaknesses. They make you who you are."

He gulps, and my fingers twitch to trace the line of his jaw and his neck the way I did the night of the party, kissing him and exploring him so brazenly. Now, in the warm glow of my best friend's dining room, I am swamped again with the desire to find out who he is beneath that smart suit and lackadaisical smile. Leaning back in his chair, arms crossed, eyes raking me like he would reach beneath my dress again, everything about him speaks of wry amusement and ease—except his eyes, and I cannot look away from him.

Georgia clears her throat. "Cooper, perhaps you could ask Papa if he will support you. There will be fundraising, but we must start with an investment."

"You must find out everything you can about Mr. Shaw's plans," I tell Matthew and Angeline. "When and where he plans to announce, for one thing. Even if Cooper decides not to run, we must gather a crowd to protest and make sure everyone knows that whoever would step up to run against him will have great support."

Cooper winks, as sardonic as ever. "If I decide not to run?" he drawls. "I don't recall being offered a choice."

Chapter 8
Cooper

After our friends have gone home and only Berger and I remain at Leo's house, I summon them to the study.

"Listen, fellows. I appreciate your support and faith in me. But are you sure we couldn't just knock that little rat over the head and leave him in a bootlegger's cart full of moonshine up in the hills somewhere? We don't drink that shit. No one would know it was us."

Berger nearly chokes laughing. "And no one would miss a class," he wheezes. "Your new-found dedication to your education knows no bounds."

"Precisely. Thank you."

"But then no one would save the trees with you." Leo caps the decanter and raises his glass to me. "Maudie got you there."

"It is a shame she could not run for office herself."

"I said the same," Berger says. "I admire her more and more every day. Has she always been like this and I just never noticed?"

Leo clinks his glass against mine. "Has she always been like what?"

"She has always been lovely in the ways girls are brought up to be. The things my sisters are supposed to do, like playing piano and embroidering and all that. She's a lady, and a fine one. A stunning one as well, my God..." He pushes his hair back from his face as though the sudden admission of her beauty shocks him. "But I got to know her a little better this summer at the shore, and she's so refreshing to talk to about anything. She takes pains to be well-informed and she isn't a parrot of other people's opinions. My sister Catherine had half a dozen friends in and out of the house all month and not one of them was worth a conversation."

Georgia pokes her head into the study, smiling. "Be nice. Girls Catherine's age have so much growing up to do. They are almost never worth a conversation."

"You were," Leo and I say together.

"In any case, Matthew, it's a very kind observation about Maudie. She really is delightful, and her fine conversation skills seem honed to push Cooper around." She squeezes my shoulders and leans over the sofa to whisper. "And I think you liked it."

Liked it?

She practically stripped me naked with her eyes with that challenge to not just love my passions but to act on them. And when she started ticking off tree facts that she remembered because they are important to me, I could have jumped across the table and kissed her—but I don't think that was the passion she was talking about.

I liked it, but this will be too much. I'll wave signs and go to rallies and wear a women's suffrage ribbon to class if she wants, but I cannot run for office, even for her. Berger hit the tip of the iceberg when he called her stunning. I am drawn to more than the delectable shape of her body or the silken curls I long to tangle in my hands again. She is luminous when she thinks aloud and likely my intellectual superior in every way.

All I would do is let her down.

"Well, since I have you both here," Berger says, gesturing between Leo and Georgia, "how do I do it? Or really, how did you do it?"

"Do what?" they ask in unison. Equally confused, I take a sip of my brandy and wait in silence.

"Leo, how did you convince Georgia to marry the man she always thought of as the foolish neighbor boy?"

I try to swallow but the brandy mixes with the bile rising in my throat. Thank God their attention is on Leo and no one sees me turn away as I vomit it all up in my glass, barely containing an audible retch.

Leo cocks a brow, amused at Berger's question. "I became a desperate flirt and brought her lots of flowers, hoping she'd get the point. She thought I was joking."

"That was Cooper's fault," Georgia adds, sticking out her tongue at me.

Still wheezing and fighting back acid, I pound my chest when they look at me. "Sorry about that," I gasp. "Sorry. Swallowed my drink wrong." I tuck the glass and its disgusting contents behind my back and edge toward a shelf to hide it.

"After that, I found that a few romantic soliloquies cleared the air and made my intentions clear." Leo pulls his wife to his side and rests his hand on her stomach. "And now I am blessed beyond measure."

Georgia kisses his cheek. "Those were a dramatic few months, but in hindsight, I suppose it's quite simple. Talk to her. That's all it came down to, in the end. No more assumptions or confusion. We had to talk about it."

"The kissing helped," Leo adds with a wink.

Berger nods. "I suppose the question is more around what to say to test the waters. We had a few lovely evenings at the ocean. Porch swings, walks on the beach, and so on. It was all just friendly, though, with lots of people around."

"Tell her what you told us," Leo suggests. "I think Maudie will appreciate a compliment on her intelligence and the pleasure of her company more than any flattery about her looks."

My stomach churns at the thought of Maudie and Berger side-by-side in a porch swing or strolling in the sand.

"Counter to my husband's advice I suggest holding off on any kissing," Georgia says. "Maudie has kissed one man in her life, and after Mr. Shaw let her down so terribly, I wonder if she's even interested in kissing anyone else any time soon."

For some psychic, sisterly reason, she turns to me, meets my eyes, and blinks.

I'm doomed.

My sister and I have gotten into too much trouble together for her not to recognize how I look when I'm hiding something. She doesn't know what happened—I can see that as plainly in her face as she can read the panic in mine—but she will not let me leave her house tonight without an explanation.

Her tone shifts. "As a matter of fact, Matthew, I question the wisdom of courting her at all right now. She told me earlier today how much she wants to build a new life for herself and explore the world a little more before opening her heart again. This might not be the best time, although I am sure she values your friendship."

"I'll take my leave now." I tug at my shirt collar and try to hide the rasp in my raw throat. "It was good to see all of you."

"It's not yet eight o'clock," Leo protests.

"Well, I may have a late night ahead of me."

Berger elbows my ribs with a lascivious wink. "Have fun."

I know what he thinks of my late nights. He's been on a few of them. I have no idea how much Maudie knows or suspects about any of it, but she's not deaf and I'm not stupid. It aches to know that she might think I wanted to touch her the way I touched those other women—and yet there's no way she could think otherwise. Because I have shielded myself so well from anything approaching a normal courtship, I call myself a rogue and laugh about it even though she is the only woman I've ever kissed and not paid.

I step back. "That type of late night is behind me. My supper isn't sitting well, though, so I'll bid you good evening."

I grab my glass from the bookshelf and head for the front door with a quick detour to the kitchen to dispose of my brandy-tinged disgrace. Georgia's skirts swish behind me but I don't turn around until she yanks on my arm.

"What have you done?" she demands.

Trying not to breathe in her face, I don't look up. "I was just washing up my glass."

"Must I go ask Maudie? What have you done?"

"Nothing."

She cups my chin in her hand and pulls my face up. "Oh, Cooper," she whispers. "This is not like you."

I shake off her grip and don't reply.

"Please tell me what happened. I love you both, brother. Please."

"We danced together at my graduation party. Talked a bit." I slouch. "When I saw her dancing with Berger, I got a little jealous. Then I punched Toby and ruined her night, and that was that."

"You didn't ruin her night. She was looking for you to be sure you were all right."

"How unfortunate I missed her."

She eyes me like I am a naughty child. "You did not just dance with her, did you?"

"I told you, we talked for a while."

"Your hands are shaking."

I shove them in my pockets and look down the hall to ensure Leo and Berger are still in the study. "Is it enough to tell you I apologized for showing her any disrespect and she countered by saying she did not feel disrespected? We are fine. Maudie and I are fine."

"You are obviously not fine. You are still jealous."

I say nothing.

"Cooper, why don't you just—"

"Because if I am to court a woman, her, or any woman, I should know what I want. And I don't. I thought I knew I didn't want any of this, and now... I must be sure, and it's unfair to pretend I am."

"That's nonsense. Courtship is when you decide what you want. It's when you get to know a friend in a different way, in this case. These things take time. How can you know if you do not try?"

"I do not like that kind of uncertainty."

"Well, I do not like eggplant, but I put up with it on my

table for my husband's sake."

"Marriage is not an eggplant."

"What an astute observation. Do forgive me for not accepting your expertise on the matter of marriage. Did you kiss her?"

"Really, Georgia. She said she did not feel disrespected and I had nothing to apologize for. Leave it at that."

"So you kissed her."

I lean back against the front door, knocking my head on its heavy oak panel. "Yes."

"Have you thought of her like this before? Why now?"

Because we danced on the terrace among the trees and the lanterns and the night air got to my head. Because something about being hurt by that toad of a man put a new spark in her eyes, and I love to play with fire. Because I'm used to doing whatever I want, and I wanted to.

Because I'm a spoiled boy, and I just wanted to.

"Perhaps I just pushed the bounds of friendly banter a little too far." Even to myself, I've downplayed the notion of wanting to touch her for a long time. "And in any case, she made it quite clear she wanted to leave that evening behind, so even if I wanted to court her, and I don't, I wouldn't."

She rolls her eyes. "Yet you vomited in my good crystal when Matthew said he wanted to."

"I didn't think anyone saw that."

"I didn't. I smelled it."

"Oh. I'm sorry."

When Georgia and Leo were first together, I struggled mightily with jealousy and spite at sharing my beloved sibling with my best friend and feeling excluded as they grew closer without me. That my sister is here comforting me and trying to talk me through this feels entirely undeserved, a thought that twists my stomach like a cramp when I think of how much faith Maudie placed in me by asking me to run for this office. I have not earned that from either of them.

Be a rogue or a gentleman. Just you. Whoever you are under this.

"Please tell Maudie she has my full support for any other candidate or cause she wishes to champion, but I will not be on a ballot come November."

"This will disappoint her a great deal."

"It will disappoint her far more if I fail and Toby gets in. I cannot do it. Georgia, please tell her. Please."

"I will tell her." She glances down the hall at the study once more, just as Leo and Berger share a laugh. "And I shall do my best to divert Matthew's hopes for as long as it takes you to get your act together."

"That is not necessary."

"You just twitched like you were about to vomit again."

"I did not."

"All the same, I shall try."

Chapter 9
Maudie

I will not make a scene.

Never mind that I am only in my best friend's dining room and no one is watching but her. I will not shout about her brother's selfishness and make a scene. We are laying out pattern pieces to start her baby's layette. This should be a joyous activity, so I must be calm.

Closing my eyes, I drag in a deep breath as though I would inhale Georgia's serenity and steady myself.

"Maudie?" she asks. "Are you all right?"

I twitch my head and perk up with a snap. "Of course. I'm so sorry, I just... well. That's quite disappointing to hear Cooper is not interested. I suppose I'm not surprised, really. Who's next on our list? Did you ask your father?"

Georgia fidgets with a bolt of fine white cotton. "I did. I saw him this morning, and Cooper and I asked him together."

"And?"

Georgia's father would be perfect for this race—for politics in general, really. Along with his local pedigree and renown, Christopher Truxton is a gentleman of middle years with graying hair and a kind, paternal smile—old enough for voters to trust his experience, young enough to have the energy for the campaign and the work that will follow. His demeanor alone will make Mr. Shaw look like an immature, unpolished rube before he speaks a word.

"He cannot do it."

I drop the scissors. "But he must."

"He told us that his early nights lately have been due to a stomach ulcer that is not healing like it should."

"Oh, Georgia."

"All will be well," she says, not looking up as she spreads the cotton over the table. "The doctor says he will be fine and he does not suspect it is anything more serious. But Papa needs his rest, and he could not handle the stress of a campaign."

"I understand completely. Are you sure he—"

"The doctor says all will be well."

I turn aside in case my eyes give away my dejection and worry. There is no arguing that an ill father should take this on, but my shrinking list of options weighs on me while Georgia places and pins pattern pieces with an expert eye. I watch her closely for any sign that she does not believe her own optimistic words about her father's health, and her face is as peaceful as it was when I arrived. Spinning her heavy silver shears back and forth from hand to hand, I judge it safe to restart the conversation. It will be a distraction if she needs it.

"I could talk it through with Matthew again," I muse aloud. "He has a heavy course load as a first-year law student, but I know he cares about the same causes we do. And Leo said he could speak to his father about Gregory."

"Who even his fiancée admits is not a strong speaker."

"Matthew might do all right. I should tell him it would be excellent practice for the courtroom. I shall call at the Bergers' tomorrow and see if he and Angeline are available to chat."

She looks up from her pins. "Perhaps Cooper might still be convinced."

"If he's not interested, he's no help." I flick a wave to pretend I don't care. "Cooper is so flighty that if he's not one hundred percent committed, I would not like the risk of him taking this on and dropping out when things get rough. He quits everything. He always has."

"He's done better lately. He stayed in school for his degree, which was a miracle. And he stayed in the football program when they did nothing but lose for a year and a half. I think he's grown up a bit."

"Football and forestry," I say drily. "The platform he hasn't quit on yet. No, I will not ask him again. Could Leo do it himself?"

"He'll be in Virginia for half-weeks twice a month during the fall. It remains to be seen whether he'll even be here on Election Day." She pats her stomach. "Dr. Everett thinks I am due in early December, so we hope he'll be home for that, at least."

"Then I will write to my brother this evening for his advice and any recommendations or contacts. I'll ask Matthew and Angeline tomorrow."

"Don't ask Matthew." Turning back to her pattern, she points to a corner where the pieces are pinned and gestures for me to start cutting. "I'll ask Cooper again. Or you can. Sometimes he just takes a little convincing."

"It is so unfair that we must convince anyone." I snip the delicate cotton. "I could do this myself if I were allowed. I listened to every word Mr. Shaw said for more than a year, and I could stay a step ahead of him for an entire campaign. I know enough to beat a faithless opportunist for a seat representing our friends and family, but politics may as well be football because I cannot do anything more than watch from the sidelines."

"It is terribly unfair."

My shoulders sag as I set several trimmed pieces aside. The cutouts are so tiny and remind me of the days Georgia and I learned to sew making doll clothes together. Cooper and Leo ran around the backyard like hooligans, climbing trees and making noise, and we stayed inside and sewed useless little doll clothes.

"Speaking of football, Cooper did help us get the team wearing women's suffrage ribbons around his campus last year," she continues. "I am surprised Mr. Shaw does not think the issue will be addressed at the state level here when it has been so many other places."

"Let's move to Wyoming. We can vote there, and I hear the great buffalo is a handsome pet." I squint to snip some corners as Georgia works down the table from me, still pinning. "Cooper thinks North Carolina is holding back on women's suffrage as part of a larger view to suppressing the black man's vote as well."

"He is a voracious reader, and his opinions on politics are always well-informed."

"I agree. It's so unfortunate he will not run."

"Just ask him again."

I look up to find her staring at me, and the knowing smile on her face unnerves me. "Oh, no. He didn't."

"He told me about the party. I dragged it out of him."

"Georgia, I am so sorry I didn't tell you. I must explain."

"You do not need to explain, darling." She smiles and bites her lip to hold back a giggle. "I certainly didn't tell you everything right away when Leo and I fell in love."

"No one is falling in love here."

"Should you wish to tell me what happened, I am terribly interested. He didn't tell me much, but he also forgot to ask me not to mention it to you."

"You'd be a splendid politician as well, finding all the loopholes."

"This is why they fear our vote so much."

"Nothing really happened at the party, though." Remembering the heat of his hands on my thighs, I turn back to my work to hide my flushed cheeks. "A little kiss. That's all."

She laughs again. "That little kiss left him quite shaken. I've never seen him so unsettled by a good-natured interrogation."

"But he is your brother and you are my best friend, so he will be impossible to escape for the rest of my life. I am not some empty-headed girl who must marry a man because he kisses her. I prefer to let it go and avoid any complications between us."

"That is the most practical thing. He is stuck with me and I am glad to be stuck with you."

My hand jitters and I snip an uneven layer, leaving a jagged edge on a tiny sleeve. He was shaken?

"And if it is as you say," Georgia continues trying to hide

her smile, "and it was just a little kiss, there is no need to complicate anything. It must not have made much of an impact, anyway, but I suppose that's Cooper for you."

"Indeed."

"My noisy, cocky brother doesn't make much of a splash, does he?"

"Of course not."

"Maudie Hamilton."

I drop the scissors and cover my face with my hands. "Georgia, it was nothing, and I don't want anything from him. This is my time to establish myself on my own terms. A fresh start at school. I don't want anything from any man, any time soon."

"Except…"

Lowering my hands, I meet her eyes. "Except this. We need him. We need someone. I'll ask him again. Then you, then me, then you again until we get him or someone else to do it."

It's early afternoon when I leave Georgia's house and stop by the Truxtons' on my way home. Mabel, their maid, invites me in and disappears to find Cooper. On returning, she informs me, to my great surprise, that he'll see me in his father's study. She leaves the double doors open and lingers in the hall as a quiet chaperone, dusting the same picture frames and wainscoting over and over for my benefit. No doubt whatever we say will make it to a Berger's ears sooner rather than later, which I don't mind a bit. Any help I can get with this stubborn man is welcome.

Cooper greets me from behind Mr. Truxton's wide walnut desk with his feet propped on the blotter. "You're late," he announces, not looking up from his newspaper. "I expected a strategy meeting bright and early this morning."

"Bright and early this morning, I was at your sister's house."

"Ah, so she will have delivered my message." He still does not look at me.

"She did."

"Then you two plotted about how to use your feminine wiles to persuade me, and now you are here to try again."

"Not at all."

He looks up and I see shadows under his eyes.

"As a matter of fact, she told me not to bother asking you again because you'll never see it through and you would do our cause more harm than good."

"She certainly did not say that."

"Well, one of us said it. Georgia loves you dearly, but she isn't blind. I only stopped by on my way home to apologize for pressuring you about this last night." I offer him a handful of lilacs I plucked from the bush in front of his house, like a penitent suitor with a bouquet. "I am sorry."

Folding his paper, he lowers his feet and leans across the desk. "Did you say I would never see it through?"

He looks genuinely hurt as he places the lilacs precariously in an empty glass on the desk, but I turn my back and help myself to water from the sideboard. After I settle on the sofa, I bring my glass to my lips to hide a smile. "We must be practical, Cooper. Votes are emotional, but platforms are practical—and like you said, you don't have much of one, anyway. You were right, and I was far too pushy."

"You were just excited. I am honestly flattered it even crossed your mind."

"Well, a great deal of campaigning is about charisma, and you have that in spades. The actual work of governing would bore you."

He shuffles through a stack of papers and holds up a recent issue of *The North Carolinian*, headlined with an article about the furniture factories in High Point. "Did you mean what you said last night about the trees?"

"Every word. Trees mean jobs in this state, jobs mean factories, factories mean workers' rights... it's all tied together. Some people just need help making the connections."

"Workers' rights are an important cause. It's time I am more active in supporting what I believe in. But it is a shame I shall not have time to run for office."

"Classes, of course."

He rakes a hand through his messy brown hair and his stern facade crumbles in a blink. "When do you move in? I am happy to assist any way I can."

"Not for a few weeks, but I shall keep your offer in mind." I take another sip of water and leave a delicate pause before dropping what I suspect will rile him a bit. "Matthew has already offered to give me a little tour of Fayetteville Street and the shopping along the streetcar line."

"He what?"

"Well, you know I have never been in the city on my own. I am the luckiest girl in the world to have such helpful friends." I rise and approach him, taking note of his flushed cheeks and the set of his jaw. He didn't like that.

Well, good.

"You're not going already, are you?"

I blink. "I came to make my apology, and I made it. Are we quite all right, Cooper?"

"Oh, dandy."

Turning to the door, I wave over my shoulder. "Then I am sure I will see you at Georgia and Leo's sometime soon."

"Maudie, wait."

I stop.

"Do you remember what I said to you the night of my graduation party?"

I whip around and meet his eyes. "You said many things that evening. I thought we agreed to leave those things alone."

"No." Cooper shakes his head and stands, holding out his hands as he approaches me. "Before all that. I said you were the only woman in the room I trusted was not after me for my name or my income." He takes my hands in his with a gentle squeeze. "You are trying to reverse me into this by saying I can't do it because you think I'll fight back and say I can. Well, I can't. And I won't be used like that. Not by you or anybody."

"I never intended to use you."

"That's all politics is, isn't it? Using people as a means to an end. I have a last name that is valuable to you. I'm the next man up since my father cannot do it."

I yank my hands away. The hurt in his eyes is at odds with his harsh words and I am not sure which to believe. "If you wish me to heap praise on you to win your agreement, you will remain unsatisfied. I can see you do not trust my motivations, and all that tells me is that you never understood why this is necessary in the first place."

"To get back at Toby Shaw for switching sides on your cause. I was listening, Maudie." He pivots away and stomps across the room to the window. "Enough. I think we have both made ourselves clear."

"If you think that's why—"

"Please go." When he turns back to me, the sunlight catches his face for the first time, and his loss of sleep shows in the shadows under his eyes and the stubble he scratches along his jawline. "I can't, and I won't."

I whisper just loud enough to cross the room. "You could."

He squints into the afternoon sun and doesn't answer, and I take my leave in silence.

Chapter 10
Cooper

"No, I can't," I grumble, rolling over in my bed as I drag a blanket over my face. "I can't, and I won't."

I've replayed yesterday's conversation with Maudie in my head a hundred times and cannot banish from my mind the disappointment in her blue eyes. My pride will not allow me to serve as the errand boy on her path of revenge. Tobias Shaw can burrow under the ground with the rodents for all I care, and I'd be happy to deal with him the old-fashioned way if she wished, but I don't need my name and face plastered across the newspapers with college friends' anecdotes about late nights at Miss Ada's and how they presume I really feel about women.

The thought turns my stomach and I smash a pillow to my face in frustration, screwing my eyes shut. My repentance is a private affair.

Maudie is not the only one who wants a fresh start. My shadows lurk in parts of Raleigh she will never visit, and neither she nor the constituents of this district need to know the extent of my youthful follies and failures. I should have applied to a program out of state—although since those follies and failures often extended to my grades, it is a miracle I have another college opportunity at all.

The harsh morning sun glares a rainbow of stars behind my closed eyelids. If it's breached the gap in my curtains, it must be at least nine o'clock. "Go away," I tell the sun, shouting through my pillow. "Go away. I hate you."

"That's no way to greet a lady."

I sit bolt upright and swear under my breath, clutching my covers to my chest.

Maudie sits on the window seat, dainty ankles crossed, a floral explosion of a hat at her side as she inspects a pristine white glove with a frown.

"How did you—why are you here?" I scrabble at the blankets and nearly dive under them like a child when I realize she's buttoned from her chin to her wrists, all business, and I'm half naked. "Who let you in? Maudie, you have to—please leave. Leave. Go downstairs and I'll be there in a minute."

"Your father is at work and your mother is at church, and Mabel and Victor are... somewhere." She flicks a dismissive wave. "I let myself in. Calm down. No one is compromised yet."

The *yet* rolls between us on the floor like a marble, waiting for one of us to snatch it up.

"You cannot just walk into my bedroom."

Arching a delicate brow, she finally looks up. "I suppose my invitation has expired."

My entire body prickles with goosebumps and I pull a quilt up to my bare shoulders. "Is that what you're here to talk about?"

"No."

"Good. Because to be perfectly clear, I will not entertain the notion of bargaining for my compliance with your virtue."

She rolls her eyes. "As always, we are of the same mind on so many important issues."

"The answer is still no."

"Except that one, I see."

"Please go downstairs. I'll be right down, I promise. We'll talk this through."

"What are you worried about?" She gestures to the space between us. "I have not even touched you."

"Yes, but you—this is my bedroom, and you're right there, and I'm not dressed, and—for God's sake, Maudie, I don't have to explain this to you."

"I bet you feel quite vulnerable right now, don't you?"

I freeze. The spark in her eyes tells me there is no right answer to that question and I had better not make a joke.

"I bet you're thinking about the rules we were raised with and what must happen if we are caught here. My innocence wouldn't survive an encounter like this with a rogue like you, would it?" She lowers her voice. "Your worst nightmare—being forced into marriage. When you're a woman, you can be forced into anything and have no say on the matter at all. And the more you are forced, the more you live in fear because you never know what man will make your life his business. Who will enforce what rules, and when? Who will leverage your reputation as a weapon and force you into a future of his choosing?"

I gulp. "I think I see—"

"You do not see! You do not understand, and you will never understand."

"If you're trying to make a point, you've made it. Please go."

She grabs her hat from the bench and flings it at me, smacking me in the arm. "As long as you refuse to run for this office, I have not made my point. You don't feel helpless enough if you can't see yet that I am doing this because I have no other choice. You and other lazy, selfish men like you have left me no choice. In North Carolina, only those eligible to vote can hold office. I cannot even be a notary public in this government."

"But do you want—?"

"I can't even certify a signature. That's how little I am worth to the state. I cannot fight for my own rights in the legislature without enlisting the help of someone like you, favored by a system that values what's between your legs more than it does what's between my ears!"

My mouth hangs open as I pull the blankets tighter.

Her cheeks flame as she steps toward me. "If you think this is about getting back at Mr. Shaw for hurting me, you're wrong. This is about men like him holding positions of power where they may lie, cheat, and manipulate the rules. And it's about men like you who will give lip service to women's rights for their mothers and sisters but won't get off their lazy asses to help us do anything about it."

I clutch her hat to my chest, silk petals tickling my bare arms as she smooths her skirts and brushes by me without another word. Scrambling to my feet, my eyes dart wildly around the room as I hop into yesterday's trousers and grapple for a shirt.

"Maudie," I shout. "Wait. Please, just wait."

Her high-heeled shoes click an angry staccato on the stairs and I dash after her barefoot, just in time to catch her at the front door and pull her into my arms. She doesn't protest when I cradle her head against my chest, the heat of her cheek and her tears seeping through my unbuttoned shirt as I stroke her back. "I'm so sorry, darling," I whisper, breathing in the scent of lilies-of-the-valley from her hair. "Maudie, I am so sorry. I didn't understand. You're right. I've been lazy and selfish, and I didn't understand."

She straightens her back and dabs at her eyes with the delicate lace cuffs of her sleeves. "I am sorry for my outburst," she says stiffly. "I will not trouble you again."

"I'll do it."

Her eyes meet mine and I brush blonde waves off her damp forehead. She opens her mouth to speak, then snaps it shut again.

"I'll do this for you. For you and for Georgia, and my mother, and..." I cannot help stealing a glance at her trembling lips. "I'll do it, Maudie, but I will need you. I don't know politics. I won't know how to take a breath in that world without you, and I will entrust my every move into your care."

"That's a very poetic way to hire a campaign manager."

"I mean it. I will be your voice, but I will be lost without you telling me what to say."

She tries to step back but I hold her tighter, and the heaviness in my heart lifts a little when she smiles. "It is a good thing we are so often of the same mind, then."

"You flatter me when you equate my mind with yours."

"Thank you, Cooper."

"Do not thank me yet. The road ahead is littered with ways I may let you down."

The churn in my stomach is more than just a rumble for breakfast. As my friends, Leo and Berger might brush off my concerns about my past behavior and say many gentlemen have indulged in a similar way. Berger was a member of our little crew a few times and has no platform to stand on if he wishes to judge me. He'd tell me if my past would doom our cause before it starts, and I know already he and his web of rumors and whispers will be crucial to checking the pulse of my campaign.

There's more to it than he knows, though. The shame of how I realized the error of my ways gnaws at me some nights when I consider how helpless I am to fix anything in this world, from chestnut trees to suffrage, let alone the moral chasm I flung myself into when I decided to pay women for their affection instead of earning it. Fixing one thing always seems to break another, and there's so little one man can do.

But at least a man can be a notary public. Maudie, however, must do what she can with the scraps we have given her.

My heart calms as she rests her head on my chest once more, and the weight of her body against mine is the sweetest comfort I could wish in this tumult. As her breathing slows, she sinks into my arms. The lazy, selfish boy in me—the one she knows well—ponders for a moment whether I could whisk her back upstairs.

"Oh my goodness." She jolts away from my embrace. "We have so much to do."

"I—I'm sure."

"We must start at once."

I bob my head obediently.

"We will meet at Leo and Georgia's, tonight or tomorrow if they can have us," she says. "I shall stop there this afternoon, and at Angeline's. She and Matthew will spread the word. We want only close friends in attendance at first, you know."

Do I know? "Of course."

"I'll send to Raleigh for the paperwork."

"Certainly."

"Cooper?"

"Maudie?"

She perches on her tiptoes to kiss my cheek. "You can. And we will."

Chapter 11
Maudie

I have only really swooned once in my life, but since it was at Tillie MacGregor's twelfth birthday party and a tiny lizard was involved, the funny story stuck in everyone's minds and I gained a reputation for wobbling under pressure.

It wasn't pressure. It was ninety degrees, three slices of chocolate cake, and and an itchy thread inside my chemise that set me scratching and twisting my new stays. I didn't even see the wretched lizard, but it all became something of a joke back when I thought it was delicate and dainty of a lady to swoon. I wanted to be delicate and dainty then—corseted and wasp-waisted within an inch of my life, smiling prettily for the boys at dancing school. I had no goals beyond being the belle of my year, which would surely net me a husband soon after my debut.

It netted me some proposals and I learned some uncomfortable lessons.

This morning, Cooper insisted on walking me home after he dressed properly. When the cool indoor air met my flushed face in the front hall, I had to clench the corner of the bombé chest to steady myself. That outburst drained me. My unbridled rage at the unfairness of my situation rose from a simmer to a screaming boil in a blink, and here at home half an hour later, I am still catching my breath. If we are to succeed in this effort, I must remain calm, collected, and upright.

The swoon at Tillie's party was real. I was so overcome by heat and chocolate I fluttered my lashes and flopped onto the divan before the lizard even escaped Artie MacGregor's jar. After that, my swoons became a joke of my own making. I cannot count the number of times I have pretended to faint on hearing important news, good or bad, just to have an acceptable outlet for how big everything feels sometimes. Newspapers and neighborhood gossip can be as jarring as any lizard, and when thing upon thing stacks up, sometimes I want a moment to take it all in. A little swoon stops time. My friends' engagements all get theatrical fake swoons from me. I daresay if Brent proposes to Emilia and I don't at least fan myself and flutter my lashes, she'll feel left out.

I have never swooned for a proposal of my own.

It should be the most swoon-worthy time in a girl's life—and yet each time, the heightened emotion I expected fell flat. Even when I was heated and furious at Mr. Shaw for his betrayal, his pretty words and the sparkle of the ring left me cold and empty.

Today, a cannon must have blasted me into Cooper's room with the strength to shout him down and leave my pride and my fear on the floor. I got what I wanted, but every joint in my body feels loose when I plod into the breakfast room and pour a glass of water.

I will not faint.

I sit up straight on the high-backed chair at the table and do not even allow myself the comfort of one of the wing chairs or the sofa in the sitting room. Gulp after gulp, the cool water races through my body, lowering my pulse and steadying my stomach.

I breathe with my shoulders, a trick Mama taught me when I started wearing my laces tighter, lifting my collarbone to fill my lungs a little deeper instead of putting pressure on my waist and causing pain in my stomach. The gasping subsides and I take another gulp of water.

Tracing the lines of the whalebone stays under my dress, my thoughts turn to another set of worries lingering in my dizzy brain. Practicalities dictate I should dress myself without anyone's help when I live in the dormitories, and that must mean I have clothes I can put on without someone else lacing me.

We really are trained to do nothing alone, and that I have such simple hurdles on the way to college is proof of how early the world is in accepting that a lady can do more than swoon, stifle her feelings, and stuff herself into a gown from La Rue de la Paix. Why wasn't this in the booklet from the school? I only have two weeks, and much of my wardrobe hinges on Cecelia dressing me. I gain at least two inches around the waist when I have to lace myself. It is certainly more comfortable, but hardly anything will fit.

I pop up from my seat and dash back to the hall where the morning post sits on the bombé chest. As I hoped, it contains a note from Victoria Harper, who Angeline recommended as a potential roommate. I tear it open and heave a sigh of relief that she agreed. Now that I have a friend to share her experience and wisdom about all these changes and new expectations, I settle back at the breakfast table to scribble a quick invitation for a shopping trip at her soonest convenience. I don't know what to buy. What does a student wear? Not the pink dress with tiers of lace I have on now, certainly.

And just like that, my mind spins again back to Cooper.

This morning, I put on this dress for a boost of confidence before I slipped into his bedroom—not that it mattered to him, and I'll wager he couldn't tell me what color it was because he was so shocked. Flabbergasted, really, but he listened, and not because I looked pretty or told him he was clever. I raged at him like a fishwife and told him he was an idiot, but he heard what was underneath all that frustration and agreed to help.

He held me close and agreed to help, but I must block out the feeling of his arms around me if I want to get anything done. Swooning can wait, and this dress and its frivolous ruffles will go back in the wardrobe. I won't be able to wear it with my stays let out two inches anyway.

I reach for paper to clear my cluttered mind with a list, starting with registering Cooper for the race. Dresses and laces be damned. Backward-thinking slugs like Mr. Shaw have no choice now but to face the indomitable, unlikely duo of Maudie Hamilton and Cooper Truxton, who are once again of like mind on all important matters.

Chapter 12
Cooper

My father accepted the news of my new political ambitions with a solemn face, but I caught him sending a *Whose idea was this?* look at Leo, who volunteered to serve as my moral support. Even before Leo was his son-in-law, Papa looked on him as one of his own children. Papa is not a fearsome man by any means—if anything, he has been far too indulgent with my shenanigans —but when he leans back in his chair and tugs at his mustache like he's doing now, the little boy in me always whispers that one day, he'll be sick of my shit.

I'll need him for this almost as much as I'll need Maudie. Still, I am shaken by the news he gave to me and Georgia the other day about his ulcer, and determined not to cause him any stress.

"Who have you talked to in the party?"

I startle. "The what?"

"Have you talked to Julius already?"

"Well, Papa, I don't know what—"

"Not yet." Leo slaps my shoulder as he addresses my

father. "But I'm sure that's in the plan." He rises from the green leather sofa and nudges the top off the brandy decanter, then lines up three glasses.

My father glances between the two of us. "Whose plan?"

"You may remember Maudie Hamilton courting with a young man named Tobias Shaw." My tongue thickens as I force out his name.

"Oh yes, I remember him," Papa says with a little chuckle as he accepts a glass from Leo. "Our unwelcome guest."

"That's him."

"He is your partner in this endeavor?"

"He's my competition. Maudie is helping me. She recruited me, really."

As Papa's mouth falls open, Leo hands me a drink. "We are all helping you. We all agree with Maudie that Shaw is an opportunist and a turncoat, and he should not be allowed to ride Ambrose Shockley's coattails to a seat in the legislature. The election is less than three months away, and the Republicans have not put forth a challenger."

"Don't tell me you are tired of agriculture already, son. Classes don't start for another week."

I tighten my hand around the glass and try to stop my nervous twitching. "I can do both. The campaign will be brief, and next semester I can schedule around sessions. It will be more convenient for me than every man in the assembly who doesn't live within shouting distance of the capitol. My studies are important to me, and I do not forget your generous support. This would not be an option if the General Assembly did not meet just across town from campus."

He sips his brandy with an appreciative nod. "Shockley's

held his seat for twenty years because Hillside likes what he stands for. If Shaw has his endorsement—"

"He doesn't. Shaw's carpetbagging. He'll fly the Democrats' banner because of his father, but he doesn't know anyone here."

"Says who?"

"Matthew Berger."

My father perks up.

I have no idea how the Bergers manage to learn everything first, aside from the sheer volume of listening ears they have in this town. Yet as far back as I can remember, a rumor from a Berger was as good as gold. Matthew is one of seven children and has fourteen first cousins on the Berger side, every one of them in Hillside or Raleigh. Maudie, of course, has the inside look at Shaw's methods to paint a clearer picture.

"Berger heard from one of his cousins who knows Herbert Spicer and Will Connelly, who lead the county Democrats. Shaw threw his hat in the ring as an unknown and they already don't like him much. He's relying on his father's reputation."

"Spicer's still alive?"

"Alive, and as ready as ever to drag us back to medieval times, if you catch my meaning."

"It will be a long shot to convince Hillside of more progressive policies."

Leo clears his throat. "Perhaps not with a name like Truxton."

"Shaw isn't the only one leaning on his father's reputation." Papa chuckles.

"A familiar name and face, though," Leo replies. He grabs

my chin and shakes me. "He even looks like you, Chris. He'll do, won't he?"

I shove him off me. "My name will get attention. My message will matter more. Shaw will parrot tired talking points and dance around anything controversial. That's why he backed off supporting suffrage. Maudie said he has some weak points where he's personally uncomfortable with the platform he presents, but he's faking it to get the vote."

Papa rises. "Let's have a look."

One of the perks of having an old family is having an old family home and all its accumulated history. Like most houses in this section of town, ours was built in the early nineteenth century and has been passed down through generations—from Charles to Chester to Christopher, and one day, if I don't screw it up, to me. Plucked from a corner of the office where it has rested untouched for decades, the map of Hillside and northern Raleigh is a relic. Papa unfurls it over his desk. Using his pocket change, he marks the borders of our legislative district.

"Gerrymandered to all hell," he says. "All of Hillside is in the boundaries, the whole of your old college, as well as this section of Oak Grove. This corner of Raleigh is where you'll find most of your progressives. Here in town you'll have to lean on our name to break the stronghold."

Leo squints at the lines. "That part of Oak Grove is mostly commercial. You won't have many resident voters there."

"What are my boundaries in the city?" I trace the street names, looking for landmarks. The old map is dated 1881, four years before my birth, and A&M didn't exist until 1887. I find a park as a reference point as Papa traces a diagonal line that carves a triangular section of the city, keeping my new boarding house in bounds. Even though I can still claim residency in Hillside as a full-time student, I'd have sought new living quarters if I'd been out of the district. Fortunately, that's one less thing to do.

Papa dots a faint boundary line on the map in pencil. "Where's he from?"

"Shaw? Wilmington. He was going to run there but accidentally ended up with residency here because he voted with his college address for a few years."

"Wilmington."

Leo and I share a glance.

"Yes, Wilmington. His father represents their district in the House, and—"

"Leo, did your father talk to you about what happened in Wilmington ten years ago?"

My friend's brows furrow as he shakes his head. Papa keeps his face turned down, still working on the boundary line.

"I should have talked to you about it, Cooper. Many parents who saw the war don't like to burden their children with these things. But Shaw is about your age, isn't he?"

"He is."

"Then he likely saw this with his own eyes, and I will hazard a guess that his feelings on racial tensions will not play especially well with Hillside families, despite their party affiliation. For better or worse, no one has rocked the boat here yet."

There it is again. *Yet.*

"What happened ten years ago?"

"It started as a war of words between the editor of a black newspaper and Democrats calling for white supremacy. That turned into mob rule and dozens of black men dead in the streets of Wilmington. Some suspect as many as a hundred more might have been killed and the bodies hidden in the river."

Leo and I stare, first at him, then at each other. My father can be a grandiose storyteller, rather like me, and his brevity says a great deal about how bad it must have been.

"How did it end?" Leo asks.

I jab him in the ribs when Papa finally looks up. The shadows under his eyes are a grim reminder of his ulcer and why I shouldn't worry him. Leo and I came by to tell him the news and talk about party leadership, and if there's an emotional story that will cause him any stress at all, I'll ask someone else to tell it.

"Never mind, Papa. Maudie can tell me all I need to know. I'm sure Shaw told her."

"They overthrew the government."

"They what?"

"Democrats stuffed the ballot boxes in the 1898 election and claimed victory, and two days later they kicked out the elected populist government and installed their own mayor and council. They blew up the newspaper office and a mob took to the streets." His shoulders slump. "I know we are insulated here. When I was seven years old, Raleigh surrendered to occupation before Sherman could put us to the torch like he did Atlanta and Columbia. The mayor did the best he could to protect the city. Only a few days later, a Union general stopped his own men from rising and burning everything after Lincoln was shot. All things considered, Raleigh has been lucky, and Hillside even luckier. No one wants to think of these things. What happened in Wilmington more than thirty years later was a harsh reminder that this country is not 'reconstructed' by any means."

Heaviness bears down on my chest, slowing my breaths. My father's tone is grave and thoughtful, and it tears at my heart. Maudie snuck into my bedroom and demanded I hear her out because she thinks I can take this on?

Papa is right to say we are insulated. Hillside began as a village of luxurious vacation homes for wealthy city dwellers after the Revolution—families like mine that later moved here permanently in the 1850s and 1860s to stay out of sight of a government collapsing around their ears. The population boomed in the decades that followed the war, with people seeking peace among our spreading chestnuts and gentle slopes after so much tumult. The town was just far enough removed from the city that hardly anyone noticed it during Reconstruction until the mayor went down the hill to ask about tying into Raleigh's electric utilities years later.

Across the South, as local governments were criticized for doing too much or too little, the citizens of Hillside seemed to collectively agree it was best to stay quiet. The tensions that bubbled and boiled over in Wilmington are as foreign to me as France, but the representatives of that city are North Carolinians, just as I am, and we will sit at the same table if I do this.

I glance at Leo as he traces the streets on the map with his finger. I have devoured newspapers since I was old enough to read, although I see now my father must have filtered my materials when I was young. But Wilmington has me racking my brain to find a time I might have read a black newspaper, and to my shame, I cannot think of one.

How am I qualified to lead anyone?

I've led football teams. I can read a playbook and I've been in my share of on-field fights. But there is no playbook for diving headfirst into a political firestorm with lives at stake when I have no frame of reference for anything outside my own small existence. What do I know of a black man's struggles or what motivates a mob to stage a coup?

Resuming my seat on the couch, I down my brandy—not a good idea since my head is already spinning, but I must fortify myself, and without Maudie's bravado to boost me, I don't know how else to tell myself I can do this.

"I would like to meet with Julius Crowley, if you would make the introduction. If it would be more appropriate, I'll reach out directly, but I have only met him twice and would appreciate your hand in this."

My father nods.

"I may not be their most traditional candidate. Some might think my views a bit radical, but they are honest, which is more than we can say for Tobias Shaw. I welcome the party's support if they will have me as I am. If not, I must run as an independent and do my best. There is a great deal I do not know, but as Maudie says, if she knew enough to help him win, she knows enough to make him lose."

"I will arrange a conversation with Crowley this week, before you move. What will you present for your platform?"

"My support for women's suffrage must be clear. I want infrastructure planned ahead for automobiles taking over the roads. I want to improve working conditions in factories, job creation, workers' rights and fair wages. I have studied enough of that in economics to speak knowledgeably. I would not like to challenge Shaw on anything regarding race relations until I have educated myself a bit more. Right now, all I have are personal feelings."

Leo snorts. "I can only imagine his personal feelings. I wonder what Maudie will have to say about him and Wilmington. My God, how did she put up with that weasel for so long?"

"He was raised to be a politician," Papa says, knocking his fist against my head as he takes a seat at my side. "And you were raised to be a fair, honest man. He put on a show for her, obviously, and I know you well enough to guess that you did not. She put her faith in you. Maudie and Georgia have always been two of a kind, so I imagine she will be a formidable ally."

I brighten. "She said I could talk about the trees."

Chapter 13
Maudie

Thanks to Victoria's guidance, my trunks are packed with clothes I can put on and take off entirely alone. She has joined my family and Georgia in throwing me a celebration dinner the night before I move. Mama conspired with our cook to prepare all of my favorites in a nonsensical menu of a cold soup, a hot soup, fried chicken with rice pilaf, a salad of greens and fresh berries, and a slice of chocolate cake the size of my head.

I knew to expect the meal. I did not expect the gifts, and my eyes well over and over as we all share hugs and kisses.

Georgia surprised me with the sweetest little nightdress and dressing gown set because she imagines we will all be roaming the halls of the dormitory with rag-rolled hair, giggling and gossiping after all visitors are out. "I am green with envy, and so delighted for you," she whispers, tracing her fingers over the pink silk ribbons she has woven through the collar of the robe. She has the finest eye for fashion, even in nightgowns. "Come home whenever you can, and tell me everything."

Papa, of course, is funding my college adventure, and gifted me with a thin leather account book to use at the bank when I need money to shop for my necessities and hire carriages to come home any time I wish. Like my clothes, it is another practicality, and another delightful surprise to come with it. I have never had access to more than a few dollars at a time before, and the sudden independence makes me sit straighter. No foolish schoolgirl gets a gift like that.

Mama hands me a jewelry box and clasps her hands over mine when I take it from her. "Maudie, sweetheart. I know that what you are about to do feels like a grand adventure, and it is. But it is so much more than that."

She nods at me to open the box. The black velvet lid pops up with a click and reveals a delicate brooch of lapis flowers among jade leaves, wrought in gold in the shape of a little wreath with tiny white diamonds scattered like blossoms. Blue and green are my new school colors, and Mama's eyes grow misty as she smiles.

"You are the first woman in our family to go to college, Maudie. And whether you love it and earn your degree or hate it and leave after one term, you are going because you earned it. Your daughters and their daughters will remember that. I have a letter for you from your grandmother in Norfolk, and I am sure if my mother and your great-grand-mothers were here to see it, they would join us in telling you how proud we are."

"We are all proud," Papa interjects, lifting his glass. "To Maud Cathleen, our little Maudie, for her accomplishments so far and the opportunities she has made for herself, and her many successes still to come."

At the clinking of the glasses, my tears finally spill. I fight a losing battle at swiping them away as my mother pins on my new brooch. Even Victoria, who has no history with my family, is hugging Georgia and my mother like a long-lost cousin and is a-flutter with the excitement of being my guide to this new world I am entering. For all that I complain about it being old-fashioned or dull sometimes, my home is warm and lovely and safe. This quiet enclave in Hillside is all I have ever known. With a stuffed stomach and surrounded by the love of my family, my heart twists with the ache of homesickness to come.

The chocolate cake weighs heavily on my belly, though, and between the sweets and the warmth of all the hugs and tears, I need to step away and collect myself. I don't want to swoon and miss a minute of it.

Leo arrives to escort Georgia home late in the evening, and when I greet him in the hall, he presents me with a large box. "I was in the city today and saw Cooper. He asked me to bring you this."

"More reading materials? He brought me a stack of newspapers the other day, and not just about trees. I was impressed."

"No, it's a gift."

Georgia peeks over my shoulder and Victoria watches, wide-eyed, as I untie the twine and lift the lid. Inside, beneath layers of paper, I find an exquisitely stitched satchel of warm caramel-brown leather, stiff in its newness but with a soft hand to the grain. I run my fingers over the stitches and the bright, brass clasp on the flap, and flick it open to find the inner pockets lined in canvas in red and white stripes like a candy cane. Tucked inside, I find a note.

Dearest Maudie,

I spotted this at a shop next to the bookstore today. You and Georgia always carried your books to school, but if we are to be on a campaign trail and trying to keep up with our studies, I thought you might like something to keep your things together easily, as I do. While I regret that it must be in my school colors and not your own—blue being entirely forbidden on this campus, thanks to our rivals at Trinity and UNC being so close by—I hope you will accept this as a token of my thanks for all that has been, and my excitement for all that is to come.

Warmest regards,

Cooper

P.S. Speaking of my school colors, I hope you've saved that red and white hat you wore to my games. I'm claiming you for a match this Saturday and will call for you at ten.

I breathe in the oiled leather and smile at his note. "How very thoughtful of him," I murmur, peering in the satchel's pockets and not entirely sure who I am speaking to. "Entirely practical, and so thoughtful of him to consider this."

When I look up, Leo is watching me as Georgia pins on her hat. "Will you need help moving tomorrow? I could come down, and I'll grab him."

"There will be porters," Victoria says. "They always staff the dormitory for move-in when we come back after every break. And I will show you everything, Maudie. I've already gone over the list of clubs you want to engage in the campaign, and I have friends in half a dozen of them."

Leo's brows lift. "Are you our first recruit?"

"Victoria is basically a Berger by marriage," Georgia says. "Her older sister Edith is married to Angeline's oldest brother, William."

"She's a plant, that's what she is." I grab my new friend in a hug. "I am certain Angeline set up our roommate situation so she'd have a source for all my comings and goings to report back to the Hillside rumor mill. Mama will get all my news and I shall never have to send a letter."

Victoria giggles. "They are such a fun family to be part of."

"And they'll report back to Matthew," Leo snorts. Georgia slaps his arm and he stops laughing.

I glance between them. "What?"

"It's one of those days, dearest. My husband thinks he's funny." Georgia eyes the satchel and a small smile creeps across her face, and I can tell she hasn't told Leo about the party. Cooper must not have told him either.

"No, what's this about Matthew?"

Victoria frowns and says nothing.

"Leo?"

"He was joking." Georgia is at my side before Leo can speak. "I know you are looking forward to a respite from courtship and suitors and all the complications. You are not so far removed from a very unfortunate heartbreak, and will be far too busy with class and Cooper's campaign, in any case."

"That's right," I say, lifting my chin as I clutch the new satchel to my chest. The leather sends another whiff of its heady fragrance at my nose. "Thank you for remembering. That is exactly what I said."

Leo nods, his blue eyes darting between us. "So any attention of that kind would be unwelcome?"

"I have no desire for a new attachment."

"Noted." He clears his throat and bobs a quick farewell at my mother, then to Victoria, then to me. "Congratulations, Maudie, and welcome to the ranks of college students. Please stop by on your way down to the city tomorrow and we'll cut you a fresh bouquet from the greenhouse to brighten your new room. The dahlias are especially lovely."

"Thank you, Leo." I blow Georgia a kiss before they leave, and the minute the door closes, Victoria grabs my arm and pulls me to the settee in the parlor.

"You are not interested in Matthew, are you?"

"I have not considered him in that way. But is that really what Leo was talking about?"

"He must have been, you ninny."

"I've known Matthew for many years and we are very friendly, but I've only thought of him as Angeline's brother, really. I can't even imagine—oh, Victoria." She is blushing and twitching her fingers on the rose moire fabric in a disjointed rhythm. "Do you like him?"

Her face flushes even brighter pink. "I danced with him at my sister's wedding and found him most agreeable." She looks up. "And attractive."

I still think of him as one of the Berger busybodies, but when she mentions it, I can see she's not wrong. His dark hair and gray eyes are quite appealing, and despite his steady demeanor, his smile is as sweet and boyish as it was when he was a child. I imagine that to someone not used to dumping sand on his head each summer, he could look rather dashing.

I clear my throat. "I agree that he's good company. Do you see him much?"

"Only once since then, and only for a moment. It's nothing."

I take her hands. "Well, I promise you I have no interest in him like that. And if he told Leo he is interested in me, I think Georgia did a fine job putting that idea to rest. I will not be an obstacle."

"Yes, but I—"

"He and Cooper are friends, and I shall be seeing a lot of both of them for the campaign. Any time you wish to come along, I could nudge you in his direction, if you like."

"You would do that for me?"

"Of course I would. As a matter of fact..." I dig into my new satchel and pull out the note. "Cooper and I are going to a football game Saturday. He and Matthew used to be team-mates, so I'm sure he'll come. Come with us."

She brushes her fingers over the soft leather. "Do you like Cooper? That satchel looks expensive. And it's so sweet he was thinking of you."

I must answer quickly before I get a stupid look on my face and give away my thoughts. "Cooper and I are a team now. He is another dear old friend and we enjoy each other's company. But I think he is still like he always was, and not interested in any romantic attachments. That suits me because I am not, either. We can have a friendship without any complications."

She nods and turns the conversation back to recruiting help from various clubs, satisfied with my explanation.

I shall have to pretend I was, too.

Chapter 14
Cooper

The wallpaper sold me on my room in this boarding house. It's blue, striped, and textured like the wallpaper in the room I shared with Leo during our dormitory days at EPC, which means I know it will hardly show a pinhole when I move out. I made the arrangements to let the room last spring when it was occupied by another student—I took one look and handed the landlord a deposit. Now, armed with a handful of pins, I squint and line up my decorations with the holes pricked in the wall by the previous resident, piecing them together like a puzzle. The resulting mosaic is as much a reflection of me as any mirror.

Mystery Disease Attacks Bronx Zoo Chestnuts. The curled edges around the headline that started my obsession two years ago wave hello like a friend when I pin it in the center of the wall.

Exciting Opportunities in Forest Service for Young Men. I'd stare at this one until my eyes crossed some nights when I couldn't study another minute. If the U.S. Forest Service didn't need me to have a college degree to build a grand national park out west, why get one? I sent away for the pamphlet and kept it on my desk for months before it disappeared somewhere—I suspect into Leo's pocket to remove it from my thoughts during final exams. The call to action is years old but the opportunity remains, and in a small way, so does the dream. I pause with the advertisement in my hands, tempted to clench it in my fist and tear it to ribbons.

But it's practically a piece of art since Hayes got ahold of it with his colored pencils and filled in the black-and-white forest the newspaper printed, so I pin it up anyway.

EPC's Truxton Stuns School, Stomps App State. God, the adrenaline rush from this one never gets old. Leo and Matthew and I played on an upstart mess of a college football team that didn't win a game our first season. The big teams nearby—Trinity, UNC, and my new home, A&M—showed no mercy that year and enjoyed trouncing us by thirty points or more. The second year, as this article says, "East Piedmont College demanded respect." The team from Appalachian State showed up at our little stadium in September 1906, and under the new college football rules, I threw the first forward pass in our team's history. And the second, third, fourth, and fifth in that same game, when we learned they weren't ready to defend it. I have five more copies of this paper at my parents' house, and Georgia knows that in the event of my death, she had better send one to the grave with me so I can brag to everyone no matter where I end up.

Another football story goes next to it, this one with a picture of Leo and me half-covered in dirt. An advertisement for the new Model T automobile. A few more about the trees in New York and Pennsylvania. Georgia and Leo's wedding photo. A cartoon of President Roosevelt on a moose. A family picture when I was sixteen and Georgia was fourteen. Post-cards from traveling friends circle the articles with bright greetings from London, Paris, and New York. A recent addition from Maudie's brother in Washington, D.C. sports a photograph of the White House and a jaunty scribble: *Vote for Trux!*

I dig my scissors from my trunk and snip carefully around an article on the front page of the Hillside newspaper's latest edition. *Truxton Announces Bid for Legislature.* My hometown editors are generous and devoted several inches to my biography and a statement about my platform. My parents' and grandparents' names are included for good measure. I asked for that.

"Hillside native and Raleigh Women's College student Miss Maudie Hamilton will manage Truxton's campaign," I read aloud. I asked for that, too. The newspaperman looked at me like I had three heads and only agreed when I fibbed and said she could earn extra credit for her course in Modern Southern Politics—but there it is, in fresh ink. Hayes will pass the article and Maudie's official press release along to his friend, an editor at *The News and Observer* in the city, along with a slick little cartoon of me announcing quarterbacks know how to get in the game.

I pin it to the wall along with the sketch, and it's official.

Outside the stadium on Saturday morning, Maudie drapes a red-and-white sash over my head and I notice Victoria handing one to Berger. The girls are already wearing theirs, and I shoot Maudie a sideways glance as crowds of students mill around us. "What are these for? I thought your suffrage ribbons were meant to be gold and purple."

"These are your school colors, and now they're your campaign colors, too. We're campaigning while we are here."

"Must we? I just want to watch. I want to be a hooligan in the bleachers, not behave like the fine, upstanding citizen you think I am."

"Cooper."

"Maudie," I whine. She pulls two pins from her pocket and stands on her toes, leaning close to pin one on me.

"Look."

I twist the little cloth button around and sigh when I see the embroidered leaves of a spreading chestnut tree in bright green over a black trunk, carefully angled to form a letter T. Hers is a perfect match.

"You don't have to give a speech or anything." She takes my arm to turn me toward the stadium. "We'll wear these and cheer like everyone else. And when we come back for another game, there will be more of us, and people will begin to talk. Your dormitories are within our boundaries. These are your voters, and they need to see you. Georgia has plans to make more ribbons with your name on them. Victoria and I just scraped this together quickly."

"It's perfect. I'm sorry I complained. Did you make the pins, too?"

She blushes and nods.

"Thank you for all of it."

"I'm just doing my job for the candidate."

"The candidate thinks you are a dream come true."

She smiles up at me as we move forward in the line. "And

I think the candidate is—oh, goodness, have we lost Matthew and Victoria already?"

"Just there." I point to where they're collecting leaflets with game information from a hawker.

"I didn't expect her to drag him away so quickly." She giggles. "She likes him, and I've decided to encourage a match. You will be my co-conspirator."

"Maudie Hamilton, you little sneak."

"Oh, she knows. Matthew's the only one in the dark. How about that? A Berger who doesn't know what's going on."

She tucks her hand in the crook of my elbow and I draw her a little closer. "His cousins are already bringing in information from every neighborhood. My newspaper profile came out only three days ago and it's already being seen and talked about in the city—and *The News and Observer* hasn't even published it yet. Someone's leaving dozens of copies of the Hillside paper in cafes and restaurants and on streetcars."

Her brows shoot up. "He's a powerful ally. Victoria is so sweet. She might be the key to keeping him in a good mood."

My thoughts race back to Leo's study and the night Berger asked advice about convincing Maudie to marry him. As I pay for our tickets, I fight back a grimace at the memory of brandy and bile coming up when his declaration made me vomit. He speaks of her warmly and often, but has followed Georgia's advice and refrained from any romantic procla-mations.

Bless my sister. We do not need a love triangle on our hands.

Chapter 15
Maudie

I don't have to feign dizziness when I flop onto my bed, but I'm not sure it counts as a swoon. Alone in the dark room, I stare at the ceiling and count backward from one hundred to slow my heart and quiet my mind. I was an excellent student in high school and expected my summer studies to serve me well in college, but since classes started two weeks ago, I wake up every morning with my mind reeling as though I haven't slept a wink.

I signed up for five classes because Victoria said everyone did, but when I pinned every syllabus side-by-side over my desk, my heart sank when I looked at my list of campaign appearances I am organizing for Cooper.

I told him I would handle everything, and I have no idea how to make good on that promise and the one I made to myself. College is supposed to be about me, not about a man. While he may be an overgrown boy at heart, he's a man and cannot be my priority.

Squeezing myself in a hug, I roll onto my side and curl as tightly as my stays will allow, like a child pretending that if I make myself very small, whatever trouble I imagine won't see me. But this is trouble of my own making, and if I do not face it by the deadline to drop classes, I will lose one of the easiest ways to lighten my load.

Victoria opens the door and shrieks, nearly startling me off the bed.

"Oh goodness, Maudie." She clutches her chest as her chemistry textbook tumbles to the floor. "Are you ill? Why are you in bed in the middle of the day?"

I sit up and rub my eyes. "I have a little headache and thought I should take advantage of the hour I have before my next class."

"I'll get my things and leave you to rest."

"No, stay. My mind was too busy to rest, anyway. Do we have anything in here to eat? I missed lunch."

"You are not taking care of yourself." She digs in her desk drawer and hands me an apple. "You hardly ate last night, either."

"My appetite hasn't caught up with all this change."

She eyes the syllabi tacked over my desk and the stack of textbooks and required novels underneath. My red-and-white sash is draped over my chair. "Perhaps since you have been out of school for a few years, you might consider a lighter course load to ease back into it."

"You're so delicate with your words, Victoria. My compliments to your mother."

She grins. "I'll tell her. But you have plenty of time to take everything in the years ahead. Why race to do it all at once and make yourself sick?"

"It's not a race." I dig into my satchel and hand her my campaign notebook. "It's this race. I signed up for school before I signed up for this, and it's complicating everything."

Sitting next to me on the bed, she flips through my lists. "You said your friends at home are all working with you. None of them have class. They could help more."

"Leo is traveling half the time, Georgia is pregnant and already straining herself with worry about her father, and Angeline is up to her elbows in wedding preparations for next week. Matthew is taking more classes than I am. Everyone is busy. Perhaps this wasn't such a good idea."

"Maudie, don't talk like that."

"No, think about it. We had so much fun at the football game having a normal day out with other students. What if that is the only game Cooper and I go to this year? Maybe this race will ruin our college experience. He loves football almost as much as he loves trees, and he won't even get to watch if he does all those things I've laid out." I jerk my head at the notebook. "I was so upset this summer when Matthew told me about Mr. Shaw's campaign that I overreacted and dragged Cooper into it with me."

"But if you drop a class, you'll have time to manage both more comfortably." Victoria hops up and scans my course lists. "Here. Drop biology and you'll free up time from the lecture and the laboratory sessions."

"If I don't take biology this year, I can't take geology or botany next year, and I want to."

"How about Modern Southern Politics? You'll be doing enough political work anyway. And what politics class assigns a paper due on Election Day?"

I grimace. "I have two papers due that week."

"Drop this class and you'll have just one."

"But Cooper—"

"Cooper is a grown man and can manage his own class schedule."

"That's not what I mean. Well. It's exactly what I mean. He's a man."

She looks at me like I'm speaking Chinese. "And?"

"He's a man, Victoria, and I cannot compromise the things I want in life for a man any longer. I won't do it."

"Pushing Modern Southern Politics off a semester will not derail your life. And it's not as though you'd drop a class to go climb trees with him. Give yourself a little credit, dear."

When I bite into the apple, my mouth waters so fast I nearly drool. I'm starving. Victoria takes advantage of my chewing to challenge me with a question.

"How does dropping this class compromise what you want in life?"

I gulp down my bite. "It's the principle of the thing. I said I was going to make school a priority. I was going to make myself a priority."

"Well, priorities change."

I freeze with the apple halfway to my mouth. "Now you sound like Mr. Shaw."

"Perhaps he's not one hundred percent stupid, then," she says, hands on her hips. "You have a week or two to think on it, in any case. What's left for your afternoon?"

"History. The French Revolution is at two. Then I'm meeting Cooper for supper and policy documents. We're looking at transportation infrastructure tonight."

"Perfect. Since you are going out, you must eat at supper."

"I will eat at supper."

I take another bite of the apple and picture Cooper's face.

Victoria's wise words are not quite enough to soothe me. I don't know if he'll be crestfallen or relieved if I tell him I cannot do this anymore. I don't know what to tell him, because I'm not sure which one I'll feel, either.

Cooper has discovered his campus library, and he is animated and excited over supper telling me he now has access to every back issue of *Forestry and Irrigation* magazine. He was always a middling student in school, but this man's passion for absorbing information is unmatched.

"How is everything sifting out for you with your classes?" I ask, spinning my spoon in my soup. We are at a noisy café about halfway between my campus and his boarding house, and I am mesmerized by this new sensation of sitting so close to the street and watching people walk by while we dine. It's too loud in here to work, so perhaps we'll find our way to the library later.

He shrugs and pops a grape from his fruit plate into his mouth. "Fine enough. Nothing insurmountable. What about you?"

"I meant, is your class schedule going to work with everything we need you to do for the campaign? It might be quite a lot, and I don't want you to fall behind."

He grins and plucks a few more grapes. "So what if I do? This is my second college degree, remember? If I have to drop a class to make this work, I'll drop a class."

"That's it, you'll just drop a class?"

He makes as if to toss a grape at me, stops, and tosses it up and into his own mouth instead. "That's right. This is important, and I made you a promise. I'll make things work to keep that promise."

I stiffen. "You do not need to rearrange your life to keep a promise to me."

"Yes, actually, I do."

"Cooper, if you want out, we can call it off now. I pressured you to do this on my behalf, and now I've put you in an awful spot having to choose between your priorities and mine. Just say the word. We can call it off."

He bursts out laughing and I drop my soup spoon into the bowl.

"What on earth is so funny?"

"Did I pass the test?"

"What test?"

"Maudie, darling, we have known each other a very long time. This is the 'Cooper quits everything, so why not just give him a way out' test." He winks. "I am not quitting. Would you like to know why?"

"I told you, you don't need to keep that promise to me."

"I am not doing this for you."

"What?"

He leans back in his chair, an amused smile on his lips. The light in his brown eyes is a tease but his tone is somber. "Everything you said about why I have to be the one to do this is now rooted in my brain. You stuck it in my head the way I stuck the idea about college into yours, and this is not just about trees or even suffrage. No one in this country has an easier road to affect change than a white man with a rich father. The rules favor me unfairly, but that means I am uniquely placed to turn the system on its head. I will see this through with you, Maudie, because I cannot quit."

I stare into my soup, cheeks burning as I try to scoot my spoon out with my fork. He tucks a finger under my chin and tips my face up so I'll look at him.

"Are you satisfied?"

There it is again. That word from his lips in such a sweet, caramel tone sets my mouth watering.

"I am, thank you."

He beams. "Excellent. If I order the whole fried chicken, shall we share it, or would you like your own? We have so much to do."

"Now that you mention it, I'm starving."

Chapter 16
Cooper

I've met a hundred people since classes started, but when I feel unmoored, as I do now, there's only one person in this city I really want to see. But I cannot pester her every day, so I'm rattling around my room in near-silence, missing the clatter of dormitory life on one hand and my friends and family back home on the other. I try humming to break the quiet, but all I can come up with is the catchy, obnoxious ditty 'Get On the Raft With Taft' for the presidential campaign. It conjures a humorous visual, because William Howard Taft is a rotund sort of fellow as likely to sink a raft as he is to get stuck in a bathtub.

Perhaps I need a campaign song. Maudie plays piano.

I cannot keep bothering her.

It's Wednesday afternoon, and I should be social on campus somewhere and build up the momentum that started when one of my professors announced my candidacy to an entire lecture hall. I shook dozens of hands after class and promised to bring pamphlets, but the idea of meandering the classroom buildings just to promote myself leaves me cold.

Flipping the pages of *Agriculture and Rural Business* for my class of the same name, I scan my syllabus for the dozenth time to be sure I haven't missed anything for class tomorrow. For the first time in my academic career, I'm not running a year behind. I got the assignment—a few questions based on the first chapters—came right home, and did it.

How rudimentary is that? Why, exactly, have I struggled my entire life not with doing things, but with getting them done?

Exciting Opportunities in Forest Service for Young Men.

I run my fingers over the yellowed advertisement. I didn't get things done because I'm a spoiled boy and I didn't want to do anything that didn't make me immediately happy.

My red-and-white sash is slung over the back of my desk chair. I undo the pin from it and place the little chestnut tree on top of my campaign notebook. How fun this would all be if Leo and I were still living together. On orders from Jeremiah Hamilton, we used to prank Shaw with all kinds of nonsense when he was calling on Maudie. I don't think he ever knew it was us gluing pages of his textbooks together or leaving crickets in his desk drawers. The man can screech like a girl. Leo heard him grumbling one day that he thought he had competition for Maudie's affections, which was enough to get us off the hook. We were just stand-ins for her absent, mischievous older brother giving his sister's suitor a hard time.

Yes, Leo and I could have been plotting my campaign until all hours. Berger lived around the corner in a hall full of our friends and teammates. And with Maudie and Georgia just a brief walk up the hill in town, we could have seen them every day if we liked. What a delightful, well-oiled machine we would be. I glance at my growing stack of notes on the articles I've dug up about Wilmington. Why didn't any of us try to fix this miserable world sooner?

I could go to the library, but it's too quiet.

I could go to the noisy but pleasant café where Maudie and I ate the other day and have dinner with a book.

I could go downstairs in the common room and read for a while, maybe strike up a conversation with the other boarder, a quiet law student. The proprietor of this house is an old man and deaf enough to make any but the briefest conversation difficult. He already loves me for my habit of leaving newspapers around when I've already read them, and when I told him of my campaign, he said I was a nice boy and he would tell everyone he knew to vote for me.

I grab my leather satchel—a near twin of Maudie's, but substantially more battered—and shove in my campaign notebook, a textbook for my class in botanical pharmaceuticals, and some homework due next week. Leo has been working on my print materials, and Maudie said Georgia will have sewn more sashes by now. It's a good enough excuse to go home for an evening.

Autumn hasn't chilled the air yet, and my sister's house is a respite from the heat of the day. She greets me with cool water and fruit even though she wasn't expecting me. Leo will be home from work in an hour, and I'm thrilled to learn our parents will be over for dinner.

"My good luck still follows me some days," I observe, and

I smile when I see the rounding of her stomach has become more noticeable in the two weeks since I moved. "How is my little niece or nephew?"

"Hungry," Georgia says. "Always hungry. I shall be the size of an elephant when the baby shows up."

"You are radiant, sister."

"And you look exhausted, dear brother. You should be jumping around telling me about everything you are learning, but here you are, dragging through my door like a tired old man."

"By all means, spare me your flattery."

"I want you to be well. I love you dearly."

"As I love you. I am finding my pace. My class schedule is palatable and your best friend could serve the army well as a drill sergeant with her orders. It is a huge change for me, but I am pleased with it all, I think."

She lifts a delicate eyebrow and gestures me to sit with her on the sofa. "Do you see Maudie much?"

"Here and there. We went to the football game last weekend and screamed our heads off together, which was a lot of fun. And of course, we work on the campaign."

"And our friend Matthew?"

"Yes, I've seen him a bit, too."

She clears her throat.

"She is encouraging a match between him and her roommate. They came with us on Saturday."

"Then it does not sound like he has spoken to her about any intentions."

My stomach churns. "I don't think so."

"Have you?"

"I did not come over to be interrogated."

"I think you wanted a little sympathy and knew just where to get it," she laughs. "Oh, Cooper. Look at your face. The more you see her, the worse this will get. When are you going to be honest with yourself?"

"I am honest. Even if I thought of her romantically, and I don't, it is a terrible idea to address right now. I value her friendship. I need her for this campaign. And most importantly, she does not want to trouble herself with a man. If I had any reason to trouble her, I still wouldn't."

"Oh, I'm sure she's already troubled by you." She snickers again. "And don't worry. I haven't said a peep to Leo. I'll leave that to you to fess up."

"There's nothing to fess up."

"What a slick liar you are, Mr. Politician."

I open my mouth to protest, but there is a knock at the door and Georgia's maid greets our parents in the hall. Once again, Papa is right on time to save my ass.

As Leo rambles about work through dinner, I second-guess my decision to go back to school again and again. I have one degree. I don't need another. But I changed majors so many times my father said he'd cut off my tuition if I didn't stick with the one I was in until I graduated. After that, I could try something new. I was an engineering student, so I got an engineering degree and am now qualified to design bridges, among other things—a thought that used to excite me as much as saving the Appalachian forests from chestnut blight and illegal logging.

I had always thought Leo and I would follow similar paths and do things at the same time, and while I am genuinely happy for his bliss with Georgia, I am selfish and want him back. We could be on this grand election adventure together if he were still in school and not at work. So much has changed since graduation, like the brother I never had is drifting away from me.

Although, come to think of it, we'd have precious little to drink if he didn't go to Virginia for work so often. Perhaps I should stop complaining and ask him for another bottle of brandy.

"I have a box of pamphlets for you," Leo says. "Three hundred of them, fresh from the press. Infrastructure, worker's rights, votes for women, and conservation. We can add and change things for the next batch, depending on how these go over. How do you want them split out?"

"Maudie wants one hundred and fifty here in town, probably a third of those at your father's bank, if he'll set it up."

"Certainly."

"The post office, drugstore, and city hall. I'll cede the rest to the Bergers to decide. I'll take a hundred. Maudie has claimed fifty."

Papa frowns. "She doesn't have voters."

"She has women who will help me get voters. She's organizing a sort of town hall next week where I will meet the leaders of a lot of her school clubs. Her plan is for them to be so charmed by my grand ideas and good looks that they'll join my team and help canvass here and in the city."

Georgia snorts a laugh. "She certainly knows how to flatter you."

"Oh, I like that idea," Mama says. "Let me help organize when they come up here."

"You have my gratitude, and Maudie's as well."

"How's Shaw doing?" Leo asks, scooping up a bite of eggplant. "I saw he had an announcement in the paper. Anything else?"

"I'm surprised you didn't see him at the press. Berger has a mole in the Democratic Party staff, you know. Some clerk."

"Of course he does."

"Thank God the Bergers are on our side. Anyway, he'll have print material coming out soon, so we are first out of the gate on that as well."

"I'm interested to see if he talks about Wilmington," Leo says.

Georgia nudges his arm. "What happened in Wilmington?"

"In brief, his father's party violently overthrew the city government. In full, the story is not for the dinner table, and I'll explain later. But we think Shaw's proximity to that trouble could be useful."

"What does Maudie think?"

Leo looks to me to answer.

"I—I don't know. It hasn't come up. We are focused more now on presenting my platform and marketing my charm and engaging personality than on attacking his lack of any of those things. Brent is working on some more cartoons to remind everyone I am far handsomer as well."

Papa chuckles as he gives me an approving nod. "You are a thick-headed dolt sometimes, son, but you are a gentleman. A clean campaign in this day and age is a rarity, but Maudie is a lady and certainly skilled at managing the subtleties of public perception. You're making a wise choice in letting her steer the ship."

"All of our classes in polite conversation, turning a table, and managing a household come in handy in the strangest places," Georgia says, winking at our mother. "In steering the ship, it sounds like Maudie has become an admiral."

I frown. "What do you mean, turning a table?"

"It's when you speak to assigned partners during each course of the meal so everyone is included at all times. So, I might talk to my darling husband during the soup course, but when the main dish arrives, I turn and speak to Mama. It's very important for a hostess to plan for this when she plans seating."

Leo, Papa, and I glance at one another, entirely confused. "But we don't do that," I say. "I don't believe I've done that in my entire life."

"Yes, but we could if I wanted to, because the ladies in the room will always know how. If we had dozens of guests to dinner and large centerpieces, you would appreciate seating arrangements more." She nudges Mama's shoulder. "What do you wager none of these men would ever notice the ladies turning the conversation between courses?"

"They would imagine everyone around them thought their company delightful," Mama says, laughing at our confusion. "And so our work would be well done. Maudie will handle your constituents the same way, Cooper, making each of them feel like you care."

"But I do care."

"You're a man. You haven't the faintest idea how to show it properly."

Leo nearly spits a bite of his supper. "Augusta, come now. I demonstrate my care for your daughter every day."

"Let us not recount the misery you inflicted on yourself by not telling me your feelings for years," Georgia says. "You are a man and you were brought up differently. If a woman approached you on the street with tears in her eyes and a hungry baby on her hip and said she was fired from her factory job and cannot feed her family, what would you do?"

He bristles. "I would buy her some food, certainly. Leave her with some money."

"What if there were a hundred of her?"

He pretends to be interested in his eggplant parmesan.

"What would you do?" I ask my sister. "For a hundred hungry women and children, I mean."

"Even if you cannot meet every need in the moment, you should do your best, of course, with what resources you have. But hope costs nothing, and your wallet never run out of it." Her blue eyes meet mine. "The people who need you must feel your compassion for their plight. They are not like you. These are women who have no rights in this system, black men who have rights but see their votes suppressed, factory workers whose bosses' money is more important than their safety. Cooper, they know you will never feel their pain, so they must feel your commitment to do something about it. Saying it is one thing. They need to feel it. A lady's skills as a hostess are about making people feel welcome, considered, and valued. And I have often thought that when we talk about equality between the sexes, that men should be taught the same."

Chapter 17
Maudie

"I tell you, Maudie, the research aspect of this campaign has been fascinating." Cooper dabs fried chicken grease off his fingers with his napkin and leans across the table like he's about to tell me a secret in the middle of the noisy café that seems to be our new campaign headquarters. "What do you know about poll taxes?"

"Not much." I give my soup a stir.

"Well, North Carolina is a sorry state for them. I saw Georgia for dinner the other night and she laid into me about everything under the sun, including voter suppression." He shakes his head as I try another sip of my soup while he catches his breath. "I am blessed beyond measure to have the friends and family I do, but I think sometimes you have all conspired to make me feel stupider by the day. Last year, I took an elective called 'The Carolinas, Past and Present,' and it covered everything from Roanoke to Roosevelt, but what a damned narrow view it all was, pardon me."

"What have you learned?"

"Don't you ever wonder why we don't have any black

legislators? We used to, and we don't anymore. Black men voted in this state, but now it looks like they do not. Why?"

"Poll taxes?"

"Poll taxes and literacy tests, and different ones administered to black and white men by whoever is running the show that day. A black man who is a college graduate must take a test to vote, and I do not have to." He stabs his knife into his fried chicken. "And I am sure you can imagine whose party is responsible for such things."

"It cannot be the Democrats. Can it? I dislike their ideals as much as you do, but they have been in power in Hillside for years, and no one has complained about suppression."

"How would we hear them if they did?"

My cheeks flush with embarrassment. "I do not know."

"Well, I do not know, either. None of it makes any sense to me, and I cannot speak on any of this until I know what the hell to speak about. But I'll wager after what happened in Wilmington with the coup, no one has complained because they are afraid."

I push my soup away and pick up a piece of chicken instead. "The coup in Wilmington was about fear."

"This is all about fear."

I am careful to keep my voice even. "So this is more of your research."

"Well, when I remembered Shaw grew up there, it seemed prudent to learn a bit about how he might perceive current affairs. I am curious about how he thinks he'll represent a town like Hillside when his father was at the forefront of an angry mob that killed men and overthrew an elected government."

"Your father is a reserved, businesslike family man, and I don't see you acting much like him."

He draws back as though I slapped him. "Maudie, you cannot be defending him."

"I will never defend Mr. Shaw's father."

"I meant Toby."

"He was thirteen years old. A child, like we were then."

"Young men have gone to war at that age."

"He didn't do anything wrong."

I sink my teeth into a piece of chicken breast and refuse to meet Cooper's eyes. We cannot start down this path. One does not choose one's parents or their political affiliation.

When Cooper speaks of Wilmington, deep inside me, a little flicker reminds me of the one good thing that always gave me hope for Mr. Shaw every time he delayed or dawdled or said 'not yet.' That one act of such humanity and kindness might not be worth anything to Mr. Shaw anymore, but if Cooper and I lose this race, we will still live in this city. Our families will still be in Hillside. We must refrain from mudslinging.

"Maudie, isn't this something we could use? Show Hillside that he may be of their party, but he comes from these radical supremacists, where—"

"There is nothing to use, Cooper. If Mr. Shaw raises the topic of the coup, we will respond. We will not raise it ourselves."

He eyes me over the chicken, lips twisted in confusion as the silence between us blurs with the noise of the cafe and the rumble of carriages on the street outside.

"Well, if you're sure—"

"I am sure."

Supper takes a more pleasant turn when we drop the election strategy conversations for a while. I share my squeamish reaction to dissecting a frog in biology and he mimics my faces as I go along. Then Cooper announces that if we're going to talk about the disgusting things we've learned lately, I should know about how much the dung of a buffalo herd is responsible for fertilizing the wild grasses the herd will consume the following year.

"What a lovely little ecosystem they've made for themselves," I muse, scraping the last bite of chicken from my plate. "Such massive, lumbering beasts. You would think them clumsy and awkward to look at, but what a delicate balance they maintain. We do not give nature enough credit for getting along just fine without our intervention, I think. And what a shame we are destroying it."

"A shame, indeed. How I would love to take President Roosevelt up on his call for young men to build his national parks."

"Is it too late?"

He taps his notebook. "It may come as a shock to you, but I must prioritize the rights of women and workers over my personal indulgence in trees and ranging herds. One day, though. There might be a way."

In September, the evenings are long and often the only time of day it is pleasant to be outside. Only a block from the busy street in front of the café, the city quiets as we approach the little park next to my campus. The main building of classrooms and dormitory suites towers over us, a Queen Anne-style castle of a place, dwarfing the smaller classroom building added recently to accommodate growing enroll-ment. My classmates are also anxious to appreciate the fine weather and have crowded nearly every bench with flounced skirts, schoolbooks, and gentleman callers, so we fall in step and start a walk around the white gravel path.

"I like seeing you wear this." He strokes the caramel leather where my satchel strap wraps over my shoulder. "I am so pleased you like it."

"It was such a thoughtful gift. I've had several compli-ments from my classmates. It seems I am fashion-forward now."

"I am glad it's to your taste. I worried a bit. You are known to be quite discerning."

"Am I?"

He holds up three fingers and winks as I swat his hand out of the air.

"I hardly think my taste in satchels and proposals is related."

"Isn't it? Maudie, if one is to be choosy about anything, that should be it. More women should emulate you."

"You may call me choosy and laugh at me if you wish. Only understand that behind each of those proposals is a great deal of disappointment, and then let's see if you tease me about it."

His smile falls away. "I meant no harm. I am sorry. Please don't call me a scoundrel. I could not handle being a varmint."

"It is so hard to stay mad at you." I don't bother to fight my smile. "You're still welcome to be my fourth proposal, remem-ber. I do my best to make my refusals painless."

"How is that possible?"

"Well, I don't throw a fit or insult anyone. There are plenty of ladylike ways to say no."

"That does not make it painless for the poor gentleman on the receiving end." He shakes his head. "No, thank you. It's bad enough to be branded a rogue. Must I be a miserable one?"

I cannot hold back a giggle. "I doubt I have left a gentleman in misery."

"I think you underestimate how tender a man's heart can be. I am in agony just thinking about your ladylike ways of saying no."

I smack his arm. "You are so dramatic. It wasn't like that at all."

"Then tell me how it was."

"Cooper."

"But it is such a lovely evening for a walk. Start at the beginning, please. Eddie Carmichael."

Shaking my head, I fight another giggle. Sometimes I forget how much of my life he's already been a part of through Georgia. I've known this man since we were in sailor suits and wagons.

"All right." I cross my arms. "Edward Carmichael. When he asked me—"

"Stop. How long?"

"What?"

"How long had he been courting you when he asked?"

"Why does that matter?"

"Details matter. Go on, please."

"Well. I suppose he'd been calling on me for four or five months. It wasn't long after my debut, so I was still eighteen, I think. And when he asked me—"

"Did he ask your father?"

"Did he—no, he said he wanted to ask me first. Why?"

He pretends to scribble a note on his hand. "Again, details. Carry on."

"He was very sweet and very shy, and he simply worshiped the ground I walked on. He was good company and everything my parents thought a good match would be."

"But?"

"I didn't love him. I didn't know him well enough. And when he started singing my praises with this long, blithering speech, I distinctly remember thinking 'well, I'm a delight, but what about you? What about us?' That's what a marriage is meant to be, isn't it? Us. Two people coming together as one."

"Of course," he murmurs.

"I told him I was honored by his esteem and affection and was open to the idea of marriage if he wished to discuss it more before actually proposing it again."

He draws back from me and winces. "Ouch."

"What's wrong with that? It's not as though I told him to go away and never return. I left the door open to get to know each other more."

"I told you, secondhand agony. There's nothing wrong with what you said, but..." He rubs his stomach like he's been punched. "It's hard for me to imagine. Next up. Wilson Brown."

I press a hand to my heart. "You know what is funny about Wilson? If he had proposed to me two weeks after I met him, I'd have leapt into his arms and followed him to China. I thought he was the most clever, charming, hand-some man I had ever met."

Cooper grabs his chest like he's been shot. "I take that personally."

"You should." I smack his arm again as we approach the far end of the park, away from my twittering classmates. "The delightful Mr. Brown left all of you silly schoolboys in the dust."

"Then why are you not the delightful Mrs. Brown?"

"In hindsight, I see very clearly that the shine wore off. He was a fine man and I have no complaints of him. Even when I grew a bit bored of him, I figured that if he asked me to marry him I would say yes because I did care about him very much. But then..."

"Mr. Shaw came a-calling."

I plop gracelessly onto a bench. What little luster was left on my romance with Wilson Brown faded quickly when I met Mr. Shaw. "I would never have met him had I not gone with Georgia to cheer at your football games. Thank you ever so much for that."

Cooper situates himself at my side and tucks my hand back in the crook of his arm. "So had you not come to cheer for me—"

"I went to cheer for Leo and Matthew."

"Had you not come to cheer for us, you might be Mrs. Brown today." I can feel his gaze on me—he's wondering how his joke has landed as I stare at my fingers. He continues with a more serious tone. "How did that end?"

"About seven months after it started—with flowers, moonlight, and another blithering speech about how lovely I am. By that time, he knew Mr. Shaw was calling on me and I think he felt pressured to act. I told Georgia once that if Mr. Brown proposed first, I would gladly accept and be content.

Yet the moment it happened—" I snap my fingers. "I couldn't do it. I couldn't just be content. He was a bit put out since he thought he won by virtue of being first in line."

Cooper furrows his brows. "I would be, too, if I spent months courting a girl and—did he speak with your father?"

"He did. And he bought a ring."

"Well, if I had gone to all that trouble and the girl I loved said no to my blithering speech, I think I'd be a bit put out as well."

"He was a gentleman about it. I was honest and kind and explained my reasoning. There is no bad feeling between us, just as there is none with Mr. Carmichael."

And no swoons, either. Flowers, lavish compliments, even a diamond ring, and this heart of mine that swells with emotion for everyone else's good news didn't even flutter from its usual pulse. Declining him was mathematical. This reason plus that reason equals farewell, Mr. Brown.

"And with Mr. Shaw?"

"I've rambled on enough." I stand and brush down my skirts.

He takes my arm to steady me. "I did not mean to upset you, Maudie. Sit back down and ask me anything. I owe you a confidence in return for all you just shared with me."

"Oh, that is too tempting." I settle back at his side on the bench. "May I ask anything?"

"Anything. You must trust your candidate."

I twitch my fingers in my lap. "You said at Georgia's house one night that you worried certain old habits of yours might become news. How did you—I mean, is it true you never courted a girl the normal way, or even wanted to?"

"That's true."

"Why not?"

"You already asked your one question."

"I gave you two proposals with all the details you asked for."

He winks. "Fair. I have never called on a girl—a woman—beyond common courtesy for two reasons. One, I think our society's rituals around courtship and marriage are barbaric. And two, even if I did meet someone I like enough to put up with the rituals for, I wouldn't ask her to put up with that archaic nonsense for me."

"Barbaric?"

"What do you call a marriage arranged by parents with no regard for love? What is a marriage forced between two parties just because they consent to kiss—or even just to spend time alone without chaperones?"

"It is rather fussy."

"Name any girl from your school and I will tell you what I thought of her at the time of her debut. Listen to how I was taught to think."

"Maybelle Howard."

"A fine hostess and planner, shrill, bossy, and probably won't let you touch her unless it's to make the annual baby. Next."

I gasp.

"Come on."

"Adeline Winston."

"Beautiful and far too aware of it, has a stuck-up mother who will be hell at holidays, and her fine piano playing makes up for none of the displeasure of her company. Will likely not be inclined to tolerate much of the marital chore but will wink at your friends on the sly."

"My God, Cooper. Mollie Caldwell."

"Delightfully well-read, studious and shy, and very willing to practice kissing if you can sneak her away."

"She didn't. You're joking," I whisper through my fingers.

"I am not." He pulls my hand away and kisses it. "And Mollie is a perfect example of the problem. What's wrong with kissing? I may not have taken her up on it, but I respect her for enjoying herself. If I were like Matthew Berger or Jacob Bowman or any of the others from my class who wanted to see what kissing was like, I would be opening myself up to the possibility of a life-long commitment if the wrong person saw us. No kiss was ever worth that to me."

"Did Matthew kiss her?"

He whistles at the sky.

"You are impossible. Didn't it occur to you to spend some time with a girl and get to know her without kissing to see if she was worth the risk? I never kissed Mr. Carmichael or Mr. Brown all those months."

"Because you are a lady and they are gentlemen." He nudges my shoulder. "And I am a rogue, remember? Perhaps only the rogues get kisses."

"I kissed Mr. Shaw, and he is nothing like you."

"Thank goodness. I wouldn't like to be a two-faced weasel." He pauses and a little smile curls his lips. "Well. Maybe if it meant I got to kiss you again."

"You and I enjoyed a few risky kisses."

"I think of them often."

He takes my hand in his and my pulse pounds at my wrist. Clamping my teeth down on my tongue, I fight to keep from asking him why it was worth it to kiss me and no one else. I cannot be the only woman he's kissed outside a brothel. There must have been someone else. Mollie, or someone like her. There had to be.

"Mr. Shaw did not propose to me until I told him I wanted him to leave," I blurt out instead.

His brows lift. "I did not know that part. The word about town was that he asked you to marry him and you turned him down because of the change in his platform."

"That's mostly true." I lean back on the bench so I cannot see his face. "The conversation about suffrage came up first. This is when he still thought he could run in Wilmington, of course, so his father's advisors were making plans. And when he told me, I…" I cover my face with my hands. "I was most unladylike."

He tickles my elbow. "I love an unladylike lady."

"It is lucky we were in the back garden, because I screamed at him like a shrew." I peek through my fingers and spy him fighting a chuckle. "Cooper. It was awful."

"It sounds fantastic. Lady Liberty standing on her principles. Oh, to have been a fly on the wall. Or a fly in the hedge."

"You would have been most helpful as a bee to sting him and shut him up before he—oh yes, this is when it happened. I shrieked like a fishwife and that man dropped to his knees, whipped out a ring he just happened to have in his pocket, and proposed."

"With a long, blithering speech about how beautiful you are when you are furious, no doubt. Believe me, the image is seared in my mind."

"Well, he blithered a bit, but more about how I should trust him and we should work together on his campaign and a future together and more nonsense."

"But not about your many virtues or how much he loves you?"

"What? No."

"And it doesn't sound like he asked your father. Ring already in the pocket, though. Impressive."

"Cooper Truxton."

"Sorry. Taking notes. As it seems there's no consensus on what to include in the proposal speech, I'd be best off with no blithering at all."

"That's not funny." I pause. "But yes. By all means, skip the blithering. It's all so very—you know, I didn't even turn him down, really. I never said no. I just walked away."

"An action that speaks loud and clear on its own." He sneaks a hand over mine again and squeezes. "Well. For whatever the opinion of a nosy, boorish rogue is worth, I'm very glad you're not Mrs. Carmichael or Mrs. Brown or Mrs. Shaw today."

I close my eyes and their faces flash before me. Edward Carmichael, embarrassed beyond belief that I declined him and unwilling to take the second chance I offered. Wilson Brown in the moonlight on the front porch with pretty words and a stunning ring, crestfallen when I said I did not see a future for us. Mr. Shaw lingers, not in the garden, but with the teasing smile he wore so often back when I called him Toby and thought I might one day call him husband. I will see him again soon, I have no doubt—without that smile and perhaps without any warmth between us at all, and my heart sinks as that view of him fades.

I open my eyes and there's only Cooper, a shy smile on his face like he's on the cusp of a laugh, his hand still curled around mine.

"So am I."

Chapter 18
Cooper

The evening before Gregory and Angeline's wedding, I make my first solo campaign appearance. Maudie has already gone back to Hillside for the weekend, so I must face a small crowd of my fellow students alone. After a quick show of hands to determine where everyone is from, I address the out-of-towners with instructions about how to register to vote in the city if they wish.

"Regardless of your party affiliation, gentlemen, if you have any political inclinations of your own, look into the residency requirements in your home districts. Full-time students are all eligible to register here. But my opponent Tobias Shaw learned to his disappointment that voting here superseded his residency in his hometown of Wilmington, leaving him unable to run for the seat his father vacated a few years ago. He is stuck with us, his second choice for a district to represent. I should hate for any of you to find yourselves in such a fix."

A voice rings from the center of the small auditorium. "He's a carpetbagger."

A plant in the audience was Maudie's idea. After the professor announced my campaign in my agricultural business seminar, several classmates offered their support. I have a few new friends in the crowd today with instructions to move the conversation along if things get dull.

A murmur of approval arises.

"A carpetbagger and an opportunist," I say. "But we are not here to talk about him. We are here to talk about trees."

My brief lecture focuses on forestry and infrastructure, the topics I thought would be of most interest to my fellow students—and the least controversial. I might drag Maudie to the lectern if I am asked to answer questions on factory conditions, but as an engineer and an amateur conservationist, I can handle questions about roads and bridges.

"Mr. Ford up in Michigan is set to ship tens of thousands of his Model T automobiles in a matter of months." I hold up a full-color ad from *The Saturday Evening Post*. "These are made for every man, affordable and easy to maintain, but outside the center of our city, our roads are rutted from carriages. Automobiles will vastly improve our lives, but only if we have the foresight to improve our roads. When every man with a little money in his pocket can buy a Model T, he wants somewhere to drive it. If our streets become mangled and perhaps impassable to those in carriages, we will lose our status as a business destination in a matter of months."

At this juncture, my new friends rise and pass leaflets to the crowd. "Raleigh, Durham, and Chapel Hill." I point to each one on the leaflet. "The three finest universities in the state exist here, with businesses booming around them, and it is my idea that we collaborate with the representatives of those districts to resurface the roads between our cities first. We will optimize this entire section of the state and show our cities the reason to invest in better local roads as well, and boost one another's economies in the process. Who would like to take their lady for an evening at the theater in Durham instead of seeing the same show for the tenth time here? Who would join friends for an away game to watch our teams play in Chapel Hill?"

That gets a murmur of approval and some applause. I bounce on my toes for a moment like an excited child with a boost of energy. Maudie will like to hear I can handle a little of this on my own.

The next morning, I am in fine spirits and ready to brag to Maudie about my success as soon as I can see her. I whistle as I hop out of the open carriage and extend my hand to Berger to help him in like a lady. Instead of the eye roll I expected, he greets me with a ringing laugh and a slap on the shoulder. "It's a beautiful morning, Trux. And it's going to be a beautiful day."

"You're in a delightful mood." I climb back into my seat.

"I'm marrying off a sister. Weren't you a little relieved to see Georgia settled? Imagine having three more after her to worry about." He narrows his eyes as the carriage rolls into motion, and we are bound for Hillside and a busy day. "A favor, please. Do not pay my sister Catherine too much attention today. Angeline thinks she has a little infatuation with our new political darling."

I bristle. "And this offends you?"

"The hellish opposite of a happily-wed sister is a heart-broken one, so yes, unless you have drastically changed your stance on courtship and marriage, it offends me."

"Ah. Well, I shall pay her no attention beyond what is required, then."

"Thank you."

"A political darling, am I? Already?"

He flips idly through the stack of newspapers I brought along for the lulls in the day's schedule. "You tasked me with managing your public relations, and it's better to stay ahead of the rumors with positive talk than try to clean up after a mess. A good story can beat a nasty rumor if done right, and I would not be surprised if your stated devotion to women's causes nets you some female attention."

"My stated devotion?"

He lifts a brow. "Must I explain the sharp divide between what you do and what you say?"

"What I did, thank you. Maudie says that although we should be prepared to steer away from my past behavior if the subject arises, it will not be an issue unless Shaw makes it one."

"And why wouldn't he? I hate to point it out, my friend, but he lived in our hall and you were not especially discreet."

"Maudie believes he will not."

"Why not?"

"I asked her twice, she demurred, and I gave up. I decided when I told her I would run that I would leave myself in her capable hands, and so I shall."

He shakes his head. "I envy the time you spend with her, Trux. I should have taken her up on the suggestion when she asked me to run first."

I forgot she asked him first.

"Angeline did me the kindness of pairing me with Maudie today," Berger continues, "so she will be with me for all activities with the bridal party and seated with me at supper."

My stomach churns and I am glad I have nothing in it to bring up. "I'm sure you'll have fun. She is delightful company."

"And the bridesmaids' dresses are pink. She looks so lovely in pink."

"Indeed, she does." I flip a few pages in my paper. "Did you see the new—"

"Do you really believe what Georgia said about her having no interest in seeing anyone?"

I glare. "My sister is no liar. We are rarely treated to a glimpse of women's conversations on private matters, so the fact that she shared it tells me she is quite serious."

"I meant no offense to your sister."

"Then do not suggest I should not believe what she says."

There's the eye roll.

"All I mean is that I wonder if Maudie might be gently convinced to give me a chance."

When I think of my conversation with Maudie about her proposals, it's plain she is still a little wistful about Toby Shaw. It stings me, and it shouldn't. While I already admire her for standing up for her beliefs, that admiration is multiplied when I look at what it costs her tender heart to stand against such a man. Beneath all her strength, she has as fragile a heart as anyone, and hearts are not always quick to mend. Her hurt shows in her eyes and the tone of her voice sometimes in a way I cannot pretend I don't see.

I cannot speak now about these feelings Georgia thinks I have for her, even if I wanted to. And I don't, so there's nothing to speak about. Maudie knows her own mind, and if she says she's not ready to love again, she's not ready. I'm Berger's friend, not his nanny, and I've said enough to make a sane man back off. If he's stupid enough to pressure her, he'll get whatever she flings at him.

I hope it's a chair.

I re-fold my newspaper and shuffle through the stack for another. "Do you know how hard it is to find a black news-paper in this city? After what happened in Wilmington, it is no wonder a black man would not like to own a printing press, but I followed some tips to find a sort of underground broadsheet and am determined to hunt down every issue from now on. They don't offer a subscription."

His brows furrow at the sudden change of subject. "Why are you looking for black newspapers?"

"Because I like newspapers and am determined to broaden my selection. I know so little about half of the citizens I am asking to represent. The rot in this state runs deep, and I am ashamed of how little I know."

"What's this about Wilmington?"

I give him the rundown of my father's lecture and watch his eyes bug out. All the parents in Hillside must have thought like mine, protecting us from anything unpleasant since they survived one war and would not like to engage in another one.

"And you think Shaw was there for all that?" he asks.

"It's where he grew up, and that's his father's party."

"It's Shockley's party, too, and Hillside loves him. But then again, he's so neutral on everything it's a wonder he even shows up to the assembly. Everyone rests easy voting for him because no matter what they believe in, he's bound to ignore it."

"It is no wonder he has not endorsed Shaw." I grab the side of the carriage as we jolt left and turn onto the road that zig-zags up the hill toward home. "Papa wonders why the Democrats did not field another candidate more like Shockley to continue their successful blandness."

"My source in the county office believes a large check from Ashford Shaw's federal campaign funds made its way to his son's local ones."

"Is that legal?"

He shrugs. "Apparently when you give money to elect a Shaw, you don't get to decide which one. I'll leave that to you and Maudie to decide if it's worth pursuing. The law is a matter of interpretation between state and federal rules."

"We are lucky to have you, Berger. You have my thanks, and hers as well."

"What's she say about the Wilmington situation? Is that something we can use against him?"

"I think so, but it doesn't matter what I think. She says we are not bringing it up." I jab a finger at him. "In any capacity, official or otherwise, so don't start anything unless you want to make her mad."

He settles back in his seat and I pass him the broadsheet. "Why wouldn't we use that information?" he muses. "Hillside doesn't like radicals on either side, really."

"She said it won't help. Just like the issue of my past behavior when I asked about preparing for that to arise—I asked twice, then left it alone. She said we'll be ready, and I trust her. She knows his methods and motivations."

"And thank goodness she does. I heard your event went well last night, by the way. Congratulations."

I stare. "How on earth do you know that?"

He bobs his finger through the air as if connecting dots. "William Hutchinson was there, and he told his brother Ernest, who works at the bank with my cousin."

"Yes, but do you all just stay up all night writing letters? How did word get to you already? Do you have a network of pigeons?"

"That's a fine idea, now that you mention it." He laughs. "You know, I am kicking myself for not approaching Maudie after she sent Carmichael packing years ago. But perhaps I needed to pass these years either alone or with boring girls to appreciate what an extraordinary woman she is."

And we are back to this, with twenty minutes to go in our ride. I must remember I am a co-conspirator in Maudie's matchmaking scheme, even if my vision is a little clouded by some leftover delusions of my own.

"Well, if she's not interested, I am sure some other extraordinary woman will sink her claws into you." I keep my tone bright. "Victoria is rather pretty, and exceedingly clever. You seemed to enjoy her company at the football game."

"Yes, Victoria is very nice," he says absently. He gives the sky another appreciative glance and smiles at the cloudless, blue expanse. "What a lovely day it is going to be."

Chapter 19
Maudie

My heart flutters when Angeline's mother and sisters slip a cloud of white satin and lace over her head, and when she emerges, pink-cheeked and smiling, we rush to smooth her skirts and sleeves. Her mama fastens heirloom pearls in her ears while the other bridesmaids and I coo at the antique lace veil her maids have spent hours whitening for the occasion of the first Berger girl of her generation getting married.

Angeline is radiant, and her smile is so broad and genuine it is hard to believe she is the same girl Georgia and I bickered with in school. She is a Berger, so I cannot fault her for being a gossip, but she used to be quite catty about it sometimes. In her case, making changes in her life for a man worked out very well, indeed. I should be less judgmental about people who do that since I see what joy it brings her. Selfishly, I am also glad to have another friend.

She comes to stand behind me at the mirror and squeezes my shoulders when I tuck in one of my curls that has come a little loose. "Look at us," she whispers. "Maudie, you will be the next bride, I guarantee it. How beautiful you look today."

"I am so happy to celebrate with you, but I don't want this any time soon."

She pouts. "You always wanted it before."

"Well, we see how wonderfully that turned out. Three times."

"They weren't right for you. Someone is."

"Later, perhaps." I pinch my cheeks to make them pink. "I am supposed to send you Victoria's regrets if she does not attend today. She said she would try, but when I left last night she was laid up with an awful cold and quite miserable."

"Poor darling. I will tell her sister Edith in case she worries."

I beckon her closer so we can avoid the ears of the other women milling about. "Victoria told me she danced with your brother at Edith's wedding and she was quite taken with him. What do you think of that?"

"Which brother?"

I pinch her arm. "Well, it was William's wedding, and it certainly wasn't little Anthony. Matthew, of course."

"Of course." She taps her finger to her lips. "I have nothing ill to say of Victoria, but I don't see a match there."

"Why not?"

I am desperate to shake the squeamish feeling that crept in the evening Leo made a joke about Matthew and me. Georgia silenced him immediately and we haven't spoken of it since, but there are moments when Matthew's smile becomes more tender and I think he is looking at me in a way he didn't before.

"It's nothing. You'll be walking with Matthew today,

though, so maybe—oh." She pops up as her mother places her veil and everyone gathers closer. The sweet scent of orange blossoms from the wreath on her head lingers over us like a perfume, and her diamond ring sparkles in the morning sun.

The scene is much like the day of Georgia's wedding, our friend Ellen's wedding, and all the other weddings where I've stood by a bride and smiled. Everything is full of warmth and love and heirloom lace—safe and predictable—only this time I am not planning my own nuptials in my head. Maybe it's just my anxious excitement to ask Cooper how his event went last night, but my mind isn't occupied with its usual things on wedding days, and I am rather proud of myself for that.

When we walk down the aisle ahead of Angeline, I spot Cooper and Leo in a pew with their parents. My heart sinks a little when I don't see Georgia with them. She was more tired than usual last night and joked that her father could use his daily allotment of energy to attend the ceremony so she could save hers for supper and dancing. I must trust her when she says her pregnancy is quite normal and nothing to be concerned about, but I miss so much down in the city that every time I see her, it's something of a shock. I always thought she and I would be doing this together, having our babies and raising them, but it must be better to do it later than to do it with the wrong man.

I scoot between Angeline's sister and their cousin when we reach the steps to the altar, and we angle ourselves to show off every flounce and ruffle of our pink dresses without upstaging the bride. We gaze admiringly at Angeline, who blushes when her new husband places her wedding band. I know this role so well I could hire myself out as a bridesmaid for women who need to make up numbers when their friends fall ill.

Gregory and his groomsmen are debonair in morning dress with orange blossoms in their buttonholes to match our bouquets. I cannot turn to face the audience, but I smile at little Anthony Berger, a stoic boy of twelve who is puffing out his chest to stand tall next to his brother.

When the marriage is pronounced and the couple has their kiss, Matthew and I are the third pair to proceed down the aisle. "You are stunning," he whispers as I take his elbow.

I don't look at him since I am supposed to face the pews and smile—and my eyes land on Cooper, who smiles back. He taps his lapel as I walk by and I spot the tree pin I made for him looking entirely homemade and out-of-place on his fine suit. The pride in his brown eyes sets my heart fluttering as Matthew tugs my arm so I'll keep up with him.

The luncheon that follows the ceremony is for the family and bridal party only, and we will not see the rest of the guests until we meet for supper and dancing this evening. My leather satchel looks entirely ridiculous with my bridesmaid's dress, but I have biology homework. I lifted a weight off my shoulders and dropped Modern Southern Politics, but if I don't stay ahead of schedule on my reading, I could find myself in big trouble when midterm exams come up in a few weeks.

"Today is not a day for studying." Matthew sneaks up

behind me and plucks at my hair. "Even I managed to leave my textbooks alone, and I am more or less required to memorize the Constitution this week."

I swat his hand away. "You manage your studies and I'll manage mine."

"But you're dressed for a party and your nose is in a book."

"I'm dressed for a picture, just like you are." I point down the hall to the parlor where Angeline and Gregory are posing with their parents for a photo. "When we are done here, I'll go to my parents' house to rest and finish my reading before supper."

"I look forward to sitting with you tonight. Even if we must talk about—" He peers at the spine of my book. "*Lucent's Biology*."

I sit up. "Would you like to? I am dissecting a frog and can tell you all about it. Victoria did hers last year and helped me get over being squeamish. She is going to be a nurse, you know, and loves her science classes."

"Are you tired of talking politics?"

"Not really. But I am training my mind to focus on one thing at a time. This morning was the wedding, and for now, it's the frog." I flip a page and show him a diagram.

"You are a rare woman, Maudie." He smiles and plucks at my hair again. "I'll see you tonight."

Chapter 20
Cooper

G eorgia is arm-in-arm with both Leo and me when we enter the ballroom, and she shrugs us both off in a blink when she sees Maudie and races to her side.

My mouth falls open when I see her.

She's done something new with her hair, twisted up as usual but with a thick curl draped forward over the curve of her neck like a fall of gold begging to be touched. And there's something different about her dress—the way it fits, the way it skims her shoulders and clings to her hips a little tighter and lower than I've seen on her before. It must be some new fashion, and that gown hugs her figure in a way that makes my hands jealous.

"Trux." Leo elbows me.

"Huh?"

"I said, Gregory's over there. Want to ask him if we can add a little contraband to one of the punch bowls?"

"How old are we now?"

He shrugs. "Not old enough, apparently."

"Maudie will kill me if I ruin this because I was caught spiking punch at a wedding, but by all means, you ask him."

He disappears to the other side of the room.

When she looks up and smiles at me, I want to race after Leo and gulp down whatever he's got in that flask. Berger lingers behind her, surveying me like a territorial cat, but her eyes draw me in.

"I saw your pin this morning." Her shoulders shake with a suppressed giggle as I twitch my fingers on my lapel to show I'm sporting it again. "Look."

Her dress has a satin flower on it with petals that drape over one shoulder. She pushes a few of the petals aside to show me she's wearing her pin to match mine.

I lift my chin. "Well, I expect nothing less from my devoted campaign manager. Although I am a little sad you must hide your allegiance."

"My allegiance to you is unchanged." Her cheeks blush a little pinker as she steps toward me. "Matthew says your event went well last night."

"It did. Are you proud of me?"

"You know I am."

Berger is breathing down her neck. If he wants to embarrass himself with these antics, I won't stop him unless she looks uncomfortable. I should step away and find someone else to talk with instead of putting her between us. She looks comfortable enough for now.

As a matter of fact, she is radiant, and when she turns to speak to him, he stops glaring at me and switches on a smile like she hung the moon in the sky for him.

Instead of vying for her attention, I beckon him over. "Do your sources have any more information on people I should not pay much attention to this evening? I've already noted Catherine."

He breathes a sigh—instantly, visibly calmer. "Tabitha Jeffries wants nothing to do with you. Consider yourself free of the obligatory dance."

"Excellent."

"You probably shouldn't dance with Maudie much, if at all."

"Why not?"

"Because you are working together so closely and no one believes a single man and a single woman can do that without complications."

I snort. "You believe people will doubt our professional relationship if we dance at a wedding?"

"It's something to think about. Maudie is in a rare enough position by working on this campaign with you. It is a little scandalous to some people already. For her sake, I wouldn't add fuel to that fire."

"Berger?"

"What?"

"Did you ever kiss Mollie Caldwell?"

He shrugs. "Didn't you?"

Catherine Berger has changed since my graduation party. When we danced that evening—a while before my botched spin with Miss Jeffries and my one-sided boxing match with Toby Shaw—she was trembling with nerves and only offered brief answers to simple questions. She must have taken lessons from her sister this summer, because she looks a great deal like Angeline now—chin held high, flaunting the curve of her pretty shoulders in a low-necked gown she knows how to pose to her advantage. What's more, she's obviously rehearsed for a conversation with me, and elbows her way to my side as a song begins so I am obliged to dance with her.

"How do you balance your classes and campaign commitments?" she asks after beginning our dance with bland pleasantries and feigned shyness. "You must be terribly busy."

"I am, but I manage with careful planning. Maudie has mapped out every appearance, so we have time to align our calendars."

"What is your favorite class?"

"Rangeland Sciences. We are learning about how the diet of the great buffalo impacts the biodiversity of Appalachian forests."

I made that up. There's not a wild buffalo within a thousand miles of Appalachia, and anyone with a passing knowledge of geography would call me out on the lie.

As expected, it flits past her like a butterfly, gone in a flutter of her lashes.

"There is a buffalo in the zoo in Washington," she says brightly. "Have you seen it?"

"No. Have you?"

"No."

She scrunches her nose. I think I can actually see her searching her brain for the next thing she ought to say, and I am tempted to break the silence with a tidbit about the fertilization properties of buffalo dung, since she pretended interest.

"Do you ever talk with your brother about his studies?" I

ask instead. "I believe the world needs more women reading the law. Men's interpretations have gotten tired."

"We studied some in history. Matthew says his classes now are very tedious, though. Not like yours, I am sure."

As if on cue, his laugh rings over the dance floor and I see Maudie smiling in his arms—amused, no doubt, by some witty recitation of the Stamp Act or the Bill of Rights.

"Well, we should study what suits us," I say. "Tedium suits him, I see."

"You are not tedious, Mr. Truxton." She bats her lashes again.

"I have many flaws, but I like to think tedium is not one of them."

"I think you are a fine man, Mr. Truxton. Perhaps not flawless." She glances up at me, eyes wide as if she's surprised by her own flirtation. "But you are lovely to talk to, and to dance with."

Will this song ever end?

"Have you considered college, Miss Berger? Maudie is enjoying it very much. I believe you would be the first woman in your family to go, as she is."

"I had not planned on it."

"What do you do with your days, since you are done with school?"

She flusters. "I—I do what everyone does. I receive callers and I sew and I garden. I do things at the church with Mama. And I play the harp."

"The harp is a fine instrument. Your brother says you and your sister Lillian are both very accomplished."

"Lillian is only fifteen, and I am much better than she is. I would love to play for you sometime."

"Hm." I look over her head as the music slows and see Maudie extracting herself from Berger's arms even though the dance is not finished. I wonder what he said to her.

"I have many other hobbies and interests, Mr. Truxton." Catherine nods at the open doors to the terrace. "Perhaps we could walk a little and talk some more."

My face goes cold.

"Thank you for the dance, Miss Berger. I hope you enjoy your evening."

A plaintive protest escapes her lips as I turn my back, the height of rudeness, but there is only one thought in my head: I am not leaving this room with that girl.

I am not walking with her onto a terrace, even a terrace full of people, because all those people may go back inside and leave us alone. Then all she has to do is complain to her father that I made a lewd joke or kissed her, two things no one would put past me, and I'm either engaged or run out of town. I cannot call a lady a liar.

In the last five years, I've smiled and shaken hands with five friends who married because the bride's father or brother said they must. Only one of those seems to like his wife after the honeymoon—Leo's older brother, who, to his credit, was a happy groom and is an even happier husband. Leave it to a Rigby to find the romance in a shotgun wedding. I want nothing to do with any of it.

Tugging at the neck of my shirt, I scan the ballroom for Leo to ask him which punch bowl has the brandy in it. He's dancing with Maudie, who appears much more relaxed now, and that means my sister is seated somewhere close by.

I find her in a quiet alcove—another too-convenient place to get in trouble. She can sit wherever she likes with whomever she likes now that she's married, but this place is full of traps.

"The baby is not much of a dancer, I see." I pull up a chair at her side.

"I think this is my last social event for a while. Maudie will make sure Leo has a partner when he wants to dance."

"Funny. I would have expected him to sit out every one to stay at your side."

She grins. "Perhaps I have it backward. Maudie would like to dance every dance, and I will loan her my husband to give her a good excuse to wriggle out of Matthew's embraces."

"You are the most delightful sister and friend."

"I am, aren't I?" She folds her hands over her belly. "And how are you managing?"

"I feel like I ought to be chaperoned like a lady so no one compromises me."

"Stay here with me. I'll protect you."

When the music ends, Leo spins Maudie right into the alcove with us. He turns to Georgia at once to ask how she's feeling and Maudie reaches for my hands.

At the edge of the dance floor, my hand shakes when I push the petals of the flower on her dress aside to see the pin with my tree on it. "Look at us, Maudie. A matched set."

"Well-matched indeed."

We begin the dance, and although I've looked forward to speaking with her all day, I can only move my lips enough to smile. I thought I would tease her a little about the last time we danced or tell her about my campus meeting yesterday. Instead, my tongue is numb and I cannot even muster a compliment or a joke.

She doesn't seem to mind my silence, casting her eyes

down and back up now and then, always with the prettiest little twitch of a smile as if to tell me she likes this rare quiet, too.

Even with the orchestra playing and dancers whirling around us, we are at peace together and all my tension ripples away with the notes of the Blue Danube waltz. She's the only woman in the world I'd venture onto that terrace or into an alcove with because I know in the deepest recesses of my cynical heart that everything my sister suspected is true. Maudie's smile is a cool breeze in this warm crowd. As long as I'm with her, I can stay in this stuffy, oppressive place as long as I have to.

She sinks into a curtsy to finish the song and Berger is already there to grab her arm.

"Matthew, there you are." Her voice shatters the bubble around us. "I dropped Leo off with Georgia so he could check on her, and Cooper was looking after her."

"He is a devoted brother." Berger grins at me like he doesn't see Maudie is walking a tightrope. She looks desperately uncomfortable glancing between us, and I'll excuse myself to make this easier on her if I must. I'll save my posturing for politics.

"And I think I'll make my way back over there." Maudie's right hand is already tucked in Berger's arm, so I reach for her left and bring it to my lips to kiss. "Thank you for the dance, Maudie. Are you coming back to the city tonight, or staying in town?"

She pulls back from him. "I hope to go back tonight, if I can find a party to get a carriage. I have three study groups tomorrow and I just know that if I sleep in my own bed at home, I'll snooze right through church and miss all of them. And I should check on Victoria since she's been unwell."

I nod at Berger, pretending deference to his position as her escort. "I'll make sure you get a carriage," he says. "I was also planning to go back tonight."

"Excellent." I slap his shoulder so hard he nearly loses his footing. "It's settled. We'll all go back tonight."

Chapter 21
Maudie

I dance twice more with Matthew, dodging compliments and longing looks, and twice more with Leo, who swoops in like a knight on a white charger and pretends to complain of his wife's disposition. I know Georgia wants to go home and I know Leo has no desire to dance with anyone but her, but they understand the problem as well as I do. Cooper has been side-stepping me all night with the exception of one dance, so I think he understands it, too.

While we wait for our turn in the line for hired carriages, he is behind us on the steps shaking hands and hopefully winning votes. I can hear his voice but I don't look back in case Matthew sees.

I tap his arm when the couple ahead of us moves forward and we have a little space.

"Thank you for arranging the carriage, Matthew."

"Anything for you."

"Well, you already do quite a lot. You are a valuable part of the campaign, but you should know I appreciate your friendship with or without an election."

"Yes, and I—"

"I am so fortunate to work with men who respect me like you do. I have no time or inclination for another romantic attachment, and it is so refreshing to work with a man who doesn't make that a condition of his friendship." I wait until he meets my gaze. "I mean it. I am grateful for you and your friendship. I always have been."

A flicker of frustration sparks in his gray eyes, but it's gone as quickly as it came. "I count myself lucky to be among your friends."

We wait in silence for our carriage, and when Cooper spots Matthew talking with the driver, he sprints down the steps after us.

Matthew assists me up the step and pops in behind me so quickly the door nearly slams on Cooper's nose. When he stations himself at my side on the bench, I peel off my elbow-length gloves and wriggle my fingers before indulging in a long stretch to nudge him away a little.

The ride down to Raleigh is so familiar I can judge our travel time at every groove and notch in the road. Every week, more chugging, metallic, automotive sounds rise above the soft whinny of horses and the steady clip-clop of their hooves. Automobiles sound at home in town and I hardly notice their strangeness anymore. Out here in the little stretch of green between Hillside and the city, the merry *brrrrrrr* of an engine shatters the quiet like a profanity.

"We'll stop at the dormitory for you first," Matthew says when the engine noise fades. "Then Trux, then me."

"That doesn't make any sense." Cooper sketches city blocks in the air. "You first, because you're closest. Then me, then Maudie."

162

"She should be escorted in. It's late."

Cooper lifts a brow and looks at me. "What do you think?"

I feign a yawn. "Matthew, it makes sense to go first because you're closest. Then Cooper, walk with me."

"You should not be alone in a closed carriage with him."

I open my mouth to protest this rule and am interrupted by Cooper's groan.

"What am I, Berger, an animal? I can keep my hands to myself for four blocks."

"Did you or did you not nearly duel Leo when you caught him alone with your sister?" Matthew throws up his hands. "You do not get to play fast and loose with Maudie's reputation. She shouldn't be alone in a closed carriage with either of us. I wasn't dragging you specifically."

I clear my throat. "Am I part of this conversation?"

They duck their heads and wait.

"As I was saying, Cooper, I will need to run in and get a stack of notes from the Arborist Society for you. My friend Jenny Bowers is part of the meeting I've arranged for you next week, and she thought you might appreciate some of her research. I'll bring that out, and then you can head home."

"The trees always keep me up late worrying about them."

"We could meet tomorrow, if you prefer."

"Tonight is fine. And if you are not concerned about those four blocks, neither am I. I trust your judgement."

Matthew fumes as I close my eyes, leaning my head on the wall and away from both of them. His attention today bordered on ridiculous, and I hope what I said to him in the carriage line makes my point kindly. Cooper was his normal self this evening, amiable and relaxed with that easy smile that made Angeline's sisters blush. I locked eyes with him a few times while I danced and he circled the reception shaking hands and accepting introductions, and each time, the pride in his smile and the little tilt of his chin charmed me a bit more.

Every blink pulled me closer to that recklessness that overtook me the last time he held me close to dance.

His devil-may-care energy has a sweetness to it now, and a polish that sets everyone but me at ease because I know that underneath, nothing is as easy for him as he makes it look. Those caramel eyes often shoot me a secret glance, but today they followed me without shame, unafraid to be caught looking, and when we danced his gaze was so penetrating I felt unclothed, yet completely safe and at home in his arms.

When we stop at Matthew's boarding house, he brings my hand to his lips. With my gloves cast aside, his warm kiss covers my fingers, and he is slow to pull away. "Maudie, thank you for such a lovely day. My sister has my gratitude for this arrangement. The pleasure of your company is unparalleled."

"I had a lovely day as well. Thank you for managing all my introductions to your sizable family."

"Your reputation preceded you. I fear Angeline and I brag about you a bit. They are all watching the campaign with great interest."

I expect Cooper to clear his throat and demand attention, but he's twitching his lips to hide a smile and staring at the ceiling like an idiot.

"Good night then, Matthew."

"Good night, Maudie." He kisses my hand again and shoots a poisonous look at Cooper as he leaves. The carriage door slams shut and Cooper's eyes meet mine. He doesn't speak until we are moving.

"Do you really have notes for me from the Arborist Society?"

"I do. Jenny led a planting event last spring."

"I would like to do something like that one day."

"I thought you might. I'm sure the success story is in her notes."

"Must I read it all tonight?"

"No." As we pause to let another carriage pass, I pull in a deep breath. "We don't need to stop at the dormitory at all."

He blinks a few times as if he's not seeing straight, then leans out the window to speak to the driver as I tuck my hands under my thighs to hide their trembling.

By the time the directions have been revised and he slides onto my side of the bench, I've fortified my resolve and can nestle against him for the rest of the ride without fear. Only when the key turns in the lock of his boarding house do I feel another flicker of hesitation. But when he presses his finger to his lips and leads me up the stairs with the wicked smile I've known since we were young, my worries melt away.

His room is well-sized but sparsely equipped with marble-topped oak furniture and burnished brass fittings, and rich with the scents of leather, oil, and paper. Stacks of newspapers and books cover nearly every flat surface, and dozens of clippings pinned to the wall flutter like leaves in the soft breeze from the window. Lit by only the glow of a bedside lamp, the hunger in his eyes is unmistakable when his lips meet mine as soon as he locks the door.

"Maudie, my darling." He breathes the words between

kisses. "I cannot believe you're here. I've thought of nothing and no one else. I have longed for you."

"You had many pretty partners tonight."

"Did I? What little sense I have left in my head did not include discretion. I could not stop looking for you." His eyes are bright as he shuffles through the satin petals on my shoulder until he finds my pin. "Did I imagine that you let me hold you a little closer when we danced?"

"I did. But dancing was not enough." When he places his hand on the side of my neck the way he did at his party, my knees weaken and I rush to undo the clasps of my cloak. His hands are on me the moment it falls to the floor. I step into his arms and kiss his lips, his cheek, his chin, then along the line of his jaw while a little growl of pleasure rises in his throat. "Cooper, I have longed for you, too."

"I love when we are of like mind on something so important. I cannot hold back another minute. I must tell you that I—"

"No, wait."

He steps back, eyes on mine, and pulls his hands away.

"I do not wish to—we cannot—" I bite the inside of my cheek in frustration. I have married friends and I know what is supposed to happen. But thanks to an education that came mostly in giggles and whispers, I can hardly summon the correct words. "What I mean is, I do not wish to be intimate with you as a wife is with her husband."

He looks away, and my next words tumble out in a rush. "And like before, we should not feel obligated to each other in any way. I know neither of us want to be confined right now."

If he is startled, he does not show it. "Despite Berger's

assumption that I am a feral beast, I am in full control of myself and I will not pressure you," he says, slipping his arm around my waist again. "I respect you, Maudie. I will not even mention it. You have my word."

"Thank you, Cooper."

I lean forward, hungry for another kiss, and he presses a finger to my lips. "But although you do not want any obligations between us, I require one promise. I must be the only one."

My head jerks up. "Do you think I have a line of men waiting on my kisses?"

"Waiting is one thing. But I must be the only one getting them." He cups his hand around my cheek. "I cannot have you batting your lashes at some weak-chinned supplicant for your hand during the day while I take you in my arms at night."

"No one is seeking my hand, and I am not looking for anyone."

"Yes, but one day, you will change your mind, and when that day comes, I must know."

Slowly, I nod. "I understand. I hadn't thought of it that way, but you are right."

"Promise me I will be the first to know."

"I promise."

His lips collide with mine before I am done speaking, and he strokes my cheeks with his thumbs to open my mouth for him so he can tease me with his tongue. I draw him in, hungry for his taste and his touch while he scatters the pins in my hair and sends them clattering to the floor. When he twists my hair in his hands, his groan sends a shiver through my body.

"Lucky for us, there is so much else we can do." He brings my shaking fingers to his tie to let me know I should undo it. "So many ways we can enjoy each other, if that is what you wish."

I wish to know everything in his heart. I want to feel everything with him. For months, I have dreamed of his kisses and already they are not enough. With a desperate ache rising in my thighs and stomach, I need to feel him.

"Show me," I whisper.

"Touch me."

His tie. His jacket. His waistcoat, his shirt—one by one, I strip each piece away and let them fall to the floor. I have longed to see him like this again since the day I found him shirtless in his bedroom and had to squeeze my hands into fists to keep from reaching for him.

He luxuriates under my touch, working leisurely at the buttons of my dress as I trace paths over his shoulders with curious fingers and linger in the dark curls on his chest. With every breath, his muscles shift and contract under his skin as fluid as water, and I am absorbed by the graceful movements of his arms as he undresses me. A thin, white scar on his left shoulder gets a kiss, then another little mark on his collarbone. Following his moans, I allow one hand to wander a little lower, then hesitate.

"What do you want me to do?"

He slips open the last button of my dress and it slides off my shoulders as he drops a kiss on my neck. "Whatever you're comfortable with. I am quite comfortable." My breath comes a little faster and he kisses my lips in reply, slower and sweeter than before. "Perhaps you would be more comfortable without this dress."

"Perhaps."

With a few gentle tugs and a flick of his wrist on the tie of my petticoat, my gown puddles on the floor and I stand before him in only my stockings, chemise and corset. He covers the tops of my breasts with kisses and reaches for my laces to begin the tedious work of loosening them one strand at a time. The rush of air in a deep breath energizes me.

"Thank you."

"Would you like to take that off, too?"

I run my hands over the thick brocade protecting me. Between this and my skin there is only a thin cotton chemise, and I am a little cold. "Not just yet."

His eyes are solemn but warm as he leads me to his bed, kissing my lips each time he takes a step. "Lie down with me so we are not limited by our wobbling knees."

I stand straighter. "I am not wobbling."

"But I am." He sits on the edge of the bed and holds out his hands. "My darling, I have been for months. Come here."

The instant I am close enough, he yanks me to the bed with a triumphant yelp and a tickle under my arms before silencing me with a kiss. I'm still giggling as he settles his body next to mine, pressing us close from shoulders to toes. Kissing me again, he moves against me and I draw in a quick breath when I feel him stiffen.

I scoot away a little and brush my hand over the front of his trousers and nearly jump when he lets out a little moan. Heart racing, I do it again and he groans deeply as he rolls on top of me. With a heavy sigh, he bears down on me, pinning me to the bed with his weight. I pull him to my chest, shaking from the unfamiliar sensation he unlocked, and when he slides down my body and unties my stockings as he goes, I cannot stop trembling.

I clap my hands over my mouth when I feel his breath on my bare thighs.

"What are you doing?"

He looks up with that wicked smile. "I told you there are many ways we might enjoy each other, didn't I?"

"Yes." My voice is barely a squeak.

He traces a finger from my knee up the inside of my leg. "Is this enough?"

"No."

He moves a little closer. I'm fluttering like a leaf.

"Is this enough?"

"No."

A little further, and the gentle graze of his finger sends a bolt of heat straight up my spine, so scorching and sudden I'm afraid I'll start sweating.

"Relax, my darling. Touch me and breathe."

Somehow I peel my hands off my mouth and lower them to his head, twisting them in his hair and stroking his ears as he rests between my legs, tantalizing me with feather-light touches. I regain my breath.

"Does it feel good?"

"Yes."

That smile again. "Is it enough?"

I already despise the boundary I had to put in place, but I must be careful, for my sake as well as his. Desire rushes over me and I want him. I want everything about him.

"Almost."

He lowers his head and kisses me. I nearly cry out, clenching handfuls of his hair in my fist, but I don't try to pull him away. The softness of his lips sets me shaking again as my thighs clench to draw him closer. With a gentle press of his hand to my belly he soothes my trembling hips, but my bones vibrate in time with his motions.

"Cooper," I gasp. "What are you—what—"

I cannot think. I can hardly will my lungs to breathe as I dig my fingers into his shoulders, grappling wildly to steady myself.

"Shhh."

That little breath ignites me and every muscle in my body arches upward and unwinds at once. A scream lodges in my throat and emerges as a deep moan that sinks me into the sheets. He blows a long, slow exhale over me as he withdraws.

I close my eyes, and I do not know if I swooned or slept for a moment, but when I open them again he is lying on his side next to me, stroking my waist and inspecting my loosened corset with a smile.

"Was that enough? For now?"

His eyes are unsure again, like they were months ago in the shadow of the forsythia. He is only himself now, stripped of the confident disguise he wears for parties and politics. A woman could trap him with this if she wanted to, and he fears that so deeply he'd rather hide from love entirely than chance getting it wrong. He trusts me to hide with him.

My lips move without a sound, then he kisses me until I can speak.

"Yes. For now."

Chapter 22
Cooper

Maudie and I are such clever spies. To hide the fact that she's sneaking into her room still in her evening wear at eight o'clock in the morning, I loan her one of my shirts to twist and tie so it looks like a tucked-in blouse. Suddenly, she is in a proper shirtwaist and walking skirt, and we look like an early bird couple out for a morning stroll. We snicker the whole way, plotting how she'll explain to Victoria that she slept at her parents' house and returned as soon as she could get a carriage. I think Victoria suspects Berger's feelings for Maudie and will be pleased enough to hear she wasn't with him. She won't tell.

When I return home, I collapse on my bed.

It still smells of lilies-of-the-valley. It smells like her hair and her skin. This whole room smells like her, and I smash my pillow to my face.

No conditions. No attachments.

It is a perfect arrangement for the man I was a year ago, and I hate it already. The promise to tell me if she wants to see other people was the only thing I could come up with in the moment.

She arranged the carriage route last night to her liking and came home with me. I didn't seduce her or entice her or even hint at wanting her for months. She chose me.

She wants me and she trusts me. That doesn't mean she loves me. What a reversal life has dealt me, like payback for the women I wanted and used and didn't love.

Many nights, I wonder why I bother trying to convince anyone I've changed. Berger is still hissing in Maudie's ear and jabbing me with my guilt as though he didn't have any of his own. Even Toby Shaw knows too much about my college years, thanks to my boyish braggadocio, and I don't know what defense Maudie has planned for that besides the truth.

I prefer to do my penance in silence. Miss Ada's income has fallen by a third since her alcohol suppliers are rarely shipping to the state anymore. To boast about the payments I make now to keep her business afloat and her girls fed would only bring down the eyes of the law on them.

My redemption for my past foolishness comes at a price, but my present foolishness and the utter collapse of my heart into Maudie's hands? I don't know if I can pay my way out of this one.

Maudie has reserved a meeting room for my introduction to the club presidents, and she and Victoria, wearing their red and white sashes, greet the ladies at the door with name tags and pamphlets. I was ordered to dress down—a college sweater and trousers. They are all in their school clothes too, walking skirts and simple blouses, and I see Maudie has taken pains to place me on the same level as them so we can see one another as equals. I'm no politician in a suit with slicked-down hair today, and when Victoria comes to the front of the room and introduces Maudie, I scoot aside.

Maudie greets her audience with a deferential nod. "Ladies, as Victoria said, thank you all for coming tonight. I know you are all very busy, and I hope this will be a productive evening. My dear friend Cooper Truxton is running for the legislative seat in our district, and I am recruiting students who align themselves with his platform to help us spread the word in Raleigh and up in Hillside, where Mr. Truxton and I are from. You all represent campus groups that might have an interest in his policies, but before I ask you or any member of your club to work with him, I want you to get to know him."

She points at me. "He is a college student like we are, and voters will wonder if he is qualified for the job. If you choose to help us, I want you to say confidently: yes, he is. He is here tonight to win your confidence. I have known Mr. Truxton since I was a little girl. His sister is my best friend and he comes from a delightful family. And with that, Mr. Truxton, the floor is yours."

I rise, clearing my throat as I look over the rows of young women seated before me, some wide-eyed and curious, others casting suspicious glances at my casual attire. Their handwritten name tags also include their club names, but I can't read them at a distance.

"Ladies, thank you for taking the time to meet with me this evening. My name is Cooper Truxton, and as Miss

Hamilton said, I am running to represent this district in the state legislature. Last year, I graduated from East Piedmont College with a degree in engineering, and I'm a student in the agricultural sciences program now at A&M. My academic passions inform some of my politics. When Miss Hamilton and I sat down to strategize my platform for this race, we did not copy a page from a party handbook. We talked about the things that matter to us, even the ones we don't fully understand from a policy standpoint. Some problems feel too big to solve. Some problems are so intertwined it is hard to improve one without making another worse. And in some cases, we simply don't know enough to offer an educated opinion yet."

Heads bob in agreement as I carry on with my introduction. "I am always anxious to learn. But the point is, my platform is what it is because those are the causes that matter the most to me, regardless of who thinks they are politically expedient. For example, both major parties in North Carolina have done little toward women's suffrage, and my opponent has tabled it entirely. I don't care if it seems hopeless. It matters, so I will keep going. Conservation is out of fashion in an age of industry, but it matters to me, so I will keep going."

I catch Maudie's eye as she pulls up a chair a little away from me. "My ticket is Republican, but my platform is in that pamphlet in your hands. Miss Hamilton here has offered to moderate, and now I will submit myself to your scrutiny on all matters, personal and political."

Maudie points to the first young woman who raises her hand and asks for her name.

"Miss Hattie Ashmead, Mr. Truxton. I am the president of the Methodist Women's Charity chapter. What is your religion?"

I breathe a quick sigh of relief that I am off to an easy start and announce I still attend many Sundays with my family at the church where I was baptized as an infant. One girl with a saucy wink has a brother at EPC and asks me about my football days. She pouts prettily when I explain why the injuries to my wrist make it unlikely I'll play again. A soft-spoken redhead raises a hand and asks about my father's business to ensure I do not have any ties to alcohol manufacturers. The president of the Horticulture Society asks me how I came to fall in love with chestnut trees, and soon I have them all laughing with anecdotes about Leo trying to throw away all my forestry magazines so I would pay attention to my engineering textbooks.

The mood is light as the discussion continues, and we begin to talk more casually without raising hands and taking turns each time. One young woman shares concerns about canvassing among strangers, and we talk through some ideas to help everyone feel safe. Another student is the daughter of a political family in Charlotte and raises questions about the integrity of our elections. Before I can respond, a murmur circles the room. It seems everyone has a father or brother who whispers about rigged ballots and the partisans who count them.

We are nearing the end of our allotted sixty minutes when a tall girl who has been quiet the entire meeting raises her hand.

"Mr. Truxton," she calls out. "I have a question."

"Please."

"My name is Jenny Bowers. I'm the president of the Arborist Society. How do you reconcile your stance on women's rights and suffrage with your habit of visiting brothels and exploiting young women?"

The room falls as silent as the eye of a hurricane, and when I move to get more comfortable, the crack of my wrist rings against the walls. The students shoot horrified looks at Maudie, then me, then back at her again. Poor Victoria is huddled against the doorframe and looks ready to bolt, but Maudie is as serene as an angel and trusts me to play my part here, just as Jenny Bowers is playing hers by asking this pre-planned question.

This is the one place Maudie conceded we should handle my indiscretions differently. These women will be the first to shun me if they hear a rumor smearing my character, but they'll be the first to defend me if they see me as an example of moral redemption more men should follow. With any luck, it will never come up, but we'll have the sweetest army in the world ready if it does. No one calls a lady a liar.

I nod at my interrogator. "Thank you for that question, Miss Bowers. It is a difficult one, but necessary, I think, when we discuss women's rights and workers' rights. You are all educated ladies. Since your belief in me is important, I will be honest and forthright, and I apologize in advance if I am indelicate."

No one walks out in disgust. I didn't expect them to. No woman in this room has set foot in a brothel, and they are desperate to know what it's really like. Many of them are leaning in to hear me better. Cheeks flushed, Maudie keeps a straight face at my side.

"I was raised in a society that expects ladies like you to learn needlework and music and expects men like me to sweep you off your feet with flowers and gifts. That society expects us to marry with little understanding of what such a commitment means. I shied away from it. It seemed unfair to me all the ways young women and men find themselves forced into marriage because some old rules say we cannot share a kiss or she'll be ruined."

A few young ladies bob their heads in agreement. I sip my water and go on. "With that in mind, I took my lofty ideals to college and learned there were women who would do as they pleased and enjoy my company while not wielding matrimony like a weapon. It came at a price, but it sounded fair and transparent, like a business deal where the parties agree on the terms, and no one is exploited or forced into a circumstance they did not choose."

A discontented murmur arises from a corner of the room and I nod that direction. "That was the logic of a spoiled, empty-headed boy. I was willfully blind and went on like this for some time, fully convinced that I was being just as respectful to the women I paid as I was to the society ladies I politely declined. I thought I was so smart. I was the gentleman gallant with my sister's friends and never led anyone on, and I had my fun on the side. This spring, something changed."

I glance at Maudie. She expects me to give a brief explanation of my change of heart, but even she does not know how it happened. This is the part no one has ever heard, not even Leo. I hate this story so much I haven't even practiced telling it for tonight.

"I've never been one for cabarets or shows. Most of the establishments I've been to function rather like a supper club. You enter like you do at a restaurant and you are given a table with your party and menus for food and drink. At some point after you are served, the proprietress assesses you and decides whose company you might enjoy, and soon there are more parties at your table. Other arrangements may or may not be made after that. This sets the scene for a drizzly Tuesday evening last March, myself and two friends stopping in only for a drink and some conversation."

I lean back in my chair, hands behind my head, and stare at the ceiling as the memory takes me. "We were one of three tables, and the other two left shortly after our arrival. We enjoyed a few drinks and chatted with some girls we knew, and a man I recognized entered. I do not know his name, but I knew his face from evenings there before—a pleasant man, a gentleman, not quite old enough to be my father. He was always jovial and good-natured, but this evening he was on the verge of breaking down. Miss Ada, who owns the house, took him to a booth where he promptly fell forward on the table and sobbed."

A lump rises in my throat and I battle it back. "She held him in her arms and let him weep. Only after several minutes of his grief could we make out that his mother had just passed away. He wept without shame. None of the girls had any customers that evening, and one by one they approached the table with kind words for this man, and several of them sat by him for a moment and shared memories of their mothers."

I swallow thickly again and allow myself a glance around the room, relieved to see I am not the only one with damp eyes. "And after a few of them came by to talk, he reached for his wallet. He came there for comfort and thought he should pay for the girls' kindness just like he paid for pleasure—as though they didn't have hearts that loved and eyes that wept like anyone else's. By engaging women the way we did, men like him—and me—made their humanity a thing to be bought and sold. My self-righteous views shattered then and there. Miss Ada shoved the wallet back into his coat herself. Then the stories continued about mothers, kind words and wise lessons, and the man even laughed a time or two."

"But there was one thing I didn't hear that night." I press my hand to my chest and steady myself. It hurts to remember how I pieced it all together, and the memory of the moment I realized how I used and degraded these women still hits me like a fist in the gut. "In all the stories about their mothers' love, not one of those girls said her mother was proud of her. Many of you in this room are the first women in your family to go to college. I'd wager every dollar I spent exploiting those poor girls that each one of you has a mother or grandmother or another strong woman in your life who's told you she is proud of you."

The lamplight catches on spilled tears and I remind myself I am not here to make them weep. I must turn this back to politics to make it make sense. "Their mothers are not proud of them, but they are doing that work because they feel they must. There are not enough safe, respectable jobs for the people who need them. Factory work kills people, or at the very least sends them home coughing up soot after twelve hours on their feet in dangerous conditions. It is no wonder some women turn to a job where their well-being is valued, even if only because they must be healthy to be desirable."

Water sloshes in my glass when I drink to soothe my raw throat, and I hear nothing but sniffles into handkerchiefs. We are almost out of time.

"In any case, ladies, I have not patronized a brothel since.

While I know there is no way to atone for my actions, I assure you that my change of heart has nothing to do with any campaign, and everything to do with this realization that if change is to come for women, it must be for all women. Those women shall have the vote just like you and your fellow students, and they are just as relevant as the factory workers in the fight for safe working conditions and fair wages."

I bring my attention back to the young woman who asked me about temperance before. "Miss O'Grady. Making vice illegal only moves it to the shadows and removes the protections the current laws bring. No one will call the police on a brute at an illegal brothel like they will in one today. Will we ask the women who work there to choose between tolerating violence and eating? I do not know what the solution is, but I have reconciled my past actions and my present course, and if I earn a seat in the legislature, I will work for women's rights and workers' safety. All women. All workers. You have my word."

The room is silent for a long moment. Next to me, tears glisten on Maudie's cheeks. If I've said too much or offended someone with my indelicate story, this race is over for her as much as it is for me, and a man who would hold her back from her dreams has a clear path into the power of the General Assembly.

"Thank you, Mr. Truxton." Jenny Bowers' voice rings out to break the stillness. "Had I a vote, it would be yours."

My heart should calm and my breaths should slow when murmurs and a little applause arise around the room, but it is only when Maudie looks up at me, a smile creasing the corners of her damp eyes, that I feel capable of a deep breath.

"Did I do all right?" I whisper when we have a quiet moment later.

"You were marvelous. I think you earned your campaign staff tonight."

My voice is nearly gone. "Can I earn one more thing?"

When I have her in my room with the door locked, I press a finger to her lips when she leans in to kiss me.

I close the space between us and bring her head to my chest, allowing myself to sink into her embrace. The scent of lilies-of-the-valley floods my senses. I should feel lighter with the weight of my confession lifted, but a part of me still writhes with the same agony I felt the first night I touched her and begged her to touch me.

"Maudie, I need you." I glide my fingers through her hair, loosening the pins. "I need you to touch me and tell me that you're doing it because you really want to. Because you choose to."

She squeezes me tight, spreading her hands on my back as I choke out the words. When she stands up straighter to kiss me, she murmurs with her lips against mine.

"I want to. I want you."

"Those words have never mattered so much from anyone but you."

She leads me to my bed and pushes my hands away when I reach to help her as she untucks her blouse and loosens her laces. After I shrug off my sweater and shirt, I lie next to her and stroke her cheek. "Thank you for coming here tonight."

"I wanted to." She cups her fingers under my chin so I'll look in her eyes. Her blue irises are as deep as sapphires in the lamplight. "I want to be here with you, Cooper. A rogue or a gentleman, remember? Just you."

"I never want to tell that story again."

"You don't have to. You can be an advocate without laying your soul bare to everyone. And I think that if you had to confess that all to anybody, that was the right group."

"Because I need my canvassers?"

"No. Because you hit them right in the heartstrings with the bit about mothers. If there is one thing that unites us all across class and race and all our differences, it's that our mothers carried us, and we will always carry a piece of them." Her eyes sparkle with unspent tears and she smiles as she taps my chest. "I know that was not calculated, and that is one of the dearest things about you, Cooper. You want so much to do the right thing it makes you almost uncomfortably honest at times, but it is what we need to hear. And now all those women who might be mothers one day can impress on their daughters and sons to think a little differently. This is how change is affected, from one generation to the next. It takes time."

"How I wish I could see you run for office, my darling. You make me want to leap from this bed and wave a banner right now."

"When we are done with this campaign, I intend to join the city Women's Club and work with the suffragettes in earnest."

"Bring me every ribbon to wear. Take me to every rally with you."

"I will." She kisses my lips, and I slide across the bed to pull her closer.

"Do you want to stay tonight? You don't have to. I could walk you home. Victoria will worry, and we don't have an excuse this time."

She yawns. "She won't mind. I want to stay."

"Only if you're sure."

"I want to. I want to be here with you."

"Hold onto me. Please."

When I nestle her against my chest and listen to her breathing slow, I can finally catch my own breath and relax until my heartbeat matches hers. She'll stay in my arms tonight. I don't know what I'll do if she ever leaves.

Chapter 23
Maudie

Victoria and I escape our science lectures at the same time, and when I catch her arm in the hall of the classroom building, we agree to take a quick walk to enjoy the sun after two days of nothing but rain. She's a year ahead of me in her studies and an eager tutor. I've already conquered frog dissection. Passing first-year biology will mean I can try botany next year.

"And you can talk about trees with our favorite forester." Victoria giggles. "Hopefully not all night again. Cooper is very handsome and wonderful company, but I would have fallen asleep talking about trees, too. You have my sympathy, but you must be more careful."

I swish my skirt, skipping a step with a little bounce. The autumn-gold wool is a bright beacon in my wardrobe, and paired with a smart new vest and my chestnut tree pin, I cannot help but admire my reflection as we pass a window. I look like an academic. I look like a lady with a brain. Skipping another step, I marvel at how far I've come from pink ruffles in only a few short weeks—then nearly trip when I realize my friend is talking about my poor excuse for not coming home last night.

"Victoria, please. I am not that careless with myself."

Her face falls. "I didn't mean you would—of course you wouldn't do anything improper. But what if someone had seen you walking home?"

"Who's to say I wasn't out for a morning stroll?"

She stops short. "That man is staring at you, and has been since we came out of the building." She jerks her head to a bench shaded by a tree. "Maudie?"

I meet his eyes and freeze.

"Maudie?" Victoria asks again. She tugs my arm. "Who is that man? I don't like how he's looking at you."

"I know him." I barely move my lips to speak. "Will you be a darling and sit on that other bench while I speak with him? I would appreciate if he did not feel very free with his words."

She bristles. "Then he should not be here."

"He might approach us if we walk away, since he knows I've seen him. I'll tell him to go."

"Who is he?"

"He is Cooper's opponent. That's Mr. Shaw."

She claps her hands over her mouth and emits a small squeak. "I'll stay, but you must tell me everything later. I'll read a book over there."

"Thank you." I hitch my satchel higher on my shoulder. He hasn't looked away since Victoria noticed him, and the amused smile on his lips sends my heart an unwelcome flutter as I approach.

He rises to greet me, dark eyes alight like we're sharing a private joke again. "Hello, Maudie."

"Mr. Shaw." I plop on the bench at the far end. "What are you doing here?"

"Why must you address me like we are strangers?"

The sight of him after so many months, so lean and dashing in impeccably tailored herringbone, has already made my ankles weak. That smile alone could drown me in memories if I let it.

When I fold my hands in my lap, I summon my sternest professor's prim demeanor. "Because the man I used to call Toby would not compromise his principles the way you did. Now, how did you happen to be outside my classroom building?"

"I saw in the paper that you attend here, and it's a small campus. I took a chance on waiting in what looked like the busiest avenue, hoping you'd pass by without Trux and Rigby and the others guarding your every move like the last time I tried to speak with you."

"Indeed, your previous strategy didn't serve you so well. Your bruises have healed nicely."

He ignores the jibe. "I thought some time might mellow your hurt. Could we take a walk?" He peers around the crowded yard and at Victoria opening her book. "Somewhere quieter, maybe."

"I prefer not to be alone with you."

"Don't be ridiculous. I would never exploit you or take advantage of you."

"I don't know what to believe of you now."

"We had one disagreement, and suddenly I am a vile scoundrel who would use you like Truxton does?"

I whirl to face him. "Tell me, Mr. Shaw, in detail, how you believe he uses me."

"I am sorry. I did not mean to sound like you would— well, I know you better than that."

He and Victoria both think they know me better than that, of course. I rather like my secret self and the man I share it with. The lock on Cooper's bedroom door unlocks something inside me and frees me from the years of shame and fear bred into me about men and my body. He is not selfish or coercive or using me for his own pleasure, as they say men do with unmarried girls. I drew a boundary and he's never questioned it. I am safer nearly naked with him than I am with Mr. Shaw, shielded by my leather satchel.

The contrast is as stark as the shadows of the oaks slicing over the white stone sidewalk.

"Cooper and I have a working partnership."

He leans back on the bench and drapes an arm over it, inviting me to slide closer. "Your working partnership concerns me. He is very popular, but he is inexperienced, and I wonder how he has gathered support so quickly. That is what I meant about him using you."

I eye his arm on the back of the bench and frown, but he smiles again like I'm playing coy and he'll tease me into scooting closer. "Maudie, sweetheart, don't be like this."

"I am not your sweetheart. What do you want?"

"I want to tell you I still have your ring and my love for you remains unchanged by any distance or time."

My cheeks go cold. Nausea grips my throat, and on my lap beneath my satchel, I pinch my thigh to keep myself looking angry and not sick.

"I'm sorry, Mr. Shaw. I am not interested."

"I know it will take some time for you to trust me again, but let's not complicate it with politics. Truxton doesn't want this. I do. You and I want this together, remember? Let's end this student farce you've started and do the work that matters, my darling. Trux can go climb his trees."

I fold and re-fold my hands in my lap, fighting the twitches that threaten to shake my entire body. "I am not your darling. And Cooper is quite serious. His platform means a great deal to him, and to me."

"Who cares about tree diseases when we have a state to run?"

"He is not as one-dimensional as that."

He scoffs. "Yes, the supposed champion of women's causes. The man is a boor and a braggart and a rake, and if he hasn't laid hands on you yet I am sure he is just biding his time. Does your father know you are running around with him?"

I grip a handful of my skirt as Cooper's wounded, exhausted face the night of his confession surfaces in my mind. "He is an old family friend and I have never known him to be anything but trustworthy. I think him an admirable man."

"Then you do not know him. You should not be involved with him."

"I beg your pardon? Who are you to tell me I should or should not do anything?"

Clenching his fists, he closes his eyes and the vein at his temple begins to pulse. All trace of his teasing grin is gone. "I cannot talk about these things delicately."

"Then don't," I shoot back. "Nothing you say about him will be a surprise to me."

"He lives immorally and doesn't trouble to hide it. Gentlemen engaged in such activities should be discreet, but

Truxton has done things that make *me* blush. We lived in the same dormitory, and he talked."

"About Miss Ada's?"

He stares, mouth agape.

"Did you think I didn't know? I vet my candidates, and I walk away from the ones who do not meet my standards. When a man shows me who he is, I believe him." No man, not even Mr. Shaw with all his political savvy, could fake a change of heart like the one Cooper had.

After a moment's slack-jawed silence, he finds his voice. "Remember what I told you, Maudie? Platforms are practical and votes are emotional. His platform is pointless and voters will feel very strongly about an immoral man like him saying he respects women as equals while exploiting them on the sly. They will talk." He lifts his hand and I freeze for a moment when he caresses my cheek. "And if you are at his side, they will talk about you. My love, of all the men to lose you to…"

I regain my senses and shove his hand away. "Have you told them about what happened in Wilmington?"

"Told whom?"

"Your father. Your party leadership in the district. Have you told them?"

"No."

"Are you going to tell them?"

He runs a hand over his sandy blond hair and looks away.

"Mr. Shaw. You told me many times that you hoped to be a voice of reform in your father's party. You said change had to come from the inside out, and what you experienced as a young man—"

"What I experienced as a young man is not a story for the campaign trail," he snaps. "Not in this party and not in this political climate. It can inform my work in the legislative session. I have not told them and I certainly hope you are not so vengeful you would do it yourself."

"What happened to your high hopes of righting your father's wrongs and fixing the world?"

He scowls. "Our hopes, Maudie. Our hopes that you ground into dust when you left me. Did you think I was flattering you when I said I couldn't do all that on my own? It was the truth. I am not ashamed to say I need you. You were my strength, and when I needed you most, you walked out and took everything I taught you to another man."

"And yet here you are to forgive me, it seems. You turned your coat completely. Why should I trust you? Why should any voter trust your promises?"

"You know me. You know more about me than anyone, and if you could have looked past your own cause that you know is hopeless for the moment, you would have seen the bigger picture and the work that must be started now. I still want to do all of it, but not yet. Sometimes we must shift our priorities."

"You must bargain away what matters, you mean."

"Women's suffrage is years away, perhaps decades away unless it becomes a federal issue. In the meantime, the people of North Carolina need jobs and security and the men in the General Assembly can do something about it. You were going to help me be one of those men, remember?"

My breath catches in my throat. "I remember."

"But if I am going to do all that, I—my darling, it will be hard to betray my father without you at my side to support me. Yes, I am here to forgive you and to ask you to forgive me. I need you."

"You do not need me. You were strong enough to betray him alone when you were thirteen years old, with his own gun. All that's left to do is tell the truth."

"I must first get to a position where I will not ruin myself politically. That means I must start quietly, which you and Truxton seem bent on preventing."

"But his causes are pointless and mine are hopeless, as you say. We shouldn't be much of an obstacle."

"Don't be surprised if he wants payment for assisting in your little scheme." His eyes rake my body. I used to tremble in his arms when he looked at me that way. He would rage if he knew what Cooper and I did the night of the party, and if he knew about anything since—well, I cannot imagine. How stark the difference is now that Cooper's kisses linger on my lips and Mr. Shaw is dangling memories in my face.

I shoot a quick glance at Victoria who is watching with wide eyes, making no pretense of reading her book.

"You have been so careful with yourself Maudie, and you should be," he continues. "I respect you, and I have always respected your boundaries. But remember, I lived in the same hall as he did for two years."

"Is his character something you plan to address in your campaign? You always looked down on muck-rakers. I believe you called their tactics cheap and vulgar."

"I have not decided. Who knows what circumstances may arise?"

"Indeed. Who knows how you will change your opinions again when it is convenient to do so?" I rise and brush down my skirts. As long as I have leverage Mr. Shaw worries about,

I will not let him force Cooper to tell his painful story to defend himself. "If you bring up his past, we will bring up yours. Cooper has plenty to do in his life without this race. You do not, so we shall see who is in a position to be ruined politically."

I spy a twitch in his clenched jaw before he shakes off his frustration, slipping back into his charming smile with a practiced ease. "Darling. You are not so spiteful as that. And on Trux's behalf, really?"

"You confuse being spiteful with being principled. If you earn the honor of representing my hometown in the legislature, I will wish you well and support you in any endeavors aligned with my causes. Until then, this is my choice."

"So if I win this race, there is a chance I might win back your favor."

I step back, glaring. "That is not what I said."

His eyes hook mine. When they crinkle at the corners, a smile with genuine warmth crosses his lips, and my breath turns to a muffled cough. He scoops up my hand and kisses my fingers as he rises. "I will win this race fair and square, no dirty tricks or mudslinging, and then we will talk about the future together. Again. Thank you for speaking with me, and good day."

After he walks a few feet away, he tosses another smile over his shoulder as Victoria darts to my side. "Oh Maudie, you're so pale. What did he say to you?"

I close my eyes and press my hands to my cheeks, willing some color and warmth back into my face. "He reminded me I was supposed to marry him."

She gasps. "Why did he say that?"

"He believes I did not have a good reason to leave him

and thinks my work with Cooper is ill-advised and will prove fruitless. And he..."

"He what?" She yanks my hands. "And he what?"

"He still has my ring and still loves me."

I nearly fall forward as the words leave my mouth.

Oh, God.

I just said all that to a girl who's practically a Berger. Related by marriage and head-over-heels for Matthew, who I must treat so gently now—my dear Victoria will talk. If Matthew knows, he will tell Cooper. My pulse thrums at my temples. He will grill me on the meeting and he will know if I hide anything—and I cannot tell him about Wilmington. He still speaks his mind a little too freely sometimes when he's excited or annoyed, and the truth about the night of the riot is fragile.

All it will take is one slip, and if Cooper mentions Wilmington he could break this wobbly truce, setting Mr. Shaw free to attack his character. Yet in the height of irony, Mr. Shaw has no idea how the shadows of his past might work to his advantage rather than against him. I was ready to use it to his benefit before I walked out. Now, he sees those secrets as a liability.

Everything could fall apart if this is not handled with the lightest possible touch, and I must keep Mr. Shaw's past hidden if I am to protect Cooper from the shame he's trying to leave behind.

"Victoria, I beg you not to tell anyone anything about this. Not that I spoke with him, not what I told you we talked about—absolutely nothing."

"But he is Cooper's opponent. Isn't this important?

Shouldn't Matthew know, in case there are rumors he needs his cousins to stop?"

"Yes, but—he only—" I fan myself as a headache attacks behind my eyes. "This is not about the campaign. It will not affect the campaign. Mr. Shaw had personal matters to address with me."

"But if he—"

"It's personal, and I don't care to be picked apart by those two," I snap. My welling eyes betray me. "Please. I am so sorry to burden you with secrets, but please don't tell a soul. I wish I had never spoken with him."

Victoria hangs her head. "Oh, Maudie. You don't have to beg. Personal talk with just us girls... it's different. I know."

"That's exactly what it is. Girl talk."

"I won't tell them. I promise." She picks up my limp hand. "Let's go back to our room and rest. I'll bring you a cold compress for your head and you can relax."

"You are a true friend, Victoria, and I am lucky to have you."

"We shall pretend we never saw him."

I won't forget, though. That visit was a warning that I have gotten too comfortable.

I did nothing wrong in speaking with him while chaperoned on the green. I told no campaign secrets and I stood up for my principles. I have no reason for shame, but as I rise and scoot my satchel forward, the warm leather curves against me like Cooper's hand passing over my hip with a quick, possessive squeeze to remind me I promised he would be the only one.

Mr. Shaw says he talked about Miss Ada's.

I bite hard on my cheek as I follow Victoria to our room

and fight back a vision of Cooper in a brothel somewhere—it was like a supper club, he said, where people came to him at a table. Girls came to him, maybe teasing him with his tie or twisting their hands in his hair while he smiled. Or worse, they made him erupt in that infectious laugh that starts deep in his chest and invites me to join him in his happiness. His laughter intoxicates me, and who knows what it did to those other women? Who knows what they did to him?

My stomach clenches and I stumble forward. Victoria catches my arm.

"We're almost home. Oh, my darling. Let's get you to bed."

"I feel a little sick." I swallow heavily but my throat remains dry.

"I cannot believe that was Mr. Shaw." Victoria huffs. "What a horrible man he is to upset you like this."

"It will pass."

"Well, it must." She cranks her key and opens our room. "Or you should tell Matthew and Cooper. Politics aside, they would be furious he treated you so disrespectfully. They adore you and would be glad to deal with him."

"It will not come to that." I flop onto my bed and wriggle for a comfortable spot, holding my stomach. "I promise you, it will not come to that."

Chapter 24
Cooper

With every passing week, this campaign becomes more surreal.

In the stands at the football games, Maudie and her friends pass out leaflets at halftime. The week after I met with the club presidents, a dozen of them attended. This week, I counted two dozen of them in bright white blouses and red and white sashes peppering the crowd with pretty smiles and fingers pointed my direction. My classmates are enchanted, and it makes for a fine boost to my confidence—which I need when I am accosted from every direction by people who believe I need to hear what they have to say on everything from taxes to temperance. Many of them are already on my side for a cause or two. My plans for roads and statewide forest conservation have gained a lot of traction in the two college communities in my district, where my father rightly noted I would find my more progressive voters.

In both Raleigh and Hillside, the older adults are a problem.

Berger and I attack a pair of mountainous club sandwiches in a pub near my campus in what's become a Monday-lunch tradition for us. Maudie's faith in me is worth everything, but Berger has his ears to the ground on my behalf, and I want to be sure he knows I appreciate it. Whatever Maudie said to keep him at arm's length has worked its magic, because he doesn't seem at all put out.

"You're going to struggle back home if you don't get up the hill and make yourself seen around town a little more," he says, tapping his knife on the edge of his plate with an ominous clink.

"I can't imagine they've forgotten who I am. Or forgotten my name, at the very least."

"If anything carries you, it'll be your name. But this is our old friend Toby's full-time job right now. He's not taking a full load of classes like you and I are. I'm told he's lugging groceries for widows and helping orphaned children to church."

"You're joking."

He pauses with his sandwich halfway to his mouth. "I have sources."

"I'll be at church every Sunday. What else can I do? Your sister's wedding was the social event of the fall, and I shook every hand in the ballroom. Didn't that net me anything?"

"It refreshed the people who would have voted for you anyway."

"So much for Angeline's brag that a Truxton would snag every vote in Hillside." My sandwich doesn't look very appetizing anymore. The idea of losing my hometown has turned my stomach. "What do I do? I'll get back up there more often. What do I need to reschedule?"

"I have an idea. And I haven't told Maudie, but I think between us, we could convince her."

My ears perk up. These lunches have an unspoken don't-tell-Maudie rule that protects us while we complain about all the things she won't let us do, like commissioning Hayes to draw a few ribald cartoons, or just spreading a little mild slander. Berger's rumor mill would be deadly if Maudie wasn't so hell-bent on telling the truth all the time.

He hasn't mentioned anything about his feelings for her since the day of the wedding, and I certainly haven't said a word to him about mine. I haven't told anyone, not even Leo, who can read my face like a book and would certainly try to smack some sense into me if he knew. He is the only person I have ever truly unburdened myself to, and now I can hardly look at him in case proof of our trysts is stamped on my forehead in invisible ink.

Leo would be sympathetic, I am sure. But he would not condone me taking her to my bed and doing everything short of actual fornication with her, dreaming that I might lodge myself so firmly in her heart she won't be able to shake me.

No, Leo did normal things like take Georgia flowers and arrange lovely outings for them. This crass stupidity is my territory entirely.

"What's the idea?"

"I think you should do a town hall."

"Another one? She already scheduled one in two weeks."

"I meant you and Shaw together. Both of you at the same event."

"You mean a debate. That's a bit unusual for a local race, isn't it? Shockley never did one."

"Not so formal." He chews another bite. "I'm picturing

something in one of the schools, maybe, where you'd each get a spot on the stage. A moderator could accept questions from the audience, and you'd take turns to answer them. Not a point-counterpoint like a debate, just conversational. And you have every advantage over him in person."

"Berger, don't make me blush."

He flicks a stray leaf of lettuce at me. "Objectively speaking, you are far more engaging and relatable than he is, so I think the contrast would play to your strengths."

"What sells him on the idea, then?" I spear the lettuce with a toothpick and consider its wan greenery. "Why would he agree to do it? I don't like him, but I don't discount him. He's not stupid."

"Perhaps he's still a little stupid over a certain lady and would like to see her a little more."

I drop the toothpick. "Do not put her in the middle of this."

"Think about it, Trux. You would shine in a situation like that. You need face-to-face time with these people and you need to create some buzz." He chomps another bite of his sandwich while I mull this over. "Maudie knows all of this," he says. "I think if we tell her together that we'd like her to approach him to—"

"Approach him? With what leverage?"

"I am not suggesting she do anything indiscreet, for heaven's sake."

"That's not what I meant. It's just that she—look, you have to know she's not over what happened with him. It still hurts her to talk about him sometimes. I can't put her in that position."

"She put herself in this position when she recruited you and hired herself as your campaign manager."

"The campaign manager's job description does not include batting one's lashes at a weasel." I push back my plate. "We would have to go with her, in any case. I have little faith in his good manners."

"I'll go with her. It would probably be better if you didn't."

"Why not?" I am ready for another tired excuse about how it looks to have Maudie at my side for this unconventional partnership, but his reasoning undercuts me entirely.

"Because Shaw will get under your skin in a matter of minutes with jibes he would never make on a town hall stage, and you will forget to mind your tongue." He shakes his head. "No. You will not see him until the event. Let me sort it out with Maudie, and we'll arrange it with his team. Trust me. You'll win this one."

I stare. "I'm not quite past what you said about me not minding my tongue. What do you mean by that?"

"You talk a lot when you get excited." He shrugs and pokes a leftover slice of tomato with his fork. "It's usually about good things, and that's what we want to show off about you in the town hall. That infectious energy for the causes you care about it. People love that. Ford should pay you a commission when he starts shipping Model Ts out here because you've sold the roads so well. I have it on good authority that people remember your passions."

"And yet?"

"And yet—" He lifts a brow and scoots the salt shaker across the table to me. "Trux, we've been friends a long time, so take this with a few grains. When you feel personally attacked, or when something you care about is personally attacked, you get a little prickly."

"I do not."

"You play it off as being sarcastic or bored until you blow up."

I cross my arms. "When have I done that?"

"Shall I begin with you clocking your opponent in the face when he made an insinuation about Maudie? You were all wisecracks until you slugged him."

"He was offensive, and you were right behind me begging for a go at him."

"Didn't you and Leo nearly have it out when he started courting Georgia?"

"That was a misunderstanding."

"A very loud one. What about when you lost your marbles at Jacob Bowman after the loss to UNC senior year?"

I grip the table and my knuckles turn as white as the tablecloth. I'm making Berger's point for him, but I cannot stop fuming. "He was asleep the entire second half of the game, so when he said I was to blame for that tipped pass, I was rightly put out."

"You punched him. Your own teammate. And then you let off a rant about every play he messed up in the previous three games. Look at you, steaming just thinking about it a year later."

My cheeks burn. "I made it up to him."

"Indeed. An all-expenses-paid evening at Miss Ada's did a lot to soothe his bruised pride, if not his face."

"I haven't put a foot wrong with this campaign, you know." I slouch forward, elbows on the white linen table-cloth. "You can name folly after folly from years ago, but people can change. I asked Maudie to nitpick every aspect of my performance, and she has been very pleased."

So there, my petulant younger self adds.

"Your temper is a liability. Even your chattiness is a liability when you start trying to prove you're smarter than someone else." He eyes me with something approaching pity. "Maudie has constructed our messaging to play to your strengths and I've run the gossip circles to do the same. Do the question and answer session, smile and wave and kiss babies, and let your team handle the logistics. It doesn't matter if whatever Shaw says feels personal to Maudie. She can handle herself. It cannot feel personal to you."

"Because you think I can't handle myself?"

"Because no one wants to find out if you can't."

Chapter 25
Maudie

Long ago, when we spoke of unconventional campaign techniques, I broached the idea of school visits to Mr. Shaw. He dismissed it out of hand for the same reason he dismissed my suggestions to emphasize suffrage and woo women to his causes. Women cannot vote, he said—as if I needed reminding—and neither can children.

On the other hand, Cooper loved the idea and saw my reasoning immediately. If Matthew thinks our town needs to be reminded who Cooper Truxton is, we will remind them with its noisiest little citizens talking to their parents about who visited their school and gave them a break from arithmetic.

If Cooper and Matthew really want me to arrange a side-by-side town hall with Mr. Shaw, I need to be more confident that it will be to our advantage. Cooper is vibrant but unpolished and excitable, and ever since my encounter with that smooth-talking scoundrel on the green, I am less and less sure a town hall is a good idea. I trace my fingers over the scheduled dates freshly inked in my campaign notebook. If nothing else, the school visits will give Cooper practice taking questions and minding his reactions, and perhaps that will make me feel better.

A visit to our old grammar school and a short discussion of how the state government takes care of roads and parks goes well, and my mood perks up. Cooper is in fine spirits when we head down the hill to the boys' high school in Raleigh two days later. The students are only a few years younger than we are, and Cooper must walk a fine line between trying to be their friend and remembering he's supposed to be giving a civics lecture.

He struggles a little, which isn't entirely concerning—I can't place him in a room of college-bound young men and not expect him to relive his football glory days a little. The exercise is as much to create buzz among the students' parents as it is for Cooper to feel a little heat from unplanned questions—and for me to calm these jitters I can neither shake nor name.

His presentation on North Carolina's budget starts off well but slips quickly from infrastructure planning to every-one's thoughts about the latest automobiles. One boy's complaint about temperance nearly becomes a brawl with his classmates until Cooper raises his voice to the harsh bark I recognize from his football years.

Settling things down, a discussion about the state's reliance on timber for the furniture factories takes a wild tangent and leads Cooper to start talking about how he's always wanted to join the Forest Service, then confessing he didn't even think about pursuing politics until a few months ago.

He cannot say that again. These casual slips are exactly what I fear if I tell him about Mr. Shaw's past. One off-hand remark about his actions in Wilmington might become a rumor, and just like that, our truce is broken and Cooper's past is fair game.

I scribble in my notebook, adding *don't say you never wanted this* to my endless list of things to tell him, right after *get a haircut* and *have you shaved at all this week?*

"Why didn't you go?" a young man with slick blond hair asks as he snaps his gum. "Sounds like a lot more fun than arguing with a room full of grandfathers." A snicker from the classmate at his left draws his attention. "I mean it, Franklin. Have you ever gone down to the assembly? A room full of graybeards still talking about the war. Hand me a shovel, Mr. Truxton. I'll build some national parks with you."

Cooper's face lights up. "You know, up in Pennsylvania—"

I clear my throat quietly without looking up.

"What I mean is, I think that combining my engineering degree with my agriculture program will position me to lead the necessary conversations about North Carolina's place in an industrialized South."

The young man glances at me, frowning with visible annoyance for disrupting his daydream by setting Cooper back on track. "Guess I'll look into it," he mumbles.

Next to him, the classmate he called Franklin looks me over and doesn't bother to hide an appreciative smile. I thought it would be a bit of a distraction to have a woman in their classroom, and since our initial introduction I've kept quiet in my seat near the teacher. With no girls in the room to set an example for, I am content to let Cooper run the show.

When I glance up from my notebook, Franklin is still looking at me, practically leering. I barely stop myself from rolling my eyes. It is laughable to think that when I was the same age as the boys in this room, I was considered ready to marry.

Cooper notices Franklin staring and smacks the side of the lectern to let him know it.

"In any case," he says, "government agencies like the Forest Service are among the many ways you can serve the country without serving in the military or holding elected office. This country depends on the citizens' commitment to our mutual betterment to grow and thrive as it already has for a hundred and twenty-five years."

"Didn't think you were a Marxist, sir," another student jokes. "We'll all be speaking Russian next."

Cooper's neck twitches with tension before he responds. "Mr. Marx has been on a few of my reading lists, and while he has some interesting ideas, I think I will never shake my love for democracy. In this country, we can balance service to the state with serving our own goals and opportunities, and we are stronger for it."

"Life, liberty, and the pursuit of happiness," Franklin adds, winking at me. "Wise words from Washington."

"Jefferson." I regret speaking when half a dozen of them look my way, but I may as well go on. "And to 'promote the general welfare and secure the blessings of liberty' is not Marxist. It's the preamble to the constitution."

"His secretary told you what's what," another student says, tossing a pencil at Franklin's head.

"As your teacher said, Miss Hamilton is my campaign manager." Cooper steps between them and scoops up the pencil. "Not my secretary. She's more or less my boss, and very used to correcting me as well, young man."

Warmth rises in my cheeks. Correcting him? Since the run-in with Mr. Shaw, I've become a shrew and a nag with my lists and constant harping, but Cooper is looking at me like I hung the sun in the sky. My fingers curl into fists as I imagine crumpling those lists with a satisfying paper crunch.

"What do you do?" Franklin asks, the slight arch of his brow and quirk of his lip speaking volumes his teacher cannot see. "For him, I mean."

The insinuation burns, and the young man's smirk is undaunted by a withering glare from me. I am so tired and not in the mood for saucy boys who haven't yet learned how to treat ladies, only that their sex isolates them from consequences. Short of a teacher's pointer to smack them with, I am prepared to cede ground and just finish this wretched visit. But Cooper's knuckles whiten when he grips the edge of the lectern, and the set of his jaw is furious at the slight. I rise before he can open his mouth.

"I oversee all strategy decisions related to his campaign platform, his policy proposals, his public relations, and his personal appearances. That includes the development of all print material and paraphernalia, aligning and managing relationships with other members of his party, opinion polls, editorial cartoons, cash bribes, and matching his waistcoats to his ties."

The room is silent. Franklin ducks his head and picks at his fingernails.

A quiet young man raises his hand and calls out. "How do you know how to do all that? Women don't run campaigns."

"They do now."

"Yes, but where did you learn? Was your father a politician?"

"I know some very talkative political families that shared their years of wisdom with me," I say curtly. "But I am sure none of that is very interesting. Mr. Truxton has only a few more minutes, gentlemen, does anyone have any questions?"

Chapter 26
Cooper

We leave the high school quietly and Maudie tucks her hand in my arm as almost an afterthought when we reach the sidewalk. Her touch is as distracted as she is, fingers tapping at random intervals over my elbow while her eyes dart everywhere but to my face. I have to yank her aside when she nearly steps in a pile of horse dung as we cross the street.

"New roads for the automobiles and farewell to horse shit. That's the Truxton platform in action. I think that went very well, don't you?"

"Did it?" She doesn't look up.

"Sure it did. They clapped, didn't they?"

"They did."

"I know we got off-topic a few times, but it was just practice."

"Corralling a bunch of boys that age would be hard for anyone," she says absently. "I pity their teacher."

"Maudie, that was practically my job for years. I was a

quarterback and a team captain. I corralled a rowdier bunch than that."

"I know."

"Then what's on your mind?"

She loses her footing on a cobblestone and clings to my arm tighter when she corrects herself. "Oh, everything. I have a history exam tomorrow and I'm just running dates and battles in my head again."

We pause at an intersection to let carriages pass and I cup a hand under her chin. "I am not convinced."

"Waterloo, June eighteenth, 1815."

"Funny."

She steers me left when we ought to turn right. I know by now that when she sets a course I would be wise to follow. Peppering her with questions at every turn just to break the silence is unnecessary and will only annoy her. Wherever she's taking us will be quiet, I think, someplace to settle her obviously unsettled thoughts.

Several blocks later, we turn once more and I know where we are bound.

It's late in the afternoon—we left the high school only minutes before dismissal—and the breeze grows crisp earlier each day now. It whisks the fallen leaves at our feet with the smell of horses mingling with streetcar oil as we cross Union Square into the green expanse in front of the capitol building.

The four pillars draw my eyes up to the domed roof, and in the corner of my eye, I can see Maudie's chin lift as well. Much like Hillside, the old building escaped the flames of Sherman's conquest without visible scars. Inside its walls I am sure I'll find that room of graybeards still grief-stricken, wounded, and angry.

Maudie slips her hand into mine as we stop near the Confederate monument.

"This was dedicated thirty years after the war," she says, noting the date in the stone. "A toast to a foolish cause built on cruelty and deception and pride. Why?"

"Pandering for votes?" It seems everything is about votes, one way or another. "Not everyone agrees it was foolish, and inside that building they're still fighting wars."

"Maybe." Her fingers dance over the engraving. "This thing, this cause—this is what our parents tried so hard to protect us from. Yet some people cling to the idea that one thing could have changed it all and vindicated their belief in it. What if a hurricane blew in and smashed the blockade? What if the Confederates never tried an offensive campaign and lost so badly at Gettysburg?"

"What if Stonewall Jackson hadn't been killed by the North Carolina infantry?"

"What?"

I squeeze her hand. "Indeed. One of the South's finest generals was killed by twitchy sentries that didn't get proper identification, not in the glory of battle like we learned in school. Yes, we've been well-protected from the unflattering truth."

"I rather like that you know that." She smiles. "You keep the most interesting tidbits from all your reading, and you always broaden my perspective."

"You trace the most interesting paths for my mind to follow." I pause and take in the pretty picture of the breeze ruffling her hair around her cheeks. "I don't think I tell you this enough, Maudie, but you are the most delightful company I have ever known, in any circumstance."

She blushes and doesn't look up. Why won't she look at me? I'm trying to be a little delicate here, but she must know what I mean by 'in any circumstance.' It's become so clear to me that we belong together—in bed or out of it, in this race or out of it—that I must grind my teeth to keep from leaping atop this monument to lost causes and announcing it. She's said nothing to indicate she's interested in romance again, so I will hold my tongue—at least until after the election when I may have worn out my usefulness to her and have nothing left to lose.

Finally, her eyes meet mine, and I lose my breath for a moment when the setting sun casts a glow over her complexion that heats the air between us. Only our hands touch. I tighten my grip on her fingers and wait for her to take a step and lead me in any direction.

She's waiting, too. That means it's my turn.

"Come home with me." I stroke my thumb over her palm. "Something is on your mind and you do not wish to tell me, but let me comfort you, if I can. Come with me."

Maudie is quiet on the walk back, and when I kiss her in my room, she twists her fingers in my hair and holds me close, prolonging the silence as I lose myself in the sweetness of her lips. When she drags her fingers over my jawline and scratches at the little bit of lazy stubble I ignored this morning, I feel her mouth curve into a smile against mine.

"Sorry," I murmur. "I was running late to class, and I—"

She silences me with another kiss. "I've bothered you far too much with foolish little things. I don't want you to be anyone but who you really are."

"Who I really am could have taken a moment to shave since we had an appearance this afternoon. I'm sorry."

"Cooper. Stop talking."

With gentle strokes on the back of my neck, she pulls me to the bed.

Undressing her is tortuously slow sometimes, an agony I prolong to make the delight of her body beneath these layers even sweeter. And when she beckons me to the pillows and sets her hands to my clothes, she teases me right back. The heat of her mouth as she kisses down my chest and stomach is nothing short of a taunt.

I dance my fingers across the front of her corset, tracing the floral embroidery. She's still never taken the wretched thing off, only loosened the laces until the busks on the front began to unclasp—then she held it to herself tighter as though the thick brocade protects her from sharing her soul with me, not her stomach. Twisting one of the ruffles in my fingers, I give it a little pull to test the waters and she ignores me.

She slides over me and rests on my chest instead, nuzzling her head into my shoulder while she shifts her thighs around my hips. When I embrace her, she sinks into me and her tension melts away, matching her breaths with mine while she dots my neck with tender kisses.

I follow orders and keep my mouth shut as long as I can. The longer I wait to speak, the more heaviness settles in my bones beneath her. She anchors me to this bed in a peace I never imagined could exist in a state of arousal, but my yearning quiets for a moment as she curls around me.

With a little twitch and a giggle rising in her throat, she shatters the stillness.

"Oh, I see." I stretch a little, pushing her up so I can see the smile she's trying to hide. "You didn't wish to tell me what was on your mind before. I wonder what is on your mind now."

A little moan squeaks out as I drag my hands down her back, fingertips pulsing to wake up every sleepy muscle and nerve. "You are very much on my mind," she whispers. "You always are."

"Good. I'm a selfish bastard, you know." That earns me another giggle. "I cannot bear sharing space in your beautiful mind with anyone or anything else."

"And what is on your mind?"

I pull her in for a quick kiss. "With you astride me and nearly naked? That is a trick question."

"Nonsense. I want to know."

"But I promised I would not even speak of these thoughts. I have a dozen seductive speeches with varying levels of desperation on the tip of my tongue." I kiss her lips again, then trail my tongue over her jawline in a quick tickle. "You will not tempt me to break that promise. You must ask me specifically if you want to breach that boundary."

"A rogue and a gentleman are a most captivating combination." She stretches back, driving her hips down as she arches away.

"I am captivated by an unladylike lady who clearly desires to ride me like an animal." She gasps when I grab her legs and pull her back against me. I hold her gaze as I pulse against her and she shifts her weight forward and back. "Stay right here. Very much on your mind, am I?"

"Yes." Her sigh is little more than a whisper as I glide my

hands over the luscious curves of her waist and thighs to lean her back a little.

"Then I want this thought to linger in that delightful mind. This feeling should beat in your heart and you should see me every time you close your eyes. You are relishing what you can to do me, aren't you?"

"Oh, yes."

"Did you know you could do this?" I ruck up the hem of her chemise so I can watch her. Every shift of her weight stiffens me further and my pulse beats for both of us. "Did you have any idea when you pulled me into the shadows that you could dismantle me like this?"

"I didn't. You told me to go exploring."

The friction of her body moving against mine like this is damn close to sending me over the edge. A slow drag of her fingernails down my chest and stomach leaves a trail of fire on my skin, and she fans the flames with a slow breath when she bends forward to kiss me.

"Everything you find is yours, Maudie."

Pressing her palm to my heart, she opens her mouth to speak.

I grab her for another kiss, but the ache rises again, turning my breaths ragged as my body tenses and strains upward. In the burst of sensation I can barely yank her off me in time to shoot a hand down to cover myself. The waves she stirred up whisk me into an airless stupor, silent and blank but for the azure glow of her eyes and a whisper of whatever I didn't let her say.

Clutching her to my side, I pant like an animal to catch my breath.

"Cooper?"

All I can do is cling to her.

The words I long to say hover at my lips, but what a pathetic time to say them. Better to lie here in silence than make such a confession as though the explosion from my body just dragged it out of me. My lungs will recover. My heart has lodged itself in her hands.

I lift my head and smash it back into the pillow, startling her.

"Are you all right?" She stretches against me, yawning.

"I—"

I love you.

"What?"

"I liked that."

Chapter 27
Maudie

I score an eighty percent on my history exam. It isn't my finest work, and my professor doesn't think it's funny that I referred to Stonewall Bonaparte in a sleep-deprived haze in the essay portion. Cooper's little remark about the South's doomed general stuck in my head. How different the world might be if Napoleon or the Duke of Wellington had twitchy sentries.

Lightened of that load, I pack my biology homework and secure a spot in a carriage to go home for an evening. I received a note from Georgia that she has a surprise for me. I haven't seen her since Angeline's wedding, which seems like months ago even though it's only been a few weeks. Perhaps time with my best friend is just what I need to escape this frustrating cycle of thoughts around the election.

Now in her seventh month of pregnancy, Georgia is relaxed and smiling when she greets me in a loose gown and robe. "I am enormous," she announces. "Dr. Everett believes I am either having triplets or a rhinoceros. Or perhaps neither of us can count and I'll have the baby tomorrow. In any case, since I've given up on the idea of fitting back into my new dresses before they go out of style, you must wear them for me."

Georgia has a fine eye for fashion and is an absolute wizard with her sewing machine. She's a one-woman couturier for special occasion gowns in Hillside and will always make room in her queue for a friend, but in all my racing about this fall, I've completely forgotten to order anything for winter events.

"I'm sure I'll manage fine in last year's gowns," I say, trailing at her heels as she leads me to her sewing room. "I've only worn my blue one twice, and I doubt I'll bother with many dances. And I have no interest in seeking a—"

I catch my breath when I see the gown on the dressmaker's form.

Georgia whirls around and grins. "I'm sorry. You're not seeking a what?"

The pale gray silk flows off the mannequin with an unearthly shimmer like mercury, tented with black lace netting over the open shoulders and gathered over the bodice at a black-and-silver medallion. Dark gray taffeta panels draw the eye from the square neckline to the waist and continue around the bodice and down the back of the dress in decadent pleats and drapes to contrast the lighter silk and wisps of fine fringe on the front skirt tiers. A loose black velvet ribbon drapes off the shoulders, still curled at the end from its spool and obviously intended to trim the waistline. Next to it on the wall, pinned magazine pages and sketches show off the process of her design.

"Skirts are a little narrower this year, there's hardly a bustle to be seen anywhere, but waists are still entirely cinched." She scoots by me to pluck her tape measure from her work table. "I have no idea if I will ever be able to wear this because I cut it back in the spring, and who knows if I will get my figure back."

"But Georgia, this fabric alone must have cost a fortune."

"And it would be a shame to waste it, don't you think? I touched it up to your measurements from your bridesmaid dress, and that one, too." She gestures to her cutting table at an elegant tiered afternoon dress of cream-colored gauze with a froth of amber ribbons and lace on the bodice. "You can layer that with the vest I made you or wear it alone. What do you think?"

"I think there is no point in trying to refuse, because you'll mail them to my doorstep if I try." I kiss her cheeks. "Thank you so much. I'll wear the cream dress to the town hall this weekend. And the evening gown couldn't have come at a better time. Cooper received an invitation from two Republican assemblymen and their wives to join them at the theater Friday night. He asked me to go with him, and I don't have a single evening gown in the city. I was going to fetch one from home tonight."

"With any luck, my measurements are correct and you can take this one. Try it on."

When I present myself in corset and chemise to be fitted, she checks my waist and hips with her measuring tape. "The cream dress will be perfect as it is. Can I take you in another inch for the gray one?"

Hands on my hips, I inhale as she gives my laces a quick pull, cinching my waist and lifting my breasts. I inspect my reflection and the little crease between my brows that doesn't entirely fade even when I relax my face.

"Georgia?"

"Yes?" Her back is to me as she unbuttons the dress on the mannequin.

"I saw Toby two weeks ago."

Her shoulders jerk a little when his first name slips out. "Why?"

"He found me on campus because my information was in Cooper's announcement. I think I handled it well enough, but it was not easy and some things he said got under my skin. Did I overreact terribly?"

Setting the black ribbon aside, she begins to gather the silvery silk in her arms. "Overreact to what?"

"I spend all this time with Cooper talking about how to play to his strengths, what to emphasize, what to conceal—that's all Mr. Shaw was doing, wasn't it? He was trying to get his foot in the door so he could get to work on the causes that matter most to him, and that meant he had to push some less-popular ideas aside. And I screamed at him for it, ordered him out of my life, and dragged Cooper into this race where I am nagging him every day about everything from shaving to sentence structure so we can win. Did I judge Toby too harshly?"

Georgia freezes for a moment with the dress draped over her arm, and the extra inch she laced me suddenly cuts into my ribs. "Maudie, suffrage is the cause that is dearest to you, and for him to drop it completely was a betrayal."

"Yes, but maybe he's right and it is hopeless in this backward state. Maybe nothing can be done here and it will have to be forced on a federal level and he should focus his attention elsewhere. He always said he was going to reform his father's party from within, and that will take time."

"He said that, and then when you asked him if he ever believed women should have the vote at all, he said nothing." She smooths the dress over her arm. "It seems to me he faked his support of the cause to please you until it became inconvenient. He thought you'd go along with whatever he wished, but you didn't. And good for you."

She holds out the gown and gestures for me to raise my arms, but my eyes well and I cannot move.

"Georgia, we were supposed to do this together. You and I were supposed to get married together and raise our babies together and have normal lives." Words tumble out in a torrent as her mouth hangs open, and I can't stop. "It was all I ever wanted before I met him. I was never political before. Maybe this madwoman I am is what I became for him, because I knew when he didn't propose after a few months that I wouldn't be able to hold onto him unless I wanted the life he wanted. I should have married Wilson and never tried to change myself for a man, no matter how exciting he made it all seem."

My breath catches in my throat as Georgia tosses the expensive silk onto her cutting table and wraps me in an embrace. Hot tears overflow and escape my cheeks, dampening her dress. "What am I doing throwing all my time and effort into trying to get back at him like this? He's not a horrible person inside. The world won't end if he wins, so what does this accomplish? What happened to me wanting a simple life?"

"What you want can change." She catches me under the chin and tilts my head up so I'll look at her. "And you are not a madwoman. You learned a lot from him and your world view shifted. You can keep the dreams without keeping the man. Sometimes we don't know much about an important cause until someone shows us. Mr. Shaw may have opened your eyes to these issues, but causes belong to the people who care about them. You care a great deal about equal rights and suffrage, and that has nothing to do with his wishes anymore."

"And now I've dragged Cooper into it. I've upset everything he wanted to do as well. He still wants to leave here and save trees in the Forest Service, you know. I told him to give up his dreams and fight for this hopeless cause with me, just to stop Toby—just to stop Mr. Shaw from getting what he wants."

My shoulders droop as my breaths finally slow, and Georgia tucks a loose curl behind my ear. Even my hair is frazzled these days, and I sniff back another burst of emotion as she shushes me like she would a child.

"Cooper decided for himself what to do. He loves you, Maudie, but if he didn't believe in what you are doing, you would not have convinced him to run. He may be a man, but he's been as sheltered as we have been in many ways, and he needed to open his eyes about what he can do that we cannot. He would not be doing this if he didn't believe in it."

"Cooper what?"

Georgia scoops up the gown and nods at me without speaking, and I lift my arms like a puppet. The gray silk ripples over me like cool water. Even the lace netting wrapped over my shoulders is gentle against my skin, and as she tuts over the draping and straightens the bodice, I ask again.

"Did you just say your brother loves me?"

"I did." She encircles my waist with the thick black velvet

ribbon just below the beaded medallion and pinches it in the back with a pin. "Do you have a narrower petticoat? I could loan you mine."

"Did Cooper say that to you? Or to Leo?"

"To me, no. To him, I doubt it. But it is painfully obvious when he speaks of you." She smiles. "And I think that when you saw this gown, you imagined him seeing you in it."

A scorching blush races over my face the instant Georgia turns my shoulders so I face my reflection in the mahogany-framed mirror and see myself as he'll see me Friday night.

He'll fight a smile for only a moment before breaking into a broad grin, and when he takes my hand to kiss it, he'll pull me closer than he should and whisper in my ear some silly flirtation about how he won't be able to take his eyes from me all night, and the show at the theater will have to do without his attention. I'll take his elbow and shiver when I feel his muscles tighten, envisioning those strong arms wrapped around me later in the evening after I tell him Victoria won't worry if I don't come home.

"Maudie?"

She snaps me out of my daydream.

"Yes, I'm sure he'll like it," I stammer, smoothing my hands over the silk and velvet. "Should I wear white gloves, do you think, or black?"

Even now, I cannot tell Georgia about the nights I've spent in his bed. She knows her brother well, but whatever she imagines she sees in his face when he speaks of me could be the warmth of friendship coupled with the fun of sneaking around and getting away with it. That doesn't mean he loves me. It might mean he's as satisfied as I am with the arrangement as it is today—or not, because lately, I am not satisfied with it at all.

He is very much on my mind, but not because of the campaign. For better or worse, the campaign will be over soon. I want football matches and fried chicken dinners and walks to the library. Couldn't we make this work in a normal life?

My logic chases itself like a cat after its tail. If Mr. Shaw wins the race, it won't be so bad. He's not as terrible as I made him seem. Then Cooper and I can go back to our student lives, going to football games and cramming for exams—but with nothing holding us together like this election does. If he wins, he will need me. He's made that clear. If he loses, we may drift apart, a worry that rumbles in my stomach like hunger when I think of his absence. I find myself wondering sometimes if the Forest Service has a place for women.

No, we must win and upend both of our lives doing it, especially his. Farewell to the old dreams and hello to resentment about giving them up... and then I think again maybe it would just be better for both of us, especially him, if Mr. Shaw won. Around and around goes the cat, night after night in my head as I try to separate these feelings for Cooper from all of my fears of losing him, losing this race, and losing myself.

"Black gloves, and don't change the subject."

"It's so complicated with him, Georgia. Even if he thinks of me like that, we shouldn't talk about it until the election is over. If we don't see eye-to-eye, this could all fall apart."

She arches a brow at me.

"I shouldn't consider anything with anyone until I sort myself out," I say, trying to sound firm but failing.

"Did you ever imagine me happily married to the neighbor boy who put live crickets in my tea set?"

I fight a giggle. "Of course not. Our dolls were mad at Leo for a week."

"Dreams change when we change, Maudie." She rustles through a pile on her cutting table and produces a length of thinner velvet ribbon she loops around my neck like a choker. "I love that about my brother, you know. No matter how foolish he is sometimes, he sticks to his beliefs and fights for them. And if he changes his mind, he's honest about why. He taught me to do the same, although I like to think I'm a little less pig-headed about it." She squeezes my shoulders and stands next to me, smiling at our reflection. "Look at us. Think of everything we thought we wanted before and where we are now. Older and wiser, and our dreams are still beautiful, don't you think?"

"Mine are a little hazy these days, I suppose. I think I know generally what I want, but the path to get there isn't so clear anymore."

"Maybe that's a good thing." She pats her stomach. "I used to get so annoyed by the rituals you and the other girls clung to. Tea cakes and dances and debutante rules for everything. I always told myself if I had a daughter she would not be trussed up and auctioned off for marriage. But did you notice, Maudie, that our parents never pushed us? Your grandmothers wanted your parents to marry because it was an advantageous match. But now, all of them would rather see you happily married than conveniently married, and all of them are happy to see you at college bettering yourself and supporting your causes without a man to support you. Everyone's dreams have changed."

"But how do I—"

"I had one very traditional courtship that went nowhere, then Leo and I chose one another out of love and bent the courtship rules to suit ourselves. Every woman's path looks a little different these days, and thank God. I got my dream, but not how I expected."

This feeling should beat in your heart and you should see me every time you close your eyes.

We have so much to do, Maudie.

My cheeks flush pink, as warm as if the whisper of Cooper's voice in my head were his breath on my ear.

Georgia smiles and brushes a loose thread off the dress. "I was a little disappointed to see this color makes my eyes look a little grayer instead of bluer. It's so much more flattering on you. Perhaps this was always meant to be your gown, and it just had to find its way to you."

Chapter 28
Cooper

My sister's house is abuzz with activity when Maudie, Victoria and I arrive Saturday morning. We'll have a luncheon with my campaign team here before the town hall this afternoon, and my energy is already ticking up. Hillside is my town, and no carpetbagger of any party will convince these people that I won't do everything in my power to give back to this community all the love and prosperity it has given me.

I should write that down. Fishing in Maudie's satchel on the sofa, I dig out her campaign notebook and scribble it on a blank page.

She and Victoria disappear with Georgia to inspect the baby's nursery and coo over all the tiny things while I join Leo and Hayes in the study.

"Here, Trux. I've got a new one for you." Hayes shows off a drawing of me towering over Mr. Shaw with a comical wink and pointing at the suitcase marked "Wilmington" at his feet. Hayes has been part of our quiet discussions about the coup and everything we learned. He is as stunned as we all are at all the things we never knew and how the events of that night have shaped state-wide politics for the last decade.

I tap the suitcase. "Talk to Maudie about that. I defer to her."

"What's wrong with it?"

"She says we won't bring it up in any way."

He furrows his brows. "But why?"

"She said there's nothing useful about his past that we can campaign with, and I guess she would know, since she knows him better than any of us."

"Huh." He accepts the sketch back and scribbles through the lettering on the suitcase. "Works without it, anyway. He's still not from here."

"Thank you."

"You'll like this one." He hands a sheet to Leo, who snorts a quick laugh before passing it to me. A line of young women wearing "Truxton" sashes and comically towering floral hats hold out their hands, palms flat like a wall, to dismiss a row of kneeling young men with rings in open jewelry boxes.

I read the caption aloud. "If you're not for Truxton, you're not the candidate for me."

"Clever, right?"

"I think so. Again, take it to the boss."

"We need it," Leo interjects. "Even if she doesn't love it, we need to keep people talking. *The News and Observer* has been a lot more generous with column inches for Democrats. Berger will tell you. There's always higher turnout in a presidential election year, and we have to keep pushing the positive name recognition so people don't just vote the whole party down the ticket if they check the box for Bryan over Taft."

As if he's been summoned, Berger barges through the study doors.

"There you are." Leo rises. "I was just telling—"

Berger crosses the room in three strides and grabs me by the shoulders to slam me into a bookcase. "You son of a bitch." His nose is nearly on mine. "What the hell did you do to her?"

I lift my hands. "What do you think I did? To whom? What?"

"What did you do to Maudie?"

I gulp. "Maybe there's been some confusion."

"What the hell did you do?"

Leo yanks him off me. "Berger, sit down. I don't care what you're offended about, you do not attack my friends in my home."

Not inclined to sit, he marches to the sideboard, pours himself half a glass of brandy, and downs it in three swallows while Leo and I gawp. "Where were you last night?"

"At the theater with some gentlemen from the assembly." I glance at Leo. "And Maudie was with me. They all brought their wives and said I should bring her to meet everyone."

"What was she wearing?"

"Um. A dress?"

"What color, smartass?"

"Kind of a silver color."

She was a goddess last night in that mercurial gown with her golden hair in a simple, loose twist held with a set of silver and black combs. The little choker my sister made showed off the lovely line of her neck to perfection and called to my hands all evening. The assemblymen's wives were decked in diamonds and fringe and looked like gaudy chandeliers next to her. Maudie stole my breath the moment I saw her, and my heart raced at odd moments all evening—a look, a touch, a smile—and didn't quiet until she fell asleep in my arms.

Leo caps the decanter and scoots Berger's empty glass aside with exaggerated, deliberate motions to slow the conversation and our thoughts. "What, precisely, is the problem?"

Berger points at me like he's tattling on a toddler. "He was seen walking with her this morning back to her dormitory and she was in a silver evening gown."

Oh, shit.

Hayes exhales a low whistle like the air being let from a balloon, and I drop onto the sofa next to him, scrambling for an excuse. "Who thinks they saw this? Which sister's cousin's friend thinks they can start rumors out of thin air? Lots of women wear silver. Or gray. Maybe it was more gray. This is preposterous."

When Berger makes as if to move toward me, Leo shoves him back and meets my eyes, dead serious. "Do not insult my intelligence with excuses, Trux. What happened?"

"My private life is private. I don't ask about your after-hours activities."

"My activities are not under public scrutiny, and they only include the woman I married. Those are crucial differences."

"And of course, it had to be Maudie," Berger interjects, still scowling. "Of all the women who would have you, you had to seduce the only one I wanted. You know how I feel about her. I would have told her long ago, but of course everyone so helpfully advised me not to, starting with your sister. Is Georgia plotting this with you?"

Leo raps his knuckles on the desk and shoots him a warning look. "Challenge my wife's integrity again and the next strike is your face," he says, cool as ice. "You'll find it hard to woo anyone without your front teeth."

"Did you know about this?"

"Leave him out of it," I say. "He didn't know a thing. Save your venom for me."

"I'd like to see what kind of venom her father has for you," Berger snaps. "I cannot imagine the leap of faith it took for him to trust you with her, and look what he gets."

"We took a walk to get breakfast at the bakery a block from her dormitory. I'm sure your little rat saw a brown paper bag the right size for three cinnamon buns. Ours, and one for Victoria. Go pester her and ask what she had to eat this morning while you were out sleuthing."

Breakfast delivery has become our go-to excuse, and Victoria accepts the pastries and sweets without questions.

Berger lowers his brows and looks ready to run me into the wall. "Even you should know the difference between a skirt she'd wear for a morning stroll and an evening gown. I have it on good authority that she was in her evening gown."

"I do not owe you details, but I will give you one." I rise and get in Berger's face like he got in mine. "I did not bed her. She can wear white at her wedding. That's all that matters to you, since you still harbor hope of being the groom."

"You selfish bastard. If you just had to treat yourself again, why not go get a girl at Miss Ada's like you always did before? Why did it have to be her?"

"Just go get a girl," I echo, digging my fingers into my thighs in a desperate attempt to keep from balling up my hands and slugging him. "You know what? There's nothing to say here. If one or two people saw us, we simply deny it."

"You can deny it to the public all you like, but you can find yourself a new public relations team. The Bergers are done with you."

Hayes makes a small yelp of concern and keeps scribbling on his sketchpad. I had nearly forgotten he was here.

"Let's not make any rash decisions," Leo says. "Gentlemen, we have known one another close to twenty years. Campaign aside, we do not fall apart bickering over a woman."

Berger crosses his arms. "I do not 'bicker' about a lady's honor, Rigby. Not Maudie's or anyone's, and especially not when the scoundrel in question is one who has always been happy to slake his thirst elsewhere."

"Must I beat this into your head?" I drive my hand into the desk, crashing my knuckles so hard it sends a painful pulse through my bad wrist and up my shoulder. "For months now, I have been repeating that I do not do that anymore, and every chance you get, you throw it in my face and in Maudie's ear like you were never at my side for a night out. People change. I have changed."

"Obviously not enough." He flops back on the sofa amid the creak of springs and leather with a groan that could wake the dead.

"Maudie makes her own choices about when to go

walking and with whom. You do support women's rights, don't you? Or are you just here to lust after the pretty ones?"

"I swear to God, Truxton, if you weren't—"

"Wait right here. I'll go get her. It's not right to leave her out of this conversation. Maudie may have some thoughts on how her honor has fared, since it is hers, after all, and I do not presume to speak for her."

"This is your new equality, and you would ruin her to make this point?"

"Ruin her?" I choke out a laugh. "I'm sorry. Does she have no value to you now? Is everything brilliant and original about her soiled by my touch?"

"Oh, that's all it was," he sneers. "A touch. I feel so much better now."

"I told you, I did not bed her."

"Splendid."

"So we are in agreement at last. Is it time for lunch yet? I'm starving."

"You are not going anywhere, you insouciant shit."

I lean over the sofa. "Do you think I owe you an apology? You came to lecture, and you've lectured. Well done. Maudie will swoon for her hero."

"Will I?" She pops her head in the room, and the smile falls from her lips when she meets my eyes. A glance at Leo, pale and drumming his fingers on the desk—another at Berger, red-faced and seething—and one more at Hayes, kicked back on the sofa, sketchbook open.

She calls over her shoulder for Georgia, and my racing heart slows a little when I see my sister. Of all of us in the room, she will be most rational under stress.

She brings Victoria in with her, shuts the door, and turns to her husband. "What's going on here?"

"Berger's spies saw your brother walking Maudie home this morning, and she was still in her evening dress."

Georgia nods like she's not remotely surprised and Victoria's mouth pops open. She yanks Maudie's arm. "But you told me—"

"Shh." Maudie presses a finger to her lips. "Matthew, what is the meaning of all this?"

"I will not support a candidate who would ruin you like this. Maudie, I am sorry you got dragged into this, but—"

"Dragged? Was I walking or being dragged?"

I can't hide a smile, but Berger doesn't appreciate her joke.

"Your reputation is damaged enough from running around with him for months. Do you want this news to get out?"

"Of course not. If it comes up, we say it's untrue. We'll say someone saw people who looked like us." Maudie lifts her chin. "This is unprovable and could easily be attributed to Mr. Shaw trying to smear my reputation."

Victoria squeaks again, holding something back as she shuffles her feet and clings to the bookcase like she might hide in it.

"What is it, Victoria?" Berger asks.

"Nothing." She looks at Maudie with wide eyes and my stomach twists. Victoria knows every night Maudie didn't come home, and I'll buy her a bakery full of sweets if she keeps that damning list to herself.

"What's wrong with letting this blow over?" Maudie asks. "Matthew, I am sorry it offends you, but for the sake of this campaign—"

"I am not part of this campaign anymore. I am sorry. I will not support Trux if he does not do the right thing here."

"The right thing?" we ask in unison.

He lifts a brow.

"I didn't think anything could be godalmighty stupider than this fake problem you dredged up, but here we are, looking at its even more ridiculous solution," I say flatly. "To be clear, you would force the woman you care about to marry a man you have no respect or friendship for, to reinforce antiquated rules we all claim to despise. You wish to punish us. You wish to punish me, specifically, with what I once called a fate worse than death. Is that correct?"

Leo falls forward on his desk, head in his hands. "You fucking idiot," he groans, and I'm not sure who he's talking to.

Hayes stops scribbling, erases something, then scribbles again.

Head bowed like a shamed child, Maudie will not meet my eyes as she tangles her fingers together, trying to fidget out a response. Her unsteadiness unnerves me, for she always keeps a cool head and makes a speedy plan where I run my mouth and spout off sarcasm like I just did.

Georgia slices her hand across her neck. "Both of you, stop. This accomplishes nothing. If this is about rescuing Maudie's honor from a rumor that might never spread, it's already too late for them to get married."

"The rumor can spread in a blink," Berger drawls. "It is not too late to distract from it. This is their mess. Let it be their distraction."

"Arson's a good one, I hear," Hayes says, chuckling. He peeks over his sketchpad at Victoria, who looks ready to shrink into the wall.

Georgia shoots Berger a glare that could wither a rose on its stem. "If they get married out of the blue, it looks like a marriage of convenience. They were not even engaged, and to elope suddenly means everyone will think she's having a baby, and then you've created an even worse rumor for them and the campaign. You can wait out anyone's guesses about pregnancy, but that takes time we do not have. We have three weeks."

"Might be funny to see who Shaw can find to marry him in a fortnight just to stay relevant," Hayes jokes. Leo flicks an eraser at him and the room falls quiet.

"Then what do we do?" Victoria asks. "Could we just deny everything and let this go, like Cooper and Maudie said?" She looks to Hayes—have they always been looking at each other?—and receives only a shrug in response.

"If your strategy is to do nothing, do it on your own. I'm out, Trux." Berger stares me down across the table. "I'm out, and I'm taking your public relations team with me."

This man is twice as stubborn as Maudie and half as smart, and I need him on my side if I have any hope of surviving the next few weeks. I need him and her both, and we must all be in agreement, not fighting. He's glaring at me and she's scowling at him, no doubt remembering the impact his chatterboxes have had on our campaign so far. And Victoria—she hasn't cracked yet, but who knows? If my old friend is so up in arms about one evening, the real scope of the situation will set him ablaze. Maudie knows this as well as I do, and when our eyes finally meet, the compromise becomes clear.

I rise and grab Leo's arm. "We'll be right back. I have an idea."

"Ominous," Hayes says, chuckling as he sketches. "I like it."

Once we are in the hall, I pull Leo to the sitting room to make sure no one can hear us. "I know precisely what to do to fix this. It might be the best idea I've ever had. Why don't you look relieved yet?"

"Because the last time you knew so well how to fix a problem with a woman, I ended up chasing you to Virginia where you had set up shop as a spy."

"It worked, didn't it?"

He groans, which I think is a bit dramatic because I did all of that for him and Georgia, and everything turned out well. It will again. I can feel it.

"Have some faith in me, Rigs. It may have taken a kick in the ass for me to get up the gall to do this, but this will placate Berger for now. The rest of it, we'll figure out after the election."

His sour frustration softens into an indulgent look I know well from my father. We've bailed each other out of so much trouble over the years there's no counting who owes whom, but in all of it, Leo is always the sensible one. I'm three months older but he's a dozen years wiser, and I need him for moral support, if nothing else, because my head is spinning with possibilities and his steady voice will keep me sane.

As understanding dawns on him, he fights back a smile. "Are you finally in over your head?"

"Not at all. As a matter of fact, nothing has ever felt better."

"And you think Maudie will understand?"

I jam my hands into my pockets. "Look, I know we haven't

really talked about how it is with her, and I should have told you. Maybe Georgia told you a little."

"No one had to say a word. I can see it in your stupid face, you know."

"I figured as much."

"Yes, you should have told me. You are closer to me than any brother, and you don't have to go through these things alone."

I brighten. "I was hoping you'd say that. Come on. We have a few errands to run."

Chapter 29
Maudie

When we hear the front door slam, Matthew pops up from the couch and paces in front of the windows again, seething.

"That's it," he says, pivoting on his heel. "I don't know what idiot plan is in Trux's head right now, and I don't care. Maudie, I am sorry. I can't support him in this race any longer."

"What would make you stay?"

Shaking his head, he stares at his feet and doesn't answer.

"Matthew, this is my fault as much as his, and I am asking you what it would take to make you stay. I told you how much I appreciate your friendship, and I—"

"Yes, right before you told me you don't wish to have a romantic attachment at all right now, and we can all see how truthful that was."

Victoria, who I had almost forgotten was here, stomps to him with a face like a storm cloud. "How dare you speak to her like that? You are not entitled to her affection. She handled your advances with a grace you are unwilling to show her. You are so high and mighty about Cooper, but you are hardly a gentleman yourself right now, and no friend to this campaign anyway if you cannot accept that Maudie's choices are just as valid as yours."

Brent's pencil skids off the side of his sketch pad and every mouth in the room hangs open. When Matthew finally recovers his voice, he addresses Victoria, not us.

"We have to play by the rules until we have the power to change them, and right now, the rule is that an unmarried man and woman do not traipse about town in the early morning like they just rose from bed together. We will have a hard enough time pulling votes from the conservatives, even with a name like Truxton on the ballot. If anyone thinks the candidate is taking advantage of his campaign manager like this, it will not matter that they love his father. And if I defend him, my family is affected."

Victoria's lip quivers and her bravery appears exhausted for the moment. I shoot her a grateful smile and she steps back against the bookcase.

"Please sit," Georgia says, scooting aside so he can sit between us on the long leather sofa. He resumes pacing instead. "I agree that Maudie and Cooper's indiscretion has put you in a terrible position, but there must be something we can do to assure you that you will not regret staying with us."

"We need you." I cannot mince words. "We need you, and I am sorry I offended you. Please, Matthew. If you are angry enough to end our friendship, I understand. But you believe in this platform as much as we do, and I am begging you to help us fight for it for three more weeks. Stay and talk with Cooper and Leo, at least. See what they've come up with."

"Whatever harebrained notion they've thought up, they had better make their case soon." He gazes out the window at the darkening sky. "And in the meantime, let's all pray my cousins aren't forging a sloppy cover-up. A broken rumor mill is the most dangerous kind. They all just repeat what they hear, and not one of them has the sense to bend the truth when we need it."

The study is quiet but for the tick of the clock on the marble mantlepiece, the occasional scratch of Brent's pencil, or the flipping of a page. Matthew plods in long strides in front of the windows, watching the clouds roll in from the east, checking the time now and then with a beleaguered sigh.

I haven't the faintest idea what errand Cooper and Leo are on, but we ladies have done our part by keeping our furious friend here, and they had better hurry up.

More than forty minutes pass. Georgia is curled on the couch as comfortably as her belly will allow, napping. Victoria is trying to read, but her shaking hands flutter the pages and obviously annoy Matthew, who keeps looking at her like he expects her to either rip the book in two or throw it at him. I want to hug her and cheer for her burst of courage, and at the same time want to hang my head in shame for weighing her down with secrets because I was careless. Georgia, too—she certainly knows how my feelings for her brother have shifted, and keeping it from him is unnatural to her.

Heavy footsteps race down the hallway, and Georgia jolts awake as Cooper and Leo burst into the study, shaking off the first drops of rain speckling their hair. Cooper's smile is one of sheer delight, and Leo looks like a naughty child with a secret. They are boys again, troublesome ten year olds climbing trees, skinning their elbows, and laughing about it. Matthew must remember his old friends like this. He was with them so much over the years, and maybe this will soften his stance.

A sharp crack of thunder rings out as Cooper, without a word of greeting, kneels in front of me and takes my hand.

"Marry me."

I clap a hand to my mouth and whisper through my fingers as everyone in the room freezes. "But Georgia is right. If we did that, people would assume—"

"Say yes. Say yes and we'll announce it tonight. A good story beats a bad rumor, right?"

"I hate that I taught you that," Matthew mutters.

Cooper squeezes my hand. "You only need to say yes today, not marry me tomorrow. We'll figure the rest out after the election."

"But if people saw—"

"We beat the gossip about our inappropriate friendship by proclaiming our love first, and everyone will smile and say they knew it was only a matter of time. Rumors about convenience are nothing if we've already announced a wedding date several months from now so it is clear we are in no rush. And in the meantime, we take a moment to breathe."

Is he joking?

He is the last man who would joke about a marriage under duress, but—*is* he under duress? Am I? I search his eyes for hesitation or fear and find none, only a mischievous pride in his plan to untangle this knot we've woven.

"This is taking the fight for your causes a little too far,"

Matthew says. "Maudie, leaving aside my affection for you entirely, this is ridiculous."

"Oh, now what's ridiculous?" Georgia asks. "They would be doing the right thing, wouldn't they? Or is it only right if the order comes from you?"

Victoria snickers.

Matthew stares out the window and resumes his grousing. "You can't just get conveniently engaged now and call it off in a month. You'll still ruin her reputation and probably your own good name, if that even matters to you. This is a farce of respectability."

"How respectable do you require?" Leo asks. "He spoke with her father."

"When?"

"About thirty-four minutes ago, before we went to the jeweler's." He looks at me and smiles. "Your mother would like to see you at your earliest convenience, by the way."

My mouth hangs open in a most unbecoming gawp as Cooper reaches into his pocket.

"I told your father of my enduring affection and respect for you," he says, keeping his voice low. "And I will not elaborate on that now, because I know you do not want another blithering proposal. Do you?"

"No." The word emerges as a tiny squeak as he places a ring on my finger but does not slide it over my first knuckle. The diamond catches the light and soft gasps from Georgia and Victoria echo mine. It is like no engagement ring I've ever seen—a pear-shaped diamond with thin baguettes radiating from the curved edge like the rays of the sun. I twist my hand a little to make it sparkle as he holds the band in place, but it is the glow in his eyes that holds my gaze.

"We have so much left to do, Maudie, and we will do it together. Say yes. Marry me."

"Yes."

I clap my hand over my mouth as if to put the word back, but it tumbles out again as he pushes the ring on all the way. "Yes. Cooper, oh my God. Yes."

He leans forward as if to kiss me in front of everyone, but only brushes my cheek with his lips before whispering in my ear. "I once thought that a declined proposal would leave a man sorely humbled. It appears an acceptance does the same. Thank you."

The warmth of his breath on my face is such a familiar, delectable sensation I close my eyes as though any moment he might kiss my neck and begin his slow descent to my shoulder. Only the rumble of a laugh in his chest snaps me back to the moment and the realization that my breath is coming short and quick like it does when he undresses me.

He strokes my cheek as Georgia orders everyone out. Hushed voices and footsteps blur around us. A burst of Leo's laughter rings out in the hall, and when the creak of the heavy doors fades, we are alone.

He brings my fingers to his lips for a kiss. "I asked Mr. Rourke for the latest style. Nothing traditional for you, my darling. In fact, I—"

I lean down and kiss him, and he meets my lips with all the need and passion I can pour into one kiss. No marriage of convenience is born of a kiss like this one, layered in desire and tenderness in the leisurely strokes of his tongue on mine.

And yet, he didn't say he loved me.

Enduring affection and respect must have sounded very nice to my father. But he didn't say *always*. He didn't say *forever.* He said we have work to do and we'll figure it all out after the election.

I twine my fingers in his hair, holding his mouth on mine as his hands grow restless on my waist and hips. I don't want to ask what he meant. I don't want to talk, and I am breathless when he finally breaks away.

"I could kiss you like that all day, Maudie. You can kiss me like that all night, if you like. We have a lot to celebrate."

My voice wobbles. "Don't you think we should be more careful now?"

"In what way?"

"We cannot be seen like that again. Matthew is right. There is only so much people will believe and forgive."

He kisses the tip of my nose. "I can manage a few weeks without you in my bed as long as I know you'll come back."

After the election, of course, when we'll figure this out.

"Will you come back?" he asks.

The joyful glint that brightened his eyes when he knelt before me fades and his gaze grows dark with worry.

I tap my ring. "You asked and I said yes. I meant it."

In a blink, his smile reaches his eyes again. "I meant it, too. What shall we do with our news before this evening?" The curve of his lips in a half-smile is begging for another kiss.

"Do we want to make a fuss of it now? You said—you said we'd figure the rest out after the election."

"We must make a fuss of it." He tangles his fingers with mine, tracing hearts on my palm. "That's the point, isn't it?"

"Is it?"

He bends his head to kiss me. "I must tell you now, alone, so there is no doubt this isn't a presentation to placate any

Berger gossip. This is what I've held back from saying every time I held you in my arms. Every night you came to me, every morning you left and wrenched my heart away with you. The fuss over the announcement is necessary for political reasons. But my darling, the fuss over kissing you for the rest of my life is entirely personal and far more important. The fuss is long overdue, yet I made excuse after excuse."

Goosebumps prickle my arms. "But—I suppose, in your defense, I said I didn't want a new romance."

"I should have said it anyway. I nearly did, so many times, and I must say it now. Since you're already wearing the ring, may I blither a bit about your many virtues?"

I nod, twining my fingers with his. "Only a bit."

"Then I will say without artistry or scripted speech that you are not the woman of my dreams because my dreams could never have conceived of a woman as remarkable as you. My heart never guessed that a partner for one dance could become my partner in dodging conventions and building a love that suits us and no one else. I admire and adore you. I love you for every trait from your brilliant mind to the beautiful curve of your neck that I wish to kiss on waking each day until I die. I will cherish your thoughts and your kisses and your companionship in equal measure and will devote myself to always sharing the same with you."

"Do you really mean to kiss me for the rest of your life?"

He brings my hand to his lips. "Do you really mean to let me?"

With one deep breath, it all catches up to me—the nerves, the weak knees, the little gasps for air and the frantic pace of my heart. The proposal that earns a swoon, finally.

It almost overtakes me.

The warmth in his eyes sets my mouth watering—that caramel color, so delectable I can almost taste the heat between us—and it draws me in with its sweetness and sincerity. Instead of wobbling in his arms, my fear and confusion fall away when he squeezes my hands and my new ring wraps around my finger like an embrace.

"I do. And I love you, too."

When we emerge from the study ten minutes later and breathless from kisses, the table is laid for lunch and more friends have arrived. Victoria approaches me with an excited hop in her step and kisses my cheek, using the moment to whisper in my ear.

"Matthew said he will stay as long as there is no more trouble. He looks like he got hit by a train, but it appears you and Cooper satisfied whatever moral objection he had."

"Hit by a train?"

"Stunned and foolish, more like. And he should feel foolish."

"Victoria, I am so sorry I dragged you into this. I was a terrible friend to put these secrets on you."

She pulls me away from Cooper and keeps her voice low. "You did what you felt you must do to be happy with him. I do not want you to get in trouble, but I would never fault you for being in love."

"So you knew—"

"And the more time I spend with you, the more I am inspired by the love you two have for one another. I wish you hadn't felt like you had to hide it. The way you look at each another is so touching. He respects you and sees you as an equal, and I've decided I will not accept less for myself when the time comes." She lifts her chin, and the same energy I saw in her face when she went after Matthew glows in her cheeks again. "So I am proud to defend your secrets."

"And I will defend yours." I shoot a quick glance at him. "All of them."

She shakes her head with a quick twitch. "I cannot think of him that way anymore. But it felt good to give him a piece of my mind. Honestly, how dare he?"

"Have you ever stood up to someone like that before?"

"Goodness, no. My ankles nearly gave out." She fans herself. "Now promise me you won't get married right away and leave me. I hate living alone. A May wedding would be perfect."

"A May wedding?"

She picks up my left hand and twists my fingers to inspect the brilliance of the diamonds. "May, but after exams."

"Make it June," Georgia interrupts. "I need time to make your wedding dress."

Another warm wave of emotion rushes past me, wobbling me again but leaving only a smile in its wake. Across the room, Leo is slapping Cooper's back and smiling as they inspect a new cartoon Brent is showing off to Ellen and Spencer Sutton, who have just arrived for lunch. The sketch is light and hasty, portraying me in my suffragette sash and Cooper kneeling before me, holding out a ring. Leo reads the caption aloud.

"In old-fashioned style, a modern proposal. Equality gets my vote." He chuckles. "It's brilliant, Trux. I can see you two taking Washington in a few years."

Matthew snatches the paper from his hand and considers it. "Georgia, Leo, I must pass on lunch. I have some work to do." He nods stiffly at me, mouthing *congratulations* before he shoots a glance at Victoria and shakes his head like he's still a little afraid she'll shout at him again. He turns to Cooper with a look somewhere between *you bastard* and *heaven help us*, and I can't make out his terse farewell.

"The nerve of that man," Victoria huffs, glaring as he turns away. "It's a little rushed, maybe, and of course it will surprise everyone and there will still be questions. But really, Cooper's solution to this so-called gossip problem was far better than Matthew's idea to force you down the aisle tomorrow like a punishment for hurting his tender feelings."

I twist my hand in a beam of lamplight and the diamond's unfamiliar shimmer scatters light around me as the man I love catches my gaze. He blows me a little kiss. "Cooper made a very shrewd political maneuver today, Victoria. And after all we've done together already, I'm not surprised in the least. I'll make one of my own now and ask you to lace me a little tighter when we announce all this, just to stay on the safe side of the gossip."

Chapter 30
Cooper

I t's hard to imagine the day getting any better, but as soon as Maudie agreed to marry me, all the stresses whirling around us began to click into place like puzzle pieces.

Berger was pacified, first and foremost, and thank God. We've got the perfect story to bury any rumors and we need him to spread it. We went from him nearly throttling me to wishing me congratulations on my engagement in the space of about an hour, due in large part to Maudie's efforts to calm him while Leo and I called first at the Hamiltons, then at Rourke's Jewelry. God bless the timing of it all—Mr. Hamilton was home and the jeweler's was open. God bless my father, his good name, and his credit for all eternity, because Mr. Rourke let me walk out of his shop with a ring I hoped would dazzle Maudie so much there could be no mistaking how serious I was. Until I knelt at her feet, I knew my plan could go terribly wrong if she thought for an instant I was proposing out of obligation.

I asked for something modern that looked nothing like

her friends' rings because she is nothing like any other woman I know. The "woman of my dreams" line slipped from my lips like only the truth can, and that diamond sunburst, coupled with the hasty visit to ask her father's blessing, said everything I needed to say—with minimal blithering, as she prefers.

We lunched with our friends at Georgia and Leo's in something of a daze, unable to stop touching one another under the table to reassure ourselves it's not a dream. The sight of that ring on her finger sparks something primal in me, and when I catch her looking at it and smiling, it's as though life has dumped a gallon of kerosene on this fire of feelings I have for her. I've finally done something right on my own—no parents bribing me to finish college, no football team depending on me to carry them. Even Berger's temper tantrum simply sped up the inevitable.

I made this impeccable woman fall in love with me. With all my shame and flaws laid bare, she chose me.

This is more than a charmed life. Is it possible to climb any higher?

On a quick visit to her parents' house after lunch, we are swamped with congratulations from her mother and father. They not only demand to know all our plans at once, they place a static-filled call to her brother Jeremiah in Washington, setting me up for an incredibly awkward conversation since he still thinks I am guarding his sister from inappropriate suitors.

"Tonight's your big rally isn't it?" he asks between bursts of static. "What are you doing at the house? Let me guess. You flattered my mother into a dinner invitation."

"It's funny you—"

"You always had a special knack for getting what you want from women. Hamilton women are impervious to your charms, though, in case you haven't noticed."

"Not exactly, which is why—"

Maudie leans close to the handset. "Let him get a word in. He's about to be your brother-in-law."

"He's what? This connection is terrible."

"He asked to marry him and I accepted."

Jeremiah is hundreds of miles away, and the scratches that break the silence on the line sound like he's pawing the ground like an irate bull. "Truxton. You were supposed to be looking out for her."

"And now I always shall."

"What the hell did you—"

I bobble the receiver and Maudie snatches it away. "Don't worry, Jer. I didn't lose my head and swoon over his many charms. I took your good advice and checked his accounts. College really is a fine place to find a rich husband."

I hang up the phone laughing so hard I can't muster words.

Our stop at my parents' house is filled with just as much love and excitement. My mother and father have always loved Maudie as Georgia's friend, and when she holds up her left hand without a word, my mother breaks into a broad smile and my father utters something that sounds like *Oh, thank God, finally* before coughing into his elbow and offering me a handshake. After embraces all around and a heavily filtered retelling of the morning's events, I elbow him into the study for a quiet word about arranging payment for the ring. The old softie hugs me again and tells me not to worry about it.

. . .

An hour later, while Hayes is on his way back to the offices of *The News and Observer* in the city to get my engagement announcement in print, complete with his sketch, Maudie and I prepare to greet guests at my first town hall.

"You are are radiant, my darling." I whisper into her hair, lips barely moving as I try to sneak a kiss without being seen by the first attendees trickling into the gymnasium at my old high school for my event. "Ethereal. I daresay you're glowing."

"Well, I'm having a very nice day today." She winks. "Thank you ever so much for noticing."

"Anything particularly fine about it? A relaxing stroll? Nice weather?"

"Not especially. I had a very frantic stroll around town today in some un-lovely rain, and I'm quite tired. Now that I think of it, I should get some rest." She pretends to flounce away.

"My dearest." I catch her as she turns and graze my fingers over the tender slope of her neck, remembering always that first caress before I kissed her and upended my world. "That was the finest stroll I've ever taken. The rain was a mist of silver. And as for getting some rest, I can think of a perfect place for that."

"You cannot lose focus, Cooper."

"One kiss."

"Not here."

She leans back into my touch, eyes darting around the room, but I nudge her toward a quiet hallway.

"I'm more focused than I have ever been in my life. You are my energy, Maudie. I know my duty to use my place to make this world better. It's not a light responsibility, and that's why I told you the very first day how much I need you. I still do and I always will. If there's ever a seat in the assembly that says Truxton, it means both of us."

Before we return to the lobby to shake a hundred hands, she grants me that kiss.

The lovely ladies of Raleigh Women's College did a fantastic job spreading the word all week. I see many people I recognize and many more I don't, which means I have plenty of chances to convert voters. At the appointed time, Maudie steps up to introduce me.

"Ladies and gentlemen, Cooper Truxton is a Hillside boy, born and raised, like his father, grandfather, and great-grandfather before him. His roots run deep here, and so does his desire to do right by all of you. No matter your party affiliation, I hope you will feel that commitment in his words and deeds and cast your vote accordingly. Improvements to our lives and the maintenance of our traditions do not need to be partisan matters. Here he is to tell you more about himself and how he plans to serve you and your families in the state legislature."

Mr. Holloway, my old high school principal and the evening's moderator, shuffles through his notes. "The first question tonight is from Mr. Harold Pitts. He is often in Raleigh on business and asks what you can do to improve the sad state of the road from Hillside to the city."

"Infrastructure is one of my favorite causes, Mr. Pitts." I drum my fingers on the edge of the podium as I talk for a few minutes about the automobile revolution. "The time is right for the legislature to commit these funds, and I am determined to be part of that conversation. As a matter of fact, I might sit on the capitol steps and pester them about it even if you don't elect me, because that's my road home, too."

I get a laugh for that little reminder that Hillside belongs to me and not an outsider like Shaw. We proceed through questions about railroads, taxes, and Raleigh's dwindling importance in North Carolina's industrial growth. When the topic of women's suffrage is raised, I take a firm stance in support of the cause and remind them that my school visits are because I believe all citizens should understand how their government works and should have the choice to engage in it. An old classmate submits a question about my conservation efforts in jest, but I am happy to spend a few minutes extolling the beauty of our state's natural resources and the importance of healthy timber in a well-regulated market to support our fine furniture industry.

When we draw close to the end of the event, Maudie joins me again to thank everyone for coming and remind them how to register to vote. As she moves to leave the stage, I grab her hand and turn her back to face the audience.

"Now that we have finished with politics for the evening, I'd like to make a quick announcement. Some very special news will be in the church bulletins tomorrow, and you ladies will refuse to forgive my mother and Miss Hamilton's if we do not tell you beforehand. Miss Hamilton and I have known one another many years, and she has managed my campaign down to the tiniest detail with brilliance and grace. I am grateful to her for organizing this event tonight, and even more grateful that she decided to extend our longstanding friendship today by agreeing to marry me."

She blushes furiously as I raise her hand to show off the

ring while murmurs and applause circle the room. Several smiling ladies press their hands to their hearts before turning to start gossip only seconds after the announcement. Even from the stage I can hear a whispered "*Only a matter of time.*"

My old principal is still chuckling when the applause finally quiets. "Then Cooper, we must ask one more thing. When is the happy day?"

"May twenty-seventh, since our semester exams will be done." If Maudie were with child and we were planning a marriage of convenience, she would be about eight months pregnant in May and not inclined to have a large wedding. Her mother already called the preacher's wife and booked the church.

"Well, it's about time you became a sensible student. I find you much improved from your school days here. Miss Hamilton, you have obviously been a steadying influence. Hillside wishes you both happiness."

Another round of applause and a few scattered shouts of "Hear, hear!" surround us as I pull her a little closer to my side. Happiness? She's smiling beside me, holding my hand where a hundred people can see us. This is exultation.

Chapter 31
Maudie

T he news spreads among my classmates like wildfire, and when we hold our weekly meeting of canvassers Sunday night, Victoria greets them all with a smile as smug as the cat who got the cream because she knows all the details and won't share them until I arrive. Although I'm greeted with squeals and demands to see my ring, several of them look askance at me when I walk in.

"I am happy for you and Mr. Truxton, Maudie, but I wouldn't have told anyone yet," says Hattie Ashmead. "It makes it look like you were just trying to get your man by helping out and devalues how much you've done to drive the campaign yourself." She shoots a quick look at my waistline, which I expected since she's devoutly religious. Just like Georgia did for the town hall yesterday, Victoria anticipated that kind of curiosity and helped me with my laces this afternoon, squeezing me down an extra two inches to fit in a snug dress I can only get into with help.

Alice O'Grady casts a longing look at my left hand. "I

suppose this means you won't be back next year. So many girls quit when they get married. It's awful, really."

"Of course I'll be back, just like you will. And I am confident that if anyone devalues my work on this campaign, Cooper will be first in line to correct them."

"I'd like to see him correct Mr. Shaw, then," Hattie says, obviously satisfied with my answer and my waistline. They know of my history with Mr. Shaw but not the story of Cooper's graduation party, and when I catch Victoria's eye, she covers her mouth to keep from laughing. Hattie pokes her. "What is it?"

"He already has," Victoria giggles, and when I give her a nod, she continues. "Months ago, long before the race, but you should hear our friends tell the story. Let it suffice to say, our dear Mr. Truxton is not the only one unimpressed by Mr. Shaw's character."

"Or the fact that he showed up completely drunk to a party looking for me," I add, glancing at Alice. She is a firm believer in temperance, and her brows knit in a disgusted furrow.

"How despicable," she says. "And how lucky for you to find a man like Mr. Truxton who is already reformed from his bad habits. I cannot imagine a man opening up to me the way he did to all of us when he came to speak. I hope this doesn't sound improper, but I feel like I know him better than William in some ways, and we are to be married in a few months."

I've met Alice's intended, a sweet young man and amateur photographer who volunteered to help canvass and submitted several photos to the newspaper of Cooper at various events. "I hope William can open up to you like that."

I squeeze her hand. "It's so natural to women and so unusual in men, but it makes me respect him a great deal, and I think that is what made me see him as more than my best friend's silly older brother."

The warmth in my chest when I speak of him now is tempered by the cold chill of being torn in two. From the moment he announced our engagement at the town hall yesterday, I felt an awkward shift in my breath, like I could only breathe from one lung at a time, never bringing in quite enough air. On my right side, the last twenty-four hours have been a whirlwind and a dream, and everything I felt for him that I denied for so long has come into focus. He loves me, and every doubt I had about loving him fell away when I looked into his beautiful caramel eyes and knew that what had grown between us was everything we were both scared to admit. The brush of his fingers on my cheek tells me I am exactly who he was waiting for, and although he is nothing like anyone I wanted before, he is everything I need.

Then a shiver hits on my left side when I remember we have less than three weeks to the election. We cannot ride off into the sunset and set up house near Georgia and Leo and make a family. One day, perhaps, but not yet. Our theater outing with the other Republican legislators Friday night all but confirmed how out-of-place he will be in the assembly. They align with our causes well enough, but Cooper and I agreed later we didn't sense much drive for change in them, only a desire to manage the status quo.

If Mr. Shaw wins, he will be a decent enough representative—I have settled that with my frustrated heart, and I am determined to see the best in his intentions now. After all, I suppose Cooper and I will find someplace else to make our mark if Hillside won't have us, and that's what Mr. Shaw is doing as well. Perhaps he'll do everything he said before and change his father's party from within. That wouldn't be so bad—but it doesn't lighten our load.

I will settle for Mr. Shaw winning, but I won't sit back and let it happen while I daydream about wedding gowns and wedding nights. If I am Cooper's energy, then he is mine—his bravado and his drive to learn from every person he meets and every page he reads reminds me to take a break from managing and just listen.

"I would like your opinions on a new tactic, ladies," I announce, gesturing for everyone to take their seats in our small library meeting room. "We are considering inviting Mr. Shaw to sit with Mr. Truxton onstage in a joint town hall the Saturday after next. Matthew Berger, who some of you know as our communications manager, suggested this to help bring out the contrast between the two candidates and highlight Mr. Truxton's strengths in public speaking and his local ties. What do you all think?"

Jenny Bowers raises her hand. "Raleigh or Hillside?"

"We are confident of his progressive support in the city at this time. Your efforts on the college campuses and in the neighborhoods have been so impactful, and it helps that they are all polling for Mr. Taft in the presidential election. Our friend Mr. Berger assures us our target should be the Hillside Democrats who are most likely to vote the party ticket for Mr. Bryan."

"We should have it at East Piedmont," she declares. "Mr. Truxton's alma mater. It's right between Hillside and the city." Murmurs of agreement fill the room.

I'm not certain the event will have the benefit Matthew

hopes—it may just be a spectacle, but he insists our good news will generate goodwill. We owe him a great deal for sticking with us, and I thanked him by telling him I'd put his idea to a vote with the ladies we'll need to get our crowd.

Hattie suggests we focus all our canvassing efforts on Hillside for another week and leave Raleigh alone, and in an instant, everyone is pairing up and comparing schedules. Matthew will win the ladies' vote on his idea tonight, which means I must put pen to paper tomorrow and find the right words to convince Mr. Shaw to join us for an evening.

Chapter 32
Cooper

With only a few days remaining before my second town hall appearance, we still have not heard from Shaw's committee about whether he plans to join us or let me have the stage and the audience to myself. Maudie's friends have papered the neighborhoods with leaflets featuring Hayes's newest cartoon: a flattering likeness of me hoisting a North Carolina flag atop a shiny black Model T laden with boxes labeled "Workers' Rights," "Women's Rights" and "American Progress." *Trux and Cars for Carolina!* it announces over the details of the event on Saturday.

I can tell she's still not entirely convinced the side-by-side town hall is the best strategy, but she trusts me enough to try. With every kiss, she buoys my confidence that one way or another, if my canvassers can draw the crowd, I will win them to my side.

Six months ago, Hayes scribbled in his textbooks and made the odd comic for a joke, and now he's in demand by the editorial staff at *The News and Observer*. Six months ago, that delightful morning of my graduation, I'd have brushed off any suggestion of a career in politics. I'd have laughed outright at anyone who said a woman would soon turn my commitment to bachelorhood on its head. In fact, six months ago I was already questioning my choice of college programs and still daydreaming about being a hero to the trees.

Raleigh is known as the city of oaks, and here on Maudie's campus, their spreading branches canopy the walking paths in a flare of fall colors, as beautiful as any of my beloved chestnuts. The saplings Jenny Bowers and the Arborist Society planted last spring have already lost most of their leaves, and a brisk gust whips up a tiny tornado of them around the bench where I sit. It brings me almost to laughter until I realize who the wind has dropped in front of me.

I haven't seen Tobias Shaw since I bloodied his face in my back garden. He offers a curt nod and doesn't move.

I don't rise and offer a handshake like I should. Generally speaking, the ladies of Raleigh Women's College want nothing to do with this man who would deny them their suffrage and other rights, and seeing him on what I've come to think of as my home turf has got my back up already. He's bold to come here, and I know from experience that men are most often bold for stupid reasons, chief among them the desire for a woman's attention.

The woman he is looking for, however, has plans for the afternoon. As soon as she's free of her biology lecture, those plans include no one but me, myself, and I.

"Have you an appointment?" I ask. "My fiancée is a busy woman."

He snorts a small puff of a laugh. "Your fiancée. I confess, you caught me off guard with that announcement. The constituency is buzzing, so you timed it well. But she assured me you had only a professional relationship, so you can imagine my shock."

"She what?"

Settling on the opposite end of the bench, he removes his gloves, shaking them out fastidiously before folding them in his lap like my mother does. "Maudie said there was nothing romantic between you."

"When?"

He frowns and turns his face skyward, giving me the perfect opportunity to wring his neck.

"September, sometime. Late September." With a little leer, he smiles. "I see she did not tell you we spoke."

"Of course she did. She just didn't waste time recounting every word of unimportant babble." I flick a wave to shoo him away, feigning indifference while I fight back a tightness in my chest. Late September, when we'd opened up to one another so much and she'd already been in my bed—she spoke with him and didn't tell me?

"We have some business to discuss around this event you've proposed for Saturday, and of course I wished to congratulate her on her engagement. I shall congratulate you as well, Truxton. She's exquisite and far too good for you."

"I wholeheartedly agree."

"It's lovely how devoted you are to her causes, and she to yours."

"Maudie and I are of like mind on most things."

"Well, she does her research and knows how to ingratiate herself into people's passions. I'm sure she's spouting forestry facts left and right to make you happy."

"As a matter of fact—"

"Will you be joining her when she comes to work with me after the election?"

"When she what?"

The sidewalks around us hush and the breeze slows to a near-whisper. Shaw pats his jacket and rustles a paper in the inner pocket.

"When I win, she said she would work with me in any of my endeavors related to her causes. I will gladly support her behind the scenes on her suffrage efforts until the time comes I can do so publicly. Oh, dear." He pulls a frown. "I can see she didn't tell you that, either. You are quite close, aren't you?"

"She promised you nothing."

"Maudie is a politician, Trux, not your secretary. You would be wise to remember she can be a cutthroat under all the silk and lace because I taught her to be one. She made a deal to keep me on my best behavior for this race, and I can see she's made one with you now as well. An engagement is an interesting way to placate a man with a history like yours, but she is delightfully creative. Of course she's fond of you, but how fortunate no one is talking about you in a way that might make her rethink this future you imagine with her."

"You're baiting me, Shaw, and I will not resort to violence again. It's not easy to refrain from ripping your head off, but I was raised right. My father is a peaceful man."

I dealt him a right hook the last time we spoke. Today it's a punch in the gut, and I haven't lifted a finger.

I don't know what the hell he's talking about. This could all be a lie to trick me into attacking him in public, but I will not stoop so low again. I won't prove him—and Berger—right about my temper. He won't use her to taunt me, and whatever Maudie and I have to talk about later, we will talk about.

266

In the meantime, I can't help but lean in and twist the knife a little to show him I will not be manipulated. "I admire my father more than any man in the world. Christopher Truxton is a fine moral example who I have disappointed many times, but his faith in me inspired me to change my life for the better. Do you admire Ashford Pinckney Shaw?"

He seethes as his father's name lands on the bench between us like a weight. After a long silence, he opens his watch. "I believe Maudie will be out of class soon and will not like to see us fighting."

"I'm not fighting with anyone." I flick a speck of dirt from underneath my fingernail. "Are you?"

Hands twitching on his watch, he doesn't answer.

"Well, I imagine my darling bride and I will—ah, there she is now."

I rise and jog a few paces to catch her before she sees him, and when her smile rounds her cheeks I can't help but kiss one. "Dearest, we have a little problem, but it will only take a moment to rectify."

He's on his feet. "I would like to speak with you, Miss Hamilton," he says with a stiff bow.

"I suppose you are here to congratulate me on my engagement." She slips her hand into mine and doesn't grant him a smile. "But the last time we spoke, I said I did not wish to see you again."

"I shall skip my congratulations on this farce and instead express my admiration for a very clever and well-timed political maneuver. It didn't seem right to wait until I see you Saturday."

She whips off her glove and my mouth twitches into a smirk when the sunlight hits the diamonds. "It is not a farce."

"It is fortunate Truxton is a wealthy man and can provide such impressive proof of his love on short notice. How beautifully you arranged it. I see I taught you well."

"Have you anything worthwhile to say to Miss Hamilton?" I drawl. "We have plans."

He waits for her to look back to him, and when she meets his gaze, the tension in her neck softens and she drops my hand. "We will see you Saturday, then?"

"I am considering it. But I see you haven't been truthful with your beloved," he says. I don't flinch as he continues. "I rather like that you kept our deal a little secret between us, although I wonder now what other secrets you are keeping."

"I will run this campaign as I see fit," she snaps, her moment of tenderness vanished as quickly as it came. "I do not bother my candidate with every little detail. He trusts me, and I trust him."

I clamp my teeth down on my cheeks to keep from breaking into a triumphant grin that will surely distract from the walloping she's about to give him.

"How can you trust a man like him?"

"Do not make this about him. You are not upset about Cooper. This is about you and me."

"You led me to believe there might be a second chance for us, and only weeks later you are engaged to a man you said you had no romantic feelings for. I suppose I should not trust you now, either."

Her eyes narrow. "I am sorry you misinterpreted my words. Trust me, or don't. I have upheld my end of the bargain."

"I only promised you a clean campaign in hopes of working with you after I win."

"How funny you admit that." The breeze whips up a sudden gust and swishes her skirt around her ankles. "I thought you promised a clean campaign because you are a decent man."

"Maudie, my darling."

The slick smirk vanishes. I remember him from those years in the dormitory—he used to be quick to laugh and make a joke at his own expense. We were never friends, but we got on all right, and six months ago, I thought he was a decent man, too. He's always disdained my choices a little, and I see now we were both wrong about one another.

She's not distracted by his little pout. "Can you pretend to be decent until Tuesday? Do not think I haven't prepared for this. And do not think I will hesitate to use what I know if you go after the man I love."

I stroke her shoulder, letting my touch linger on the strap of the satchel I gave her. It's my armor as much as it is her shield, and seeing her tear into him calms every jumpy, over-protective nerve in my body.

He sniffs a little laugh as he re-situates his hat. "Then I see I have no choice but to accept your invitation to this town hall arrangement on Saturday. I shall try to mind my manners, but I might have no qualms about shaming this self-righteous, pompous ass publicly like he deserves. Or I could simply wait until Wednesday and do it as a victory celebration."

"Try it." She adjusts her own hat in a broad gesture, mocking him. "There is more to him than meets the eye. Just like there is more to you, and more to me." She takes my arm and we step away, then she looks back. "Goodbye, Mr. Shaw."

Chapter 33
Maudie

I lift my chin and stretch my throat, sucking in air through my nose so I don't pant like an animal. I cannot fill my lungs.

"Maudie?"

Cooper's grasp is firm on my elbow as I pull in another breath, counting to five. It seems to lodge on my tongue like I'm breathing pudding, and I start to cough.

I cannot believe that after our last meeting I harbored a sliver of hope that Mr. Shaw might do the right thing. I only wanted him to know I still believed that if he won, he would do the things he once promised. In my foolishness, I thought my faith in him still mattered.

Everything I said to Georgia, every way I tried to convince myself he wasn't so bad and all would be fine if he won—I was wrong. If he plays dirty enough to attack Cooper when he knows it will shame me, the hopes I had for his decency were entirely wrong.

The betrayal hits me again like a cramp. Mr. Shaw will never change his father's party as long as its power structure supports him, and whatever good was in his spirit years ago might already be singed at the edges by corruption.

"Maudie, darling, come here." Cooper's voice is soft. "Let's sit for a moment."

I can't turn around. "Is he gone?"

"He's gone."

We reach the bench just in time. I collapse onto the wooden slats as though my joints have all come loose and my clattering bones can no longer hold me up. That man's mockery and the memory of my foolish love for him pinches me tighter than any corset as I try again to take a deep breath.

Cooper rubs my shoulders and upper back with a steady hand. "He's gone," he whispers again. "I'm here."

"I don't know what's come over me."

"He was baiting you, darling. Both of us. You slaughtered him like a lady. I am in awe."

My heart slows. "What did he say to you before I arrived?"

"Fake congratulations, as expected. He implied that you were using me, couldn't possibly have love for such a low creature as myself, and so on. And of course, the implication that you would go work with him if he won."

"Oh, Cooper. You must know how wrong he is."

He stares at his lap, bouncing his knees in a nervous jitter. "I know, my love."

"What else?"

"What?"

"You're tapping like a telegraph. What else did he say?"

"What bargain did you make with him?"

A chill grips me. "It wasn't really a—well, I suppose you could call it that, but I—"

"He said you spoke with him back in September and

made a bargain of some sort to keep us both on our best behavior. What happened?"

The college green and the sidewalks around us hum with activity and classmates passing by and I press my fingers to my temples. "Could we walk, please?"

"You're still trembling a little. I don't mean to upset you, but—"

"I would rather not talk about it here."

The afternoon sun is still high, so we don't need to fear a scandal when he escorts me to his boarding house in silence, eyeing me with anxious glances until we reach his doorstep. The decision to keep all this from him seemed so wise at first, and so reasonable—but seeing it now through his pained gaze it is obvious I was mistaken. Only when he locks the door to his room and beckons me to sit next to him on the bed do I nearly burst into tears.

"Cooper, I am so sorry. I was trying to protect you."

"Protect me from what? What did he say? Why were you speaking with him at all?"

"He found me on campus not long after the newspaper profile came out. Victoria was with me. I made her stay, but I don't think she could hear us."

He stiffens. "What did he say to you?"

"Just some—some personal things he thought he must get off his chest." My cheeks flame at the memory. "His hurt feelings about how I was helping you and not him, and so on."

"Maudie. You should have told me."

"He thought I should give him another chance and asked me to forgive him. Obviously, I disagreed, but I did not wish to share that. It was not really about you."

"And yet somehow I ended up the subject of a deal."

I fidget with my engagement ring and say nothing.

"Maudie, he just got some sick pleasure out of making me look like an ass for not knowing what the hell he was talking about. He was flaunting the fact that you kept it secret from me. I need you to tell me."

"He made some unkind observations about you in hopes of shocking me." I twist my ring again. "None of what he had to say about your college days was a surprise to me. This conversation happened right after you met with the club presidents, so to hear him speak of you like you are some amoral degenerate upset me a great deal. I asked him if he was planning to attack your character in his campaign, and he said he had not decided."

He draws in a quick breath.

"So I told him that if he brought up your past, we would bring up his. And that includes what happened during the coup in Wilmington."

"You told me weeks before there was nothing to say about that. Berger and I thought we could attack him with it, and you—"

"You thought you could attack him because you don't know what happened. It's not as simple as him being a bad man because his father is. He is afraid of what people will think about what he did that night. He thinks it will ruin him politically. I leveraged his fears to protect you, Cooper, but the truth is, I don't think he did anything wrong. And if I were running his campaign, I'd shout to the skies what a good man he is for what he did in the face of a murdering mob."

Two tears seep out the corners of my eyes and I brush them back into my messy hair. "The truth can be to his detriment in Wilmington, but it might make him a hero to Hillside voters."

"Lie down," he whispers, pulling me next to him. "Just hold my hands and tell me what happened."

I start with the printing press and the inflammatory column in the black newspaper that the white supremacists decided was the last straw. Ashford Shaw, Mr. Shaw's father, represented the Wilmington district in the state house at the time and was part of the local Democrats' decision to seize control of the city government.

"The night they blew up the press, everything escalated. It was no longer about who controlled the newspapers or the city council, it was who controlled the streets with guns and torches. Armed gangs were going door-to-door looking for black men to hurt or kill. Some were taken right from their jobs and dragged away. And Ashford Shaw was among the men leading the mobs."

Cooper tightens his grip on my hands.

"Toby was thirteen years old, and when he heard the noise in the streets, he didn't know what was happening at first." I don't even mind that I slipped and used his first name again. It comes more naturally when I remember how he shivered telling me this story. The boy named Toby was inno-cent. Mr. Shaw is a varmint.

"A neighbor boy came running from a few blocks away telling everyone to shut up their houses and put out the lights. Toby loaded one of his father's pistols and waited on the porch alone. When his father approached with armed, angry men at his back, he ordered him to go with them. Toby defied him and said he had to guard his mother and sisters since the servants ran off when they heard a commotion. But even his mother and sisters did not know that their valet, their carriage man, their cook, and their two maids were huddled in the cellar under potato sacks."

"Oh, Maudie."

"The mob moved on, and for three days, he took as much food and drink as he could to the cellar. He emptied the buckets they used to relieve themselves while his mother and sisters complained about not having hot meals and pressed linens, thinking the servants really had run off. A day after Toby heard from his father that other families' servants were returning, he took that news to the cellar and offered to help them either resume their work or run away, however they chose."

I close my eyes. "He thinks we can destroy him with this because his party leaders might disown him—not to mention what wrath his father might lay down. Voters in Wilmington might hate him for betraying his party like that. Imagine common decency being something to hide. He always promised he would change the party from within, but now I wonder if he even wants to. The first time I visited his family and heard his father run on, I faked a swoon to go to bed. He promised me he would stand against his father, but I never heard a peep."

"Maudie, I—"

"I used his fear to protect you. I'm sorry I didn't tell you, but I thought I shouldn't take the chance that anyone would say something about this or bring up his stupid father by accident."

Cooper's eyes go wide. "Did you hear that?"

"Hear what?"

"I asked him if he was proud of his father."

I flop my head against the pillow. "Oh, you didn't."

"I wouldn't have said anything if you'd told me not to."

"I did tell you not to. Over and over, I told you not to, and I told Matthew not to. I told everyone to leave it alone."

He sits up, scowling. "You should have told me why. I would have been more careful."

"It's not enough to follow the simplest directions from the person you said you trust to lead this campaign?" I pop up on my knees, pillow clutched in my fist. "Hillside leans Democrat, but they don't like radicals like Ashford Shaw. Toby doesn't realize the advantage of proving he's not like him and I do not want anyone breathing a word of it."

"You don't trust me."

"I have proven my trust in you many ways. I thought it best to reduce risk in this matter. If we paint him as a radical white supremacist, an extension of his father, he can hit us back with the truth when he sees that go over poorly. It's best to let people make their assumptions. The truth is very sympathetic to him. We cannot tempt him to use it."

He shifts away from me as I scoot closer. "So you think like Berger does. I can't handle myself when I feel insulted, is that it?"

"Mr. Shaw jabbed at you today to make you feel insecure about me, and what did you do? It sounds like you grabbed for anything that looked like a sword and you swung it. I told you we were not bringing it up, and you brought it up anyway."

"I was upset." He buries his hands in his hair, tugging the brown curls into an unruly mess. "You didn't hear the whole thing. He made all these implications like you were working with him behind my back, that your feelings for me were all false and just an act for the campaign. It hurt, and I just reacted."

"You did exactly what he knew you would do." I rise. "So thank God I got there when I did."

"Oh, nicely timed, just like everything else."

"What's that supposed to mean?" I swish down my skirts and draw back from him. "I didn't plan to see him there."

"Didn't you? How does he know your class schedule?"

"I have no idea. With all I've just told you, why on earth would I want the two of you talking at all?"

"A trial run for next week?" he sputters. "I don't know. But I've failed miserably, I see. You should have told me weeks ago. I could have handled this better."

"I told you weeks ago there is nothing we can use from this matter."

"And what were you going to do if he broke his word and attacked me at this stupid town hall I agreed to?" He clutches the bedclothes in his fists. "Have you so much faith in his promises that you would send me out there defenseless while you sit on a pile of ammunition?"

My ears ring with his unfamiliar, angry tone, and I step back a few paces. "You are not helpless to defend yourself, you know. Your truth is your defense, and so is his. I used the only weapon a woman usually has with a man—his pride. A scoundrel and a rogue, and both of you so unhinged that you'll turn on me rather than look at your own fault in creating this situation. It is Mr. Shaw's fault he lies to his father and his party about his plans and shuffles his platform to suit the day's needs. It is your fault you not only went to brothels, you bragged about your adventures loudly and often."

"I have changed and Shaw has not." His forearms are corded with tension as he yanks at the quilt like he means to tear it.

"Yes. I held you in my arms while you were shaking the night you told that story. It broke a piece of me to see you so vulnerable. I promised myself I would do everything I could to keep us from a situation where you had to confess all that again. I know now that how I did it was a mistake, but I did the best I could for you."

My pulse pounds at my temples. I have never seen him so physically angry, and terrifying memories of the fights he was in on the football field chase back through my mind. Flying fists and furious glares, a Cooper I hardly recognized when it was done.

I take another step back.

"He said you were a cutthroat beneath the silk and lace," he says, softer but still tense. "And my heart nearly stopped when I wondered how much of you he really knew beneath the silk and lace."

I open my mouth to speak, but he raises a hand and looks up with damp, heartbroken eyes. The tilt of his head wrenches my heart. "I know you never let him touch you. And even if you had, I know you would not lie to me about it. But the idea of any man knowing your heart and mind better than I do is like a knife in my stomach. That he should know anything about your thoughts or plans that I do not know twists that knife."

"Cooper, I am sorry."

"You said my proposal was a very shrewd political move. I suppose your little bargain was one as well."

"They are not the same at all."

"But they are. We both found ourselves in a position that demanded we act on feelings we were trying to deny, and at the moment of truth, you made a bargain to protect me and I forced myself out of my fear and asked you to marry me. And here we are—" He chokes on his words. "Here we are fighting, and when I look at you, I already don't know what we're fighting about."

"I hurt you by not telling you the whole truth right away."

"You were right to keep it from me and right to believe I wouldn't keep my mouth shut if I knew. I begged you to guide me through this race and then refused to trust your strategy. I don't know why, because I knew before you came home with me that what I felt for you was exactly what I never thought I'd feel for anyone. I made every excuse and I denied it to myself, but I knew. And now I have shouted at you and accused you of betraying me when I should be comforting you after you had to stand up to him on my behalf." He stares at his hands, unclenching his fingers from the quilt one by one. "I am so sorry, Maudie. You knew just what to say to him. You fought for me, and what did I do in return?"

"Cooper, don't." I close the space between us in two strides and take his shaking hands in mine. "I love you, and I am so very sorry."

"I forgive you, my love. What you have done pales beside my pride and foolishness. I flouted your guidance and the care you have taken with this campaign, and I am so sorry. I beg your forgiveness in return, for that and for one more thing."

"For what?"

He draws me close and kisses me. "For needing to feel close to you right now," he murmurs against my lips. "I am unmoored, my darling, and lost between these depths of love for you and shame at all my failings. I don't know how to feel just one thing. I don't know how to love you without fear that I am doing it wrong. I need you to—"

"I'll hold onto you. I will not leave you." Pulling him back onto the bed, I kiss him again. "Always remember, I want to be here with you."

"You did not trust me, and I deserved that. I will do better." He covers my cheeks with kisses. "Maudie, do not give up on your sad wreck of a lover. I will do better for both of us."

Loosening his tie, I tilt my head so his lips find my neck. "You are mine and I am yours, and I will not keep things from you again. I'll tell you everything he said to me that day, if you wish."

"Perhaps later." His fingers fly over the buttons of my dress. "I don't want to think of him anymore. I want to lose myself in your arms right now and think of nothing else. I want to be as close to you as I can."

I need it, too. The warmth of his body and the smell of his skin mingle with mine in a closeness that heals us and tucks us away from the world. It hides us in a place where we are always of the same mind as lovers and friends and husband and wife, and everything else slips away.

We struggle through one another's clothes, sitting up and wriggling things off piece by piece, interspersed with quiet laughter until he reaches for the laces to loosen my stays. I bend forward, take a deep breath, and unclasp the front so the corset falls away, leaving nothing between us but my thin linen chemise.

He holds his breath as I draw it over my head.

"Can you lose yourself in me like this?"

"Oh God, yes." His breath is warm on my breasts as he draws me close, slipping out of the rest of his clothes before his hands find my waist. The hard edge of his teeth startles me before the tender pressure of his lips follows, teasing me as tension rises from my toes to my neck under every intimate graze of his fingers. But when he lowers his head to my stomach, I catch him under the chin and meet his gaze.

"I'm ready."

Panic fills his eyes. "You do not need to do this as some sort of apology or show of faith, Maudie. I respect that you don't want to yet, and there is nothing to prove."

"I want to. I want you." His weight warms me as I pull him up to me and kiss him again. Caressing his cheek, I bring my left hand to his mouth and press my engagement ring to his lips. "And I would like my seductive speech, please. You said you have a selection prepared."

The caramel sweetness of his eyes takes me back to the hush that fell around us when we danced at the wedding—surrounded and yet entirely alone. In silence, he tangles his fingers in my loose hair while a smile threatens to crease his cheek with a dimple.

"This one starts very simply. I love you, and I desire you with all my heart."

"Show me."

Bending forward, he presses his lips to my collarbone. "You will understand when you touch me. You'll feel my love in my breath and in my bones. Savor what you can do to me while you think of all the things I could do to you. I have brought you pleasure already, but there will be nothing more delectable than taking you while you take me. Every time you touched me, I know you imagined it."

My breaths go ragged and I caress his face as his mouth meanders my neck and breasts. Just like the first night I touched him, a tender stroke of his ear and tug of his hair set a satisfied smile on his lips as he slides down my body.

"Your kisses alone are like no other, and you struck something deep and primal in me when you offered those kisses free of obligation. Yet in the cruelest irony, you shackled my heart to yours that night and I have never been the same."

I suck in a sharp breath but he quickly moves on, tracing his fingers over my stomach in wide loops and spirals, dipping closer and closer between my thighs as he sets every nerve aflame. "You are the only woman who was ever worth that risk. And perhaps I did it all wrong by not asking to court you properly, but everything since that night had made me surer that our friendship and respect for one another will carry us further than any flowers or poetry or a courtship played by the rules."

I stroke him again as he moves between my legs, and as he nudges gently to position himself, I spread my hands on his back, raking him a little with my nails when a quick break in the rhythm of his breath tells me he's ready.

"It has carried you into my arms and this hunger in me will not be satisfied until I can possess you and give myself to you body and soul. Break the rules with me again. You cannot tell me this is enough anymore."

"It's not enough. It will never be enough again."

Inch by inch, I take him in, curled forward and trying to watch. He pauses every time I gasp, pulsing against me until I nod for him to continue, over and over until he's fully inside me and the tension as I stretch around him is almost more than I can bear.

"Cooper?" My voice is weak as I squeeze his backside, holding him down. The warm, pleasant ache spreading in my belly overpowers the slight sting from when he entered me, and I sink into the mattress under his weight. Brushing my face against his chest, I breathe in the heat and the smell of his skin.

"Are you all right?"

"Go slowly."

He withdraws enough to kiss me before he slides back in, and my hips arch off the bed to welcome him. "I have tortured myself with dreams of this since the first night I kissed you," he says. "My resolve to never trust a lady's intentions fell apart then and there."

"I could not stop thinking of you." I brush his hair back from his face as our breath and kisses keep time with our bodies. "For all my resolve to not seek anyone new, there you were. I wanted you that night and I never stopped."

"You wanted me like this?" He smiles and rolls us onto our sides, sliding out and pressing deeper as steady as a heartbeat. "Even then?"

"I wanted to uncover everything about you. My favorite rogue is so much more than he seems."

"My unladylike lady." With a jerk of his hips he touches someplace new inside me, setting my bones trembling with a familiar heat. "And, not soon enough, my wife."

Chapter 34
Cooper

We make it to the day of the joint town hall with no further scandal, only a slew of notes and cards congratulating us on our engagement and piling up in our parents' homes. Georgia writes thank you notes for Maudie and me to sign when we have a few minutes between school papers and practicing the questions we anticipate for the evening. As usual, we have a few plants in the audience, but only to make me sympathetic and nothing that could get us accused of targeting Shaw. I have adopted my love's resolve to run a clean campaign.

What else Maudie has up her pretty sleeves is anybody's guess, and perhaps it's best I don't know. Thoughts of more stolen moments with her chase me all day and wake me every night, and I can only turn my mind back to my schoolwork or campaign events when I picture my ring on her finger and the promise that those intimate embraces were the first of a lifetime to come.

"We have one more potential problem besides the town hall tonight," I announce. Ten curious pairs of eyes around

Georgia's dining room table turn to me as I point to a stack of newspaper clippings as my evidence. "Remember, Shaw's father's party stuffed the ballot boxes in Wilmington to make a bogus claim to victory and justify their overthrow of the government. We haven't addressed this yet, and I cannot help but wonder if they will resort to similar tactics since Ashford Shaw is funding this venture."

Leo shoots a curious glance at Berger. "What do you hear from the county offices? Who manages the ballot boxes, and how are they counted?"

"Partisans," he says, his voice as sour as the lemon in his tea. "Officially, a member of each party is present to oversee and certify when each box is counted."

"What about during the voting process? Is anyone making sure the ballots are legitimate and all registered voters are allowed in?"

"North Carolina gives election boards broad discretion to impose poll taxes and restrict entry for all sorts of reasons," Berger says, nodding at a notebook crammed with his scribbles and research. "It's tricky to manage in the moment. The polling stations are staffed by volunteers from the parties, but of course, they all have their motives. Still, I have hope that since it is also a presidential election, Shaw's party will play a little more cleanly because they want the expected votes for Mr. Bryan to be counted. You're on the same ballot, Trux. Legitimizing the presidential counts means that by default, they legitimize yours."

"Do we offer some volunteers?" Angeline asks. "Some of our cousins not named Berger, from Mama's side, perhaps. They could at least appear neutral and report back if anything is amiss."

Victoria raises her hand. "How many polling stations should we consider, and where and when are the boxes counted?"

"Ten," Berger replies, just as my father begins to speak. He's joined us today because my mother is tending to Georgia, who Leo insisted stay in bed because she's been so tired. She didn't seem tired to me when she ordered Maudie and me to continue on without her and quit fretting, but we obeyed.

"Since there are no government offices in the Raleigh portion of the district, the count will happen in Hillside City Hall," Papa says. "The polls will close at five and the boxes will be brought up from the city. They may count well into the night, and may recount if someone objects to the results. When the counts are agreed upon, they are notarized and submitted back to the Assembly the following day. They may be recounted even then if the presidential counts are close. Those results go to the state electors and aren't official in Washington until January."

"But we'll know by Wednesday, most likely?" I ask.

"The only time I recall that we didn't know Wednesday morning was Shockley's first re-election campaign. They counted three times because it came down to five votes."

I gulp.

"Who brings the boxes from the city?" Victoria asks.

Papa furrows his brow. "I don't know. I expect it's whoever was staffing the polls."

Victoria scribbles a note and passes it to Maudie, and whatever is in it makes her smile.

The sheer volume of carriages outside the largest lecture hall at East Piedmont College shows a great deal of turnout from the city. The auditorium's ninety seats fill quickly as Maudie and I circle the lobby shaking hands and making introductions, and by the time we are summoned backstage, the crowd is standing in the back of the hall and even sitting on the steps.

Two Windsor chairs sit a few feet apart at center stage, separated by a small table with a water pitcher and glasses as though we really are going to have a friendly conversation. Shaw and I greet each other in front of the audience with a cordial handshake and take our seats.

"Fine turnout," he mutters as he pours a glass of water. "How many are on your father's payroll?"

"Let's not start on our fathers' contributions." I smile through clenched teeth and wave at the audience. "I'll be decent tonight even if you will not."

Dr. Rutherford Williams, a silver-haired professor at Berger's law school, introduces himself as the evening's moderator and explains the rules. "Most questions have been submitted in advance," he says, pointing to a large box of folded papers. "Questioners were asked to indicate which candidate they would like to answer the question. After that candidate answers, the other will have the opportunity to provide their own response if they wish, provided they do not attack the other candidate in doing so. This is an informational event, not a debate."

Murmurs of approval circle the auditorium.

"The questions will be selected at random. Additional questions can be submitted throughout the evening as time allows." He clears his throat and introduces us briefly with text provided by our campaigns—Maudie will not join me in the spotlight tonight, although she is just behind the curtains to my side in case of some disaster that requires her to shove Mr. Shaw off the stage. We decided in advance that while it's an extreme measure, it's not unthinkable and will look far better if she does it.

Most of the first questions are directed at Shaw because the voters haven't heard as much from him yet. Maudie's hectic schedule dragging me up and down the hill every week has succeeded in making me something of a household name. Shaw talks about infrastructure with broad, vague terms, and I use my allotted two minutes to emphasize my more specific plans for the Raleigh triangle and the commuter roads to Hillside and Oak Grove. He is pleased to spout his devotion to temperance measures and even gets a little applause. I am forthright about my disagreement due to the economic impact and the lack of education and support we should offer those who indulge too much.

Dr. Williams unfolds the next paper and his grave demeanor cracks. "The next question is from a young man named Anthony, aged twelve, and directed to Mr. Shaw. Anthony would like to know your favorite cookie from Miss Cinnamon's bakery in Hillside."

Snorts of laughter erupt from the spectators as Mr. Shaw twists his lip and searches for an answer. "I have never been to Miss Cinnamon's bakery, I confess, but I have a fondness for the classic chocolate chip cookie."

"Mr. Truxton, would you also like to answer Anthony's question?"

I squint into the audience. "Like most Hillside natives, I always look forward to Miss Cinnamon's seasonal special. Strawberry jam sandwiches in the spring, iced lemon puffs in the summer, maple spice snickerdoodles in the fall, and my particular favorite will be starting in December, cranberry walnut cakes."

I don't know who put Anthony Berger up to that excellent reminder that I belong here and Shaw does not, but if anyone asks, it wasn't me.

The next question is mine and the name is unfamiliar, but when the young man in the audience stands, I recognize him immediately. I wonder if Maudie can see him.

"Mr. Freddie Hudson will turn eighteen years old tomorrow, Mr. Truxton, and is excited to vote in his first election. You visited his school in Raleigh and talked about the importance of civic engagement. He would like to know how you decided to enter a political race instead of other, more exciting opportunities in your areas of study."

I smile, wishing I had more than three minutes for this one. "Mr. Hudson, it is nice to see you again, and happy birthday. Thank you for bringing it to my attention that I never fully explained why I did not pursue a life with the Forest Service and changed my course so rapidly. My love for our country's natural resources is what drove me to study agriculture in the first place. I have a true passion for conservation. But I realized not long ago that my vision of that life was to escape responsibilities and a society where I didn't think I fit in."

I catch Leo's eye and get an encouraging nod for finally

admitting what he's been saying for years. "It may be an adventure or a dream of service for you and other young men, but for me, it was a dream to run away from the rules and live a bohemian lifestyle on my own whims. In moments of clarity, when I am most honest with myself, those desires were selfish. This world has afforded me many unearned privileges, chief among them my sex and race. If I despise the rules, I must act with the power I have to change them. A seat in the legislature is a great opportunity to serve others whose needs are far more pressing than any chestnut blight or illegal logging. I will make the most of this opportunity for all of us if you allow me to represent you."

I sneak a glance at Maudie offstage and catch her bobbing her head in agreement.

"Mr. Shaw, do you have anything to add?"

"I have never sought any career beyond public service," he says, lifting his chin a little as though it's worth bragging that he hasn't an original thought in his head. "So while I do not have anything to say that is specific to Mr. Hudson's question about changing course, I will agree with Mr. Truxton that a seat in the legislature is a powerful opportunity to serve. It is one that I have been raised to hold, and my experience in clerkships and other legislative offices prepares me with an understanding of lawmaking, ways and means, and the workings of the government that will allow me to serve you efficiently from my first day in office."

Slick. Imperious, but slick.

"Another for you, Mr. Truxton," Dr. Williams says. "Dr. Edwin Mullins is a physician in Raleigh. He says that while your support for women's suffrage is consistent and clear, he is interested to know how you view women's labor issues, specifically dangerous working conditions."

I take a long drink of water and pray no one sees my hand shaking. Maudie and I wrote scripts of how I could handle any planted personal attacks by Shaw's minions or even snide remarks onstage if he were so bold, but no one from Shaw's side put Dr. Mullins up to this. I suspect I know who did. I may be Miss Ada Butler's ally, but I have been a silent one, and she might see this event as a way to test my promise to advocate for women like her.

Shaw will latch onto this like bait on a hook if I tempt him with it.

"Dr. Mullins, thank you for broaching this topic. My belief in women's suffrage stems from my conviction that all adults in this country should have the opportunity to participate in the government and speak for their interests. Women cannot. Women who work in unsafe conditions have no voice in the government that could change those conditions. Every day, thanks especially to the ladies at Raleigh Women's College who helped with my campaign, I learn more about what it is to be helpless and voiceless in this world. At the deepest core of my being, I know this is unfair, and I will not waver in my commitment to be a voice for causes that matter to women. Working conditions. Care for widows and orphans."

I stare at Mr. Shaw, daring him to react to the direction of my words. His chin twitches.

"And that even includes women in brothels." I push on and ignore the audience. "Just like the women in factories, none of them are there because they wish to be, and just like the women in factories, they should have a safe way of earning money. They may not be coughing up soot and dying of lung disease after being worked to the bone for pennies, but they are often subject to violence. They are often malnourished and ashamed to seek care if they are with child or have hungry children. Even church charities look down on them with pity and judgment. All women's safety and suffrage matter. This is my moral conviction. I won't waver on that to win votes."

The auditorium is quiet when Dr. Williams turns to Mr. Shaw and asks for his contribution.

He uncrosses his legs and indulges in a stretch, then leans forward and squints at me like he's eyeing a science experiment.

I tilt my head to invite the weasel to speak.

Do it, you cocky bastard. Show everyone how stupid you think I am.

"Forgive me if I beg a quick deviation from the format here, but does your fiancée know where you were Thursday afternoon, Mr. Truxton?"

The crowd protests and Dr. Williams tries to talk over him, but Shaw raises his voice. "Does she know that despite your fine words about respecting and valuing all women, you were on Grosvenor Street at a house of ill repute just two days ago?"

Chapter 35
Maudie

My cheeks and lips go cold.

"Mr. Shaw, you are out of order," Dr. Williams booms in his best courtroom voice. "Mr. Truxton, you do not have to respond to that, and we are out of time."

The noise in the auditorium is lifting from whispers to chatter to angry hisses, and when I peek through the curtains I spy several men donning their hats as if to leave. People standing behind the seats are turning to the door.

Cooper meets my eyes for a split-second, then raises his voice over the audience. "Yes, Mr. Shaw, she knows where I was. She knows what I was doing on Grosvenor Street, and she knows who I was with."

Everyone leaving turns back around and Cooper beckons me to his side. "Fish on a hook," he murmurs without moving his lips.

I clasp his hand. "What he says is true. I know my fiancé better than anyone, and I am proud of him for being there, because that means he is a man of his word."

Mr. Shaw's mouth goes slack and I have to bite the inside of my cheek to keep from smiling. Did he expect me to cry or faint or use some underhanded means to ruin his credibility? When men use words as weapons, they speak them aloud. A woman's subtlety is a whisper in this world.

Cooper squeezes my hand. "Miss Hamilton knows I used to visit brothels, and she knows that long before this campaign began, I not only stopped doing that, I committed to make amends for exploiting those women. I cannot just wash my hands of my mistakes and walk away. My past choices were despicable, which is why I was with Dr. Mullins that day to collect receipts from the proprietress and pay from my own pocket for every call to that house and the homes of the women who work there. I don't have the means to send them all to college to train for better jobs, but even without the support of anyone in this room besides Miss Hamilton, I will support these workers' well-being and safety as long as I have the financial means to do so."

He turns to Mr. Shaw with fierce disdain shadowing his eyes. "I am not ashamed to help people in need, even if I am judged for the people I choose to help. We will all have to answer for our moral failings, but valuing human dignity is not one of mine."

From my place at his side, I scan the audience for familiar faces, smiling to show my approval. All we have left now is his character and the voters' trust—and although I'm not a voter, whoever doesn't trust him just might trust me when I lift my chin and give him an admiring gaze.

We defended the high ground and didn't attack. Mr. Shaw shrinks back in his chair, out of ammunition.

The voters may never know what Mr. Shaw had the

opportunity to tell them tonight. He was so intent to make a fool of Cooper that he missed his own chance to brag on his good deeds and tell the story himself instead of waiting for someone to use it against him. What will resonate with the voters is anyone's guess now—a reformed sinner or a slick talker—but I will rest a little easier knowing we did this right.

As Dr. Williams dismisses the audience, I twist my hand just a little to show off my ring in the lights. After all, if there's a seat in the assembly that says "Truxton" come January, it's for both of us.

Our ride back to the city is exhausted and joyous. I think the day Victoria stood up to Matthew on my behalf flipped a switch in her, and lately she is possessed of a boundless energy not only for the campaign but for all of her future plans. Today, she treats us to a string of ideas about forming a campus club so she and other nursing students can engage in issues around public health.

"Did you see Alice O'Grady tonight? I sat with her and she told me all you have to do to charter an official club on campus is submit a form to the mistress of student affairs with ten signatures of interested parties," she says, a little breathless. "I am so excited to get started. I'll get all the signatures tomorrow and hand it in first thing Monday morning."

In between sideways, stunned glances at Victoria, Matthew is entirely complimentary of Cooper's performance and even apologizes for his lack of faith in how we managed the attack on his character. "Maudie, when you said you were prepared for it, I believed you. It was still quite a fine spectacle to see it in action. I do not know how it will land with the voters, Trux, but for whatever it's worth, you've convinced me of your good intentions."

"It's worth a lot," Cooper says. "I appreciate everything you've done, of course, but no matter what happens on Tuesday, I'm glad we survived with our teeth and friendship intact."

"I suppose I can keep May twenty-seventh open for groomsman duties, if I must." Matthew rolls his eyes as though the role will be a great burden, then smiles at me. "You are well-suited for one another, and I am happy for you."

"That's very sweet of you, Matthew. Thank you." I lean my head on Cooper's shoulder as the carriage jostles around a bend in the road. "I cannot even think of wedding planning right now. Win or lose, I have no space in my brain for that until after Christmas. I am sure my mother and Mrs. Truxton will love to help however we will have them. I did the difficult part and found the groom."

"What do we have left, Berger?" Cooper numbers our next steps on his fingers. "Church tomorrow, everyone will be talking, and everyone we know will push the reformed-sinner angle. Monday, we've got one last spot in four newspapers. Tuesday?"

"We just show up Tuesday. All the signage will be for Taft and Bryan so there's really not much point adding to the noise. By now, we're either in or out."

I rap my knuckles on my forehead. "Oh, boo. I heard the funniest thing the other day and I meant to tell you to use it tonight. Someone was joking about how Mr. Bryan had already run for President and lost twice and this is Mr. Taft's first try, and they said 'Vote for Taft, because you can always vote for Bryan next time.'"

Matthew snorts a laugh. "Get that to Hayes immediately. Maybe it's not too late to switch up what he has for Monday. We all know that if Trux is in, Shaw's not out by any means. They can vote for him next time. It fits."

"He'll find a favorable district for the next election and smooth-talk his way in," Victoria says. "Cooper, I imagine you and he will have an interesting time in the assembly together."

He smiles. "And to think Maudie said the work of governing would be boring compared to the campaign trail."

The carriage jolts again and knocks Victoria into Matthew's shoulder. She sits bolt upright.

"I hope you are able to start on the roads quickly." She brushes down her cloak and skirts as though he covered her in dust. "This one really is quite awful."

Chapter 36
Cooper

A series of sharp bangs on my bedroom door wakes me from a restless sleep Tuesday morning. Untangling myself from my quilts and pile of pillows, I hear the muffled voice of my landlord.

"Your friend's here, Truxton!"

"My what?" I peer blearily at the clock. Maudie and I were supposed to meet after class for lunch. It's certainly not her. "Who's here?"

The man is half-deaf. He never heard Maudie here with me at night and certainly doesn't hear me now. "He's waiting downstairs for you," he calls. "Said it was important."

I dress with haste, a tiny worry in the back of my mind about Georgia's perpetual tiredness and my father's health. Leo wouldn't be here in either case, though. He'd be with them and send a messenger to fetch me if I was needed. I yank my tie a little too tight and loosen it with another quick tug when I remember it's Election Day.

I slip on the hardwood in my stocking feet and swing around the newel post, jumping the last two steps and nearly colliding with Berger in the front hall. He's suited in somber gray wool and eyes my disarray in confusion. "Haven't you been to the polls yet?"

"No."

"Why not?"

"It's eight a.m." I yawn. "I was going to go after my nine o'clock lecture. William what's-his-name was going to meet me so he can take a photo for the children I don't have yet. I'm not so haughty I have to be first in line to vote for myself, you know."

"Did you know what Victoria was up to with the poll watchers? Did Maudie?"

I rub my eyes. "What are we watching?"

He smacks the back of my head. "Get dressed in something that matches and come with me."

The closest polling place is a local post office branch and the steps are full of sign-wavers for every party and cause imaginable except mine. I'm relieved we didn't try to make our mark in these crowds—it's bedlam in some areas.

Berger leads me past a short line of gentlemen waiting to receive their ballots at a desk staffed by old men in spectacles. Behind them, between the desk and the curtained voting booths, two young women in white dresses and orange-ribboned hats sit side-by-side, watching every move.

"Who are they?" I whisper. "That blue and green pin they're both wearing is from the Women's College, but I don't recognize either of them. What are they doing here?"

"I only had a moment to ask after I came out of the booth. They shoo you on out pretty quickly. They said Victoria

Harper was working with their club to send election watchers to every site."

"Can she do that? What club?"

"Can she?" He gestures broadly. "I have no idea. I asked if they knew Maudie, and they only said Victoria sent them."

"Are they at all the polling places?"

"I've only been here and at the grammar school on Ninth. I didn't get close enough to ask those ladies anything, though. What the hell does she think she's doing, not taking this through Maudie?"

I scratch my head, a wry smile spreading when I think of mouse-like Victoria so recently empowered to do anything that pops into her head. "She was asking my father about the polling places the other day, remember? If I had to guess, she's separating this effort from my campaign entirely."

"To what end?"

"Maudie and I plan to meet at ten-thirty so I can vote and get my photograph, and then we'll have lunch. Join us, and we'll see what's happening with Victoria's ladies."

"Trux?"

"Huh?"

"Has Victoria always been like this and I just never noticed?"

"You do like a strong-minded woman, don't you?"

He coughs to hide a laugh. "I suppose I do."

"A word of advice?"

"From you? On this matter?"

"Well, I have some experience."

"Spare me."

Voting for oneself is a little surreal. I check my ballot half a dozen times before emerging from the little booth and smiling for the camera. Two women in college badges and orange-flowered hats keep a watchful eye on me as I drop it in the locked box.

Maudie is bright-eyed and giggling when she meets us outside the polling place. "Matthew, you will call this plausible deniability. Cooper can honestly say these women are not working for his campaign and that he had no idea there was a women's effort in place to assist with election security today."

"How did they even get in?" I ask. "You can't just walk up to the officials and ask to watch them work."

"They didn't ask. They claimed their right."

"Their right?"

"Each political party with a candidate on the ballot can send volunteer observers to vouch for the integrity of the ballots and the process."

"But the Republicans and the Democrats already—"

"They are not the only parties on the ballot." She grins. "Ladies may not vote, but we love to volunteer. It is our good Christian spirit to help those in need. And in this case, Victoria quickly convinced the local Socialist Party that her friends would be overjoyed to represent them at the polls so their candidate Mr. Eugene Debs is afforded the same protections as Mr. Taft and Mr. Bryan. The party is very small in North Carolina, so you can imagine they were excited to increase their visibility."

Berger lets out a long, low whistle as I gawp at my fiancée.

"Furthermore, Victoria had so many ladies interested in helping, they have taken up posts at polling places outside our district, so the effort is obviously not focused on a single local race."

"Socialists?" is the only word I can squeak out.

"They have women in their party ranks and a few good ideas we can support with a clear conscience. She didn't say a peep to me about it until last night. You'll have eyes on your ballot boxes, my darling, just in case."

"What about the counting process tonight?" Berger asks, regaining his voice. "Can the volunteers be part of that, too?"

"They can. And they will."

"What if they see something suspicious? Do we—well, I guess we don't do anything. Do they file a complaint on behalf of their party?" Berger's legal brain is kicking in and looking for loopholes and precedents.

"It might be gray area, but if there is trouble, we think one thing will work in our favor with the stodgy politicians who cling to the old ways."

"And?"

"A gentleman does not call a lady a liar."

Chapter 37

Maudie

C ooper and I skip our afternoon classes and make our way around the polling places one by one, peeking in where we can to see the newly-minted members of the Raleigh Women's College Social Progress Club serenely overseeing the men at the tables and in the booths. Each of them flaunts an orange flower or ribbon in her hat—an instant army of petticoats and stern gazes just daring the men around them to misbehave or raise questions.

"Who are they?" he asks as we ride up to Hillside. "Are they my canvassers?"

"They are your canvassers' roommates and friends who can say they never campaigned for you."

"Victoria thought of everything. I see she learned from the best."

"I am so proud of her. A woman who can be that sweet, smart, and determined all at once is a fearsome weapon for any cause."

He cups his hand under my chin and turns my face to his for a kiss. "My dearest, darling fearsome weapon," he murmurs. "Do you remember when I said I did not know how to love you without fear?"

"Yes."

"Well, it's partly because you're terrifying."

I slap his arm and snuggle close to his shoulder as he opens the carriage window. Crisp autumn air fills our lungs and chills our cheeks, and we are both nearly asleep when we arrive at his parents' house. Georgia, Leo, and my parents will join us for supper and hopefully distract from this waiting game we must play tonight.

It lifts my heart to see Georgia pink-cheeked and glowing with energy after the last few weeks of tiredness. She greets us with tight embraces and immediately hustles me upstairs to look at fabric samples for my wedding dress.

"Georgia, I haven't even begun to think about—"

"Hush. I have nothing but time to think, lazing about in bed all day. Leo has hardly let me rise to change my clothes since I complained of being tired last week." She presses a catalog to my chest. "I sent away for new fabric samples as soon as you were engaged. Let's just look."

I flip the pages as she settles on her old bed, wedging herself upright with the pillows. "I had no idea there were so many shades of white. How do you—Georgia, darling. Are you all right?"

"I'm fine."

"You just—well, you just held your stomach for a minute."

"You try gaining sixty pounds in a matter of months and see if you don't hold your stomach a bit." She fans herself. "Bring that over here. There are some silk taffetas I think would be lovely under light netting for spring, and if I combine those with a—"

She presses her hand to her stomach.

"A what?" My eyes widen. "Georgia, are you all right?"

Taking my hand, she guides it over her rounded belly to where the baby is kicking. "There, Aunt Maudie." She smiles. "The baby has been so quiet since I got up this morning. I was a little worried."

"She's kicking like a swimmer. Or he. Have you settled on names yet?"

"Every time we think we have it, one of us has another idea. It would help to know if we are having one child or ten so I can rest easy putting some names to the side for now without offending anyone."

"Don't name anyone Maudie. I despised being 'Muddy' as a girl."

"Yes, and years of begging to be called by your middle name never caught on. I tried, though."

"Cathleen was far better than Muddy, and isn't Kitty the sweetest nickname? It was only when Queen Victoria's grand-daughter Maud got married that I decided a tiara made everything better."

"Georgia Victoria and Maud Cathleen. We were fine royalty, weren't we?" She turns a page in the catalog and winces. "Let's see which of these swatches looks best with your complexion. Give me..."

She grimaces, trying to sit upright and catch her breath. Her lips twitch as she fights a pain, but she brushes my hand aside.

"Georgia?"

Closing her eyes, she blows out a long, slow exhale as she

sinks back into the cushions. I pat the blanket next to her, unsure what else to do with my hands.

"I'll get you some water, darling. You look a little flushed."

"Water would be nice, thank you."

I dart down the back stairs to avoid the hall in front of the study where I'm sure the men are chatting. Augusta spies me in the kitchen and reads my face immediately. Five minutes after she follows me to her daughter's room, she sends me back down to dispatch Mabel for Dr. Everett and the midwife.

The first time Georgia cries out without muffling her face with a pillow, Leo thunders up the stairs. Swinging on the doorframe by his fingertips, he nearly launches himself to his wife's side in a panic.

"Go back downstairs," she says. "I have enough people fussing over me."

He plops in the chair at her bedside like an obstinate child. "Is the baby coming?"

"I just had some pains, but it passed."

Undeterred, he turns to Augusta and asks again. "Is the baby coming?"

"It's rather early to know. Go back downstairs and let them know everything is fine. We'll tell you what the doctor says when he gets here."

He crosses his arms and doesn't budge.

"He can stay until the doctor comes, at least, Mama." Georgia rolls her eyes, fighting a smile. "It's this or he's camping in the hall."

Mabel must be faster than a Berger rumor mill because the midwife and the doctor arrive in less than twenty minutes. Dr. Everett quizzes Georgia about every step she's taken and every bite she's eaten for the past few days, shaking his head as he presses his stethoscope to her belly. Just as he sits up to speak, another pain grips her. She clamps down on Leo's hand and grits her teeth, a sheen of sweat glazing her forehead as his face goes white.

I press myself against her dresser, tightening my fingers on the brass drawer handles as she fights back a moan. I have no sisters and have never attended a birth, and I cannot imagine I'll be much help. With the doctor, the midwife, the maids, and her mother in attendance, Georgia has all the skilled care she needs. Leo, if he can keep himself upright, is far more important to have at her side. When the pain eases and he helps her recline more comfortably, I ask whether I should leave and give any news to Cooper and his father downstairs.

Dr. Everett holds up a finger to bid me wait, then presses his stethoscope to Georgia's belly again, first one side and then the other.

"It's too early," Augusta says. "Isn't it? I had early contractions with Cooper for two weeks."

A smile crosses the doctor's lined face. "I remember, Miss Augusta. But there are many factors in play. Your son took two weeks, and Miss Georgia here took only two hours. I barely made it in time." He offers a handshake to Leo. "Are you ready to be a father tonight?"

He gulps. "Tonight? You're sure?"

"Tonight, or early tomorrow."

I clap my hands over my mouth, bouncing on my toes to contain a squeak as Georgia pats her husband's arm. "He's ready," she says, already calm and collected again. "We're ready."

I am nearly shaking when they finally send me downstairs a few minutes later to share the news. Cooper and his father are bickering over something in a newspaper and he drops his glass on a tray with a clatter when he sees me.

"How is she? Do we need to get her home?"

"She's well." I take his hands in mine. "And she's staying here for the time being. Dr. Everett says you will be an uncle tonight, or early tomorrow morning."

Christopher sips the last of his brandy and chuckles. "That'll be five dollars, son."

"Is everything all right?" Cooper asks. "It's earlier than she thought it would be. And it sounded—well, she sounded very uncomfortable."

"It's an uncomfortable process, you know."

"But it's going how it should? You know, nothing to worry about?"

I have no frame of reference for normal childbirth, but Cooper's grip on my hands is so tight I must reassure him. "The doctor and your mother are both smiling."

"Then that's our cue," Christopher says, rising and patting Cooper's back. "This is the part where the menfolk go for a long walk."

Chapter 38
Cooper

We call first at the Hamiltons to cancel the invitation to supper. Maudie's mother fans herself frantically before disappearing to retrieve baby gifts she's obviously been stockpiling for some time. I lug them dutifully to our next stop, Georgia and Leo's house, where Maudie has instructed me to gather certain things from the nursery.

"Twenty diapers?" I squint at the list she pressed in my hand as we left. "At what point do you just put the baby in a tub and hope for the best?"

"You can speak such thoughts freely here, son, but I advise you to hold your tongue on all matters of baby preparation and nurturing around a new mother." Papa locates a valise in the wardrobe and plops it on the chair. "If your sister asked for twenty diapers, we will bring twenty diapers. What else?"

"Ten blankets? Do you and Mama not have blankets? Are they moving back in?"

He thumbs through a drawer in the bureau and counts under his breath. "Ten."

"Do you see any hats or bonnets? Eight of those. All right, come now. The child might be spitting on blankets and shitting in diapers, but what baby needs eight hats the day it is born?"

"This one, obviously." He chuckles and flings a knitted bonnet my way, catching me square in the face. "And when you hold your new niece or nephew for the first time, Cooper, you will not care that your sister asked you to count hats and diapers. Thank goodness Georgia is doing this first so you can mock Leo for being an emotional sap. You'll be even more of a puddle when your own children are born. I will delight in that."

"I'm glad you're well, Papa." My breath catches in my throat as I drop the pink bonnet into the valise. "I'm so glad you're well. I'm glad we can do this for Georgia."

He tosses me another bonnet a little more gently. "I was never at death's door."

"I know."

"I would have run for this office if I could have. And for a short while I regretted that you felt you had to do it because I couldn't. It seemed like an unfair burden with you so young and inexperienced—and aimless, I thought." He folds a tiny sweater and squeezes it tight. "I thought wrong. Win or lose, I am deeply proud of you. The self-awareness and humility you displayed Saturday night should cause others to reflect on themselves the same way."

"I didn't follow your example well enough when I was young, and I am sorry for that."

"You challenged me in a way I never challenged my

father." He gives me a rueful laugh and tosses another little hat my way. "I was raised to be very careful in a time my parents thought it was necessary to stay a steady course. That strategy of my father's brought our family a great deal of social and financial security, but when you showed up, born backward and squalling about how annoyed you were with the world already, my first thought was not that I would have to break your spirit and teach you to keep your head down."

"No?"

"I remember thinking that times change quickly but people do not, and while it may be difficult to change an old man's views—my father's views—a baby doesn't have those old views to let go of. I was perhaps a little too permissive with you sometimes because I wanted to see you challenge things I was never bold enough to consider. You've made me proud, and I am glad to see our family fortunes in such thoughtful, capable hands."

"Better correct the will, then, because you've threatened me a few times with leaving it all to Leo and Georgia."

"Ah, yes. I'll check on that tomorrow and try not to die tonight."

"Thank you, Papa."

"My point is, I think you won't sit on this family's years of good fortune and hoard money and power like a miser for our advantage. What we have protected so selfishly, you might dismantle entirely one day." He takes a deep breath and draws a weathered hand across a simple flannel blanket draped over the end of the cradle. It is a little threadbare in places and I recognize its embroidered rabbits—it was one of my sister's.

He clears his throat. "And if you run our family's finances

into the ground when I am gone, I know you will have done it for the right reasons if you follow the heart and the conviction you have shown in this race. What you have done for our name and integrity will never have a cash value."

With a valise stuffed with enough baby items for an infant army, we return to the house by the light of the street lamps. Maudie informs us things are progressing nicely—whatever that means —and pulls me around the corner of the hall for a quick kiss.

"What a surprising night this has turned out to be already," she says, resting her head on my shoulder. "Dr. Everett thinks it will not be long now. Is there any news from the polls?"

"We've just been to your parents' house and Leo and Georgia's, so I haven't seen anyone. Remember, Papa said we might not know until morning. Berger knows we're here, so I imagine he'll send a pigeon or smoke signals if he has news."

She giggles, pushing damp curls off her forehead. "I suppose if this is the Lord's way of tempering disappointing news later, I'll take it. Georgia is exhausted, but she's so excited."

"And Leo?"

"Oh, he's near death."

I send her back upstairs with a kiss and a glass of his favorite brandy.

At just past eleven o'clock, Papa is asleep on the sofa in the study and I am shaking like a leaf, knees bouncing and feet tapping with a rush of anxiety I never knew existed. Can a twenty-three year old man have a heart attack? When a baby's thin cry pierces the silence, I fling aside the newspaper I was pretending to read and jump to my feet, ready to sprint for the door.

"Sit down. This is the worst part," Papa says, still reposing quietly with his eyes closed and a smile on his face. "Now we must wait our turn."

The baby cries again.

"Surely we can just run upstairs and see that Georgia's well and find out if it's a boy or a girl."

"And just as surely, your lovely bride-to-be will shoo us both back down here to wait." He yawns as the baby lets out another fantastic wail. "It sounds like whoever was just born has a fine, healthy set of lungs. That is enough to be thankful for and will keep us until your sister is ready to receive visitors."

Half an hour ticks by and we are subjected to several more impressive infant squalls before Maudie and Mama enter the study giggling like schoolgirls. Without a word, Maudie clasps my hand and we follow the new grandparents up the stairs.

"Are you going to want me in there with you when it's our turn?" I ask. "I've always admired your independent spirit, you know, and I believe ladies are entirely capable of handling any situation without men's interference, so—"

She silences me with a kiss. "When it is our turn, I will give you the choice. And you had better choose right."

I nearly swallow my tongue.

"Now, come meet your new niece."

My face warms. "I knew it. There are far too many men in the world already. I knew it was a girl. I just had a feeling."

"You were half right."

"What?"

She opens the door to my sister's room. Georgia is sitting up in bed, her hair a wavy tangle around her glowing cheeks as she cradles a tiny blanket-wrapped bundle to her chest. "Hi, Uncle Cooper." She beckons me over, as if I could look anywhere else. "Meet Cathleen Augusta Rigby."

She's so tiny. I don't know how to hold a baby and am afraid to reach for her, so I tap her little button of a nose and nearly jump when that triggers a wide yawn with a whisper of a squeak.

I am enchanted. How on earth did this petal of a mouth and these angelic cheeks release those ear-splitting screams?

Leo clears his throat. "And here's her noisy scamp of a little brother who hid from us all until tonight, Christopher Cooper Rigby."

I grapple for the bedpost for a moment, and my mouth hangs open like a fish as Maudie collapses into giggles. "The doctor told us when he first checked Georgia this afternoon and she swore us all to secrecy until they were born. I nearly burst."

Leo has always been closer to my father than his own, and Papa chokes up when he hands him his namesake. The instant the baby leaves Leo's arms, I smack him. "You can't name your son for me. I'm not naming anyone Leopold."

"Leopold is a fine name," Maudie argues as Leo smacks me back.

"The men in my family all have names that start with C, and every son has his father's first name for his middle. It goes back more than a hundred years. My son has to be something-or-other Cooper Truxton."

Papa bounces his grandson and smiles. "What did I tell you about old men and old ideas?"

"I happen to like this old idea."

"It's really only first sons that do that," Georgia says. "None of Papa's brothers has a C name. Your second son can be Leopold."

I turn to Maudie in desperation. "But I don't want to name anyone Leopold."

"All right, my love. You win." She pats my chest and I stand straighter, pleased to have an ally. "We'll call our first daughter Leopoldina, then."

"Leopoldette would be pretty," Mama suggests.

I throw my arm around my best friend, truly the brother I never had, and draw my fiancée in close. "Listen, both of you. Since I am about to make a fine political career out of shrewd bargaining without moral compromise, I know everyone will be pleased with my solution. We will name our first dog Leopold or Leopoldette. How's that for statesmanship?"

Leo jumps back. "Jesus, Trux, I forgot what day it is. Have you heard anything?"

"Yes."

Maudie freezes in my arms. "What?"

"Well, Papa was asleep and the rest of you were delivering babies, so when I caught Berger lurking on the porch in a fierce dilemma about whether to knock so late, I told him we weren't really—"

She yanks my tie. "What did he say? Did they count everything already?"

"They counted, my love." I bend my head to her ear so

only she will hear it first. "On January fourth, 1909, there will be a seat in the assembly that says Truxton. And that means both of us."

Epilogue: Maudie
August 18, 1920

My ten year old daughter Emmeline grips my hand tightly and makes both our palms sweat as we make our way toward the capitol building in Washington, D.C. On my other side, Cooper swings little Calvin up onto his shoulders for a better view of the crowd that stretches up the Mall waiting for the nineteenth amendment to be signed into law, legalizing the vote for all American women. My darling husband offered to stay at our Georgetown home with our son today, saying he didn't want a man's presence to undercut the spirit of the celebration, but with a quick flick to the back of his head, I put that notion out of his mind. We needed men to get this done, and men like him came through. From the floor of the North Carolina General Assembly to marches in the streets of Washington, Cooper has done his part a thousand times over these last twelve years, and he deserves his celebration.

Emmy tugs my hand. "Will someone come tell us when Congress is done?"

"After Congress passed the amendment last year, their

part was done, sweetheart." I crouch a little to her level. "Then it went to the states to ratify. It took a long time. Do you remember how many states we had to wait for?"

"Eleven!" Calvin sings out, and Cooper swats his foot.

"Thirty-six," Emmeline says, sticking her tongue out at her little brother.

"And today, the last step is for the Secretary of State to sign it. Then it becomes part of the Constitution."

Cal gestures to the crowd. "What are all the flags? Those aren't American flags."

"They're state flags," Cooper says. "I see several from states that ratified the amendment already. Who remembers which one made it thirty-six so it passed?"

"Texas!" Cal throws his hands in the air and nearly flings himself from Cooper's shoulders.

"It's Tennessee, you ninny." Emmeline's dismissive wave at her little brother is so like my own I fight a giggle when I see it. She has her father's brown hair and my blue eyes and looks so much like Georgia did in her girlhood I've called her the wrong name more than once. Calvin is Cooper's little twin in looks and in spirit. The Truxton genes are so strong, I told him, that if I want a child who looks like me I shall have to make it myself without any assistance from him.

Cooper, of course, latched onto that as a line to use when he wants a little affection. *Darling, let me assist you tonight.* After more than ten years of marriage, even with a lull during the sleepless, stressful nights with colicky children, it is still delightfully difficult to say no when he invites me to bed with that mischievous smile that will never age.

I pass my hand over my stomach as it churns with my worries even on this glorious day.

"What's North Carolina?" Cal asks, scanning the crowd. "I forgot."

"A red stripe over a white stripe, next to a blue band," Emmy says. "The blue has *NC* on it."

Cooper glances at me. "We might not see North Carolina's flag here today. They were trying to broker a deal with Tennessee where they'd both hold out, but it didn't stick." He ruffles Emmy's hair. "That means North Carolina can ratify it or ignore it and it doesn't matter anymore. Federal law overrules state law. They've made themselves irrelevant."

"Is that why we moved here, Papa?"

"We moved here because your mother and I still have a great deal of work to do for this country, and we are legally obligated to bring you along."

She scrunches her nose, then drags us to a bench so she can pop up next to him and match his height. "But since we won, will we go back to Hillside now? We could live with Grandmother and Grandfather since you said it will be our house one day, anyway. I miss Kitty and Chris."

"You are named for a great suffragist, Emmeline Georgia." He pokes her nose. "She was a fighter, a brave woman who knew that to best affect change in the world, she had to go where the battles could be won." He stomps his foot. "Perhaps Hillside is our fort and we will return one day, but this is our battleground now. We can breathe easier about suffrage, but the world is an unfair place, and we have much more to do."

"Are you going to be in Congress?"

"Your father did enough legislating in ten years to sustain us for another fifty," I say, meeting his eyes as I speak to our daughter. "Too long in public office leaves you bitter and ineffective. Papa's new work allows him to make his mark in other ways."

"What about you, Mama? What will you do now that we've won?"

"Mama's going to be President," Cal announces, nearly swinging his foot into my neck.

"Correction, son." Cooper shackles our little boy's ankles to keep them still against his ribs. "Mama is our general. Our admiral. She's always been my commanding officer."

Cooper was thirty-two when America joined the Great War and narrowly missed being called from service in the legislature to service in the Army. When he declined to run for re-election in 1918, he followed a trail of introductions from my brother Jeremiah, who works for a senator's office, and eventually landed a political advocacy role at the Department of Natural Resources that he describes as 'half-scientist, half-environmentalist, half-busybody.' We visited Pennsylvania this spring so he could see a stand of chestnuts suffering from the blight and he spent an hour talking to the trees before he spoke to the arborists.

Washington is teeming with opportunities for me in philanthropy and activism, and new causes beckon me at every turn. The losses suffered by war widows tug at my heart as I write letter after letter to representatives for government assistance. The ratification of the eighteenth amendment establishing nation-wide temperance last year has not only made some of our friends into first-class bootleggers, its economic impact hurts the poor far more than the rich. The selective, unfair enforcement of the laws infuriates us both, and we are already collecting contacts and ideas for launching the first-ever movement to repeal a constitutional amendment.

I run my fingers over my belly again.

The heat in Cooper's gaze crosses the air between us. I am already warm from this late August sun, but my cheeks flush when he looks at me like that. He is still such an old-fashioned man at heart. He loves my pregnancies like he loves my wedding ring—outward proof that I am his. The man is so doggedly devoted when I am with child it verges on embarrassing, but the thought of another spell where we welcome each other to bed only out of exhaustion tickles under my skin like an itch, like my irritation at my softening waistline and the crinkles at the corners of my lips. I am only thirty-three and use my cold cream religiously, but I suppose these are the marks of a woman who smiles a great deal and carries large, healthy babies.

I meet my husband's eyes again and my heart fills with gratitude. We managed twice before, and we will manage again.

He swings Cal down from his shoulders and stands him on the bench next to Emmy before sneaking a kiss on my cheek. "Do you need to sit, my love? Or would you like a drink? I could go back to the lemonade stand we passed."

"I am well."

The steady thrum of his heart whispers around me when I lay my head back on his chest and turn my face to the sun. Pulling me closer, he crosses his arms over my stomach.

"I love you, Maudie, and I know when you are worried. Don't be."

"I hate that I feel so conflicted. Our children are my delight, and I should be overjoyed to grow our family."

"You should be exactly as you are." He lowers his lips to my ear. "You are the dearest, most desirable wife and a superb mother in every way, but you are only those things to me and our children because you are true to yourself first. This is not what we planned, but we will adjust. If you ask me, and you didn't, feeling a little put out by a disruption of this scale is to be expected."

"A disruption of this scale." I place my hand over his on my belly as a murmur sweeps through the crowd. "Do you hear that, little disruption? This is an important day you're witnessing."

Emmy jumps on the bench to see better as Cooper tightens his hold on me. "What a fine day for another Truxton girl to experience."

"I think we have another Truxton boy."

He furrows his brows. "How do you figure?"

I point at Calvin. In a rare moment of patience, he holds Emmy's hands and helps her balance as she finds her footing on the arm of the bench. She is perched just high enough to see over the sea of people but blocks his view entirely. Cal doesn't complain, and when he spots a little boy next to them casting an eye up his sister's skirt, he delivers a swift kick to the gawker's stomach.

"I just know. The world needs more Truxton men who will lift up the ladies in their lives. And we are calling this one Leopold."

"I really think it's time we get a dog."

The air is thick with humidity and the thrum of the growing crowd. Isolated groups erupt in hymns and chants as we wait, voices soaring one moment and falling to a near-religious hush the next. Everywhere, the mood is one of celebration and cheer, and I'm certain I am not alone in supposing that this is the day I will remember more than the day I finally cast my first ballot. Votes are emotional—and isolating, alone in a little booth. Platforms bring people together.

After Mr. Shaw decamped to Wilmington to re-establish himself and run after Cooper's first victory, their bickering on the assembly floor was a source of newspaper fodder for years. We have an entire album of Brent's cartoons, including an especially fine imagining of Cooper lashing Mr. Shaw to the Confederate monument with a purple and gold suffrage ribbon after they had a heated debate about poll taxes.

Hillside loved its renegade assemblyman, but North Carolina did not. The Democrats still control the legislature, so we came after them with the power of the federal government since they wouldn't do the right thing themselves.

The suffragist Emmeline Pankhurst was a militant activist, a far cry from my army of vote-getting college ladies, and she fascinated me to no end when I was finishing my degree in American History and Government. I wrote Mrs. Pankhurst a letter and sent a picture of my Emmeline when she was four, passing out leaflets for Cooper's 1914 re-election campaign. Next to her, a hand-lettered sign read *Vote for my Papa because Mama and I can't.* I didn't expect a reply from someone of her stature, but two years later, I was astonished to receive two letters from the great woman herself, one addressed to me with words of encouragement, and one to my daughter.

I've kept Emmy's letter at home unopened and will give it to her tonight.

She shades her face with her hand as she scans the crowd, lips moving quietly as she reads the banners under her breath. North Carolina has no flag here today but us. Our home state taught us all too well that equal rights under law do not guarantee equal treatment, and as Cooper and I still say, we have so much work to do.

A shout rings out down the Mall, closer to the capitol. Our daughter rests her little palm on my shoulder to keep her balance and doesn't look down.

Next in the Series

After three proposals and three rejections, their romance ended in 1913. Four years later, Matthew Berger, a communications specialist in the U.S. Army, and Victoria Harper, a Red Cross nurse, meet again in France and rekindle an old flame in **DON'T ASK ME AGAIN**, testing the limits of what a war-torn world will allow.

Afterword

A RACE WITH A ROGUE reflects the U.S. political landscape in North Carolina in 1908, when positions taken by Democratic and Republican officials differed greatly from the more modern platforms of those parties. The Democratic Party was the more conservative of the two, and the Republicans, the party of outgoing President Theodore Roosevelt, leaned liberal. Most of this book presents a heavily-fictionalized portrait of the 1908 state legislature races based on a loose framework of local politics around Raleigh, NC. The Socialist Party did run a presidential candidate, Mr. Eugene Debs. The varmint Ashford Pinckney Shaw is not based on any historical person.

The Wilmington Coup of 1898, also known as the Wilmington Race Riots, is a true historical event that led to only the second successful government coup on U.S. soil and the deaths of an unknown count—maybe hundreds—of black citizens. Every effort has been made to portray it with sensitivity and accuracy the way characters like Cooper and Maudie might have been taught in 1908. They are at the very beginning of their awakening about American injustice. The "Lost Cause" narrative had already begun to form Southern education and policy, so white characters coming from privileged families may well have been sheltered from what contemporary audiences know to be uncomfortable and dangerous truths.

NCpedia, an online history project about North Carolina's politics and culture through the state's long existence, is a wealth of information and primary sources used by the author. This resource includes the original publications in the Wilmington newspapers that triggered the conflict, eyewitness accounts from both black and white citizens, documentation of the state constitutional amendments relating to poll taxes and black suffrage, and more. For more information, visit https://www.ncpedia.org/anchor/1898-and-white-supremacy.

The Series

The Truxtons

How to Measure a Man

A Race With a Rogue

La Croix-Rouge

Don't Ask Me Again

Dance Around the Rules

Reader reviews help authors gain exposure in search rankings in a saturated market. Your reviews on Amazon, Kobo, Goodreads, and any platform of your choice are always appreciated.

Acknowledgments

Danielle and Kaitlin, your thoughtful insights and feet-kicking comments bring joy to the tedium of editing. Thank you for your unflinching honesty and encouragement.

Mac, I'll get to the choose-your-own-adventure version eventually. Thanks for putting up with these pesky linear timelines.

Jess, thanks for every late-night message and every emoji when there were no words left. I appreciate you and your patience with my endless redemption arcs :)

To The Writerly Ladies' Brunch Club, another round soon.